BLOOD TIES

LUCAS KNOX #2

BLAKE HUDSON

To my beautiful wife, Stephanie, the heart and soul of my world. For ten years, your humour, kindness, and humility have filled my life with a love so perfect, it feels almost undeserved. You've given me not only endless joy and laughter but the greatest gift of all—three wonderful children who light up our lives. My story truly began the moment you welcomed me into yours, and for that, I am eternally grateful.

This is for you, with all my love.

ONE
HARD DRIVE

The nest, the double cross, and now the gun aimed at his head. Not exactly the day Knox had planned to be his last. He had dreams of beating the odds and dying of old age in a cabin back home, somewhere in the remote highlands he loved. There was always a bottle of scotch on the shelf, just at the ready for his last days on earth.

But fucking this? He gritted his teeth with a mixture of disbelief and anger.

A fucking traitor who clearly had no fucking idea what shit storm she had gotten herself mixed up in was pointing a gun at his head. It was no doubt some twisted form of revenge on Daddy dearest, or something worse perhaps. Knox needed to find out, if it was the last thing he did, he needed to know just how deep this shit ran. Which was when he turned slowly and faced his fate.

"Isabella? What are you…?" Knox said, taking in the frantic gaze of someone unsure what to do next.

Whatever the plan had been, in her mind it was clear she wasn't following it. Perhaps this was something Knox could use to his advantage? But as his eyes tried to subtly scan the surrounding area, wondering if Harris would stumble across them in time, she was quick to react in her manic state.

"Don't move, Lucas! I will shoot you! I am not as weak as you all think," Isabella screamed with wild ferocity, making the gun in her hand start to tremble.

"Why?" Knox asked calmly, in hopes to defuse the situation enough before acting against her. Isabella was clearly emotional, and even seemed desperate and unhinged. There wasn't anything he could do other than stall her enough in hopes she let her guard down to give him the opening he needed.

"Why?" Isabella repeated, followed by crazed laughter before continuing on. "He wanted to let you go, out of some form of twisted loyalty. You men are so stupid! You have no idea!" Isabella exclaimed, telling Knox all he needed to know about which side she was on.

A fact made even more evident as she pushed the gun forward, her face screaming at how badly she wanted to pull the trigger. Yet her body wasn't up to the task and it shook with fear. Taking that first step towards killing someone for the first time wasn't as easy as the movies made you believe.

"It's a mistake, you are dangerous and a threat. I can't have that. Goodbye, Lucas Knox!" Isabella said through gritted teeth, gearing herself up to take that step after all, meaning that Knox had to think fast to stall her further. Because he had spotted something that she hadn't and now all he needed was a few more precious seconds.

"Wait, Isabella, what about the hard drive?!" Knox asked, making her frown in question.

It was as if she was replaying in her mind all Mac had asked her to do and was worried she had missed something.

Well, she was about to find it. Knox held back a knowing grin.

"The hard drive?" she questioned. However, it was someone else that answered her from behind.

"Yeah, this hard drive, bitch!" The voice was followed by a loud crash echoing with a high-pitched woman's scream before impact.

Knox ducked and spun around at the same time, his reactions triggered on a hair pin. He watched as Isabella fell right in front of him, the gun flinging from her hand and skidding across the floor. She was knocked clean out before she had even hit the ground. And there was his saviour, panting and still clutching her now broken laptop. Rose held an expression of purpose as she continued to breathe heavily, staring down in disgust at the body on the floor.

"Rose? Now you are a sight to behold lass," Knox said, looking up at the tech geek as he got up and dusted his knees down. Then he placed a hand on her shoulder and added, "Thanks, you were right, you really can do some damage with just a laptop."

Taking the broken case from her with a gentle hand, he examined the exposed circuitry. A big smile spread across his face as he shook his head lightly at Rose in disbelief. She had finally torn her gaze from Isabella's slumped form and her breathing evened out as the adrenaline high waned.

"I was due an upgrade…" Rose said with a dryness that cut and one that brought a chuckle from Knox's lips, just before a body bust through the medical tent's entrance.

"Is everything alright? What happened to her?" Major Harris asked as he arrived, brandishing his weapon. One that he lowered when seeing Isabella sparked out on the floor and being assured that Rose and Knox were okay.

"It is now, Sir, as for this one, she got hit with more tech than she could handle, thanks to Rose," said Knox as he winked at the cute technician, who was fixing her blonde hair back into its messy bun.

Harris glanced down at her broken laptop before he picked up the handgun next to the unconscious prisoner.

"What was she up to?" questioned Harris.

"I don't know, but I intend to find out… Is the Brig okay?" Knox asked, concerned about Carter and the state he was found in when they first arrived on scene.

As for Isabella, Knox grabbed the back of her designer dress and used it to heave her up into his arms, before making his way out of the medical tent. There was only one place where she was headed, and that was straight to interrogation, making Knox wonder what he would find when opening the door. Would her arsehole fiancé still be there or had Mac busted him out?

"The Brig is sleeping, I patched him up best I could, but we need to… whoa, Knox, hold up, it may not be best… *to take her in there…*" Harris called out, but it was too late as the rest of his sentence trailed off sarcastically in sight of Knox kicking open the door. A door that should have been locked and secured but had instead been left ajar as if someone had already made a hasty exit.

"Shit!" Knox shouted when he saw Howard sitting in the chair still bound by tape.

The only difference now was that his brain-matter decorated the wall behind him. There wasn't much left of his head to distinguish him as Howard. Someone, most likely Mac, had used a shotgun at close range to devastating effect.

"Yeah, that," Harris commented dryly, having previously discovered what was left of the prisoner.

"Can't say I'm surprised, the pompous scumbag had it coming," Knox commented with a sneer.

"Shall I take his body out of here before you wake her up?"

Harris suggested as he walked over to Howard's fly attracting corpse.

"No… she needs to see it; can you fetch a bucket of water?" Knox said with a level of rage building in him he was desperately trying to control.

Harris looked in thought for a moment, then nodded before he left to get the water. However, the major bumped into Rose on the way out and quickly made a move to spare her the gruesome sight of slaughter. He took hold of her hand and blocked her view into the room, ushering her away with him. The last thing he wanted was for Rose to see the horror that sat slumped in the room, after all, she had seen enough already.

As for Knox, he dumped Isabella in the opposite chair before he dragged it into position. Then before she could wake up, he snagged the tape off the table, left over from when they had secured Howard. His movements became methodical and well-practiced as he bound each skinny limb to the chair, making sure that she wouldn't be going anywhere when she came to. And waking the bitch up was his next move, as Harris walked in with exactly what he needed.

Knox took the bucket and enjoyed every moment as he threw the ice-cold water over Isabella. She came round instantly, disorientated and coughing up the fluid she had swallowed when gasping for air. Knox had made sure there was enough left over and didn't wait for Isabella to collect herself before tossing the rest in her face. She was about to speak, when she finally noticed they weren't exactly alone. A haunting scream erupted from her the second she saw the horrific remains of the last person T.I.7 had bound to a chair.

Knox then dropped the metal bucket in front of him before kicking it away, the sound of which being enough to bring her attention back to him. Isabella's wide eyes, frantic and afraid, stared up at him just before he took hold of her face. His fingertips dug in painfully as he kept her jaw in his grasp, telling her before uttering any words that he wasn't fucking around here.

"Fucking talk, woman! Tell me everything!" Knox bellowed furiously, all feeling of protection he had once felt towards her had long disappeared after the sound of her cocking the gun in his direction.

"I… I… oh God… No, no…" she mumbled, shaking her head as if this was all some horrible dream she would soon wake up from.

Well, it was time for this Spanish princess to get a reality check, and Knox knew exactly how to do it.

"Oh, it's very real, Isabella. Here, let me show you," Knox said, before grabbing the back of her chair and tipping her forward, instantly making her scream,

"NO! Get me away! GET ME AWAY!" she pleaded as, inch by inch, the space between her and the bloody mess that was once Howard closed between them.

"What's wrong, Isabella? Don't you recognise him? Don't you recognise your dear fiancé *now his fucking face has been blown off?!*" Knox sneered before adding, "Well, let me tell you, sweetheart, that whatever brains he once had are now painting the fucking wall. And guess who will be joining him? Unless you start talking and tell me what I want to know!"

"I'm not telling you anything!" she snapped, not shocking Knox with her defiance.

"Wrong fucking answer!" Knox thundered before grabbing her chair once more, this time tripping her face right into the bloody stump.

She turned desperately to get away from the horror, but Knox took a fist full of her hair at the scalp and forced her face into the raw flesh, smothering her for a few seconds. The moment he pulled her face away, she instantly vomited all over the floor and continued to wretch up whatever food she had recently consumed.

Knox didn't relish in being the driving force behind this brutal type of integration. But he knew that for someone like Isabella, who had led such a privileged upbringing and let it shape her attitude towards life… well, then shocking her into facing her new reality was the only way to deal with the spoilt bitch. Knox knew that people like her believed nothing could ever touch them, and it was time for that to change. It was time to let the filth of the corruption she was a part of coat her pretty little head, until it became as ugly as she was on the inside. Until the rot of her world could be there, on her face, for all to see.

Knox released a frustrated sigh when she wouldn't stop screaming, knowing he was going to have to get more physical as she wriggled and squirmed in vain to get free.

"Stop screaming," Knox ordered, but it fell on deaf ears and Knox took action.

He let swing an open palm, slapping Isabella crisp and tenaciously across her face. It stunned Isabella into silence, no doubt the first time she had ever been struck in her whole life.

After this she watched in repulsion as Knox simply wiped the blood on his hand that had been transferred onto her face from Howard's pant leg. Her wide eyes took stock of how unaffected Knox was around a dead body, despite how revolting it was.

"Now start talking," Knox said through gritted teeth, looking at his hand as if silently telling her that he was willing to strike her as many times as it would take to get what he wanted.

However defiant to end.

"He will kill you for this!" Isabella screamed venomously.

"Who will kill me… your father? He's dead! Howard? He's dead! Their men? All dead!" Knox fired rapidly back.

"My Nicholas! That's who!" she sneered with a bloody smile.

"Mac… What the fuck?!" Knox asked, his mind now making sense of her involvement, especially when she said,

"He might be Mac to you, but to me he is… *everything.*"

TWO
KOKKINA

"Your everything, Mac is your everything?"? Knox questioned incredulously, thinking how quickly she had got over Howard.

"Yes, my Mac, my Nicholas! And when he finds out you have struck me, he won't be so foolish as to just warn you off," Isabella snapped out with malevolent tones of intent, her eyes burning holes through Knox's skull as she continued. "He will kill you and I will be by his side when he does. Who knows? He may even let me pull the trigger!" Isabella exclaimed, telling Knox all he needed to know about their affair.

Mac was only ever known as Nicholas to the women he was fucking. The man Knox once called a friend wouldn't have had only one woman warming his bed though. Not that Isabella's delusional mind would have seen it that way, no doubt believing the man was capable of such loyalty. A loyalty Knox was actually surprised she possessed, because it was clear Mac had put her up to all of this.

"What, like he killed Howard?" Knox mocked, despite the images of Dani flashing in his mind's eye, and the warning from Mac in the medical tent playing through his thoughts.

"You liar! You killed him, *cerdo!*" she spat, just missing him.

"Call me a pig all you want, lass, but this bloody mess that used to be your fucked up fiancée is the handy work of your precious Mac, and trust me when I tell ya, he wouldn't blink a fucking eye before pulling the trigger on you too."

"He loves me and I…" Isabella was quickly cut short by Knox's mocking laughter.

"He loves you? Can you hear yourself, Isabella? I think it's time to wake up, girl. He has used you and you are a fool if you think otherwise," Knox threw back at her, his impatience quickly morphing into anger. Especially when he thought back to all the unnecessary killing. Something that she was a part of because she had been feeding Mac everything he needed and more.

Knox clenched his fists, every fibre of his being wanting to vent his rage on her.

"Don't say that, you know nothing!" Isabella snapped back, her tone full of venom.

"I know that I would never put the woman I love in danger."

Isabella homed in on his slip up and like a shark to blood in the water, she made a target of his words.

"Oh yes, your precious Dani, how could I forget the bitch?"

All of Knox's composure left him as he reached out and grabbed Isabella by the neck, applying enough pressure to get his threat across.

"You keep her name out of your fucked up head and from your dirty fucking mouth. If you think that Mac loves you, then tell me, why hasn't he taken you with him?!" Knox roared out before letting her go. Isabella's head dropped and she stared at the floor as Knox's words began to sink in.

"Face it, he has used you from day one. He fooled you into

believing he gave a shit, when you were only ever a means to an end," Knox continued to push, driving his point home with every hardened word.

"All this killing, it is blood that's not only on his hands but yours too, just like he intended."

"No… no," she stammered, the unshed tears in her eyes proof that he was getting somewhere.

"Yes, Isabella, yes… he wanted you to take the fall."

"Stop! He loves me!" Isabella cried out, her tone hopeless and full of longing despite Knox's words. It was surprising to him that Isabella seemed to love someone more than herself as she begged him to stop going on at her, but Knox wasn't yet finished.

"Would a man that loves you leave you here, leave you to face me, to face the full wrath of T.I.7?" Knox raged as he took hold of Isabella's head, forcing her to look up at what was left of Howard's mutilated face.

"This right here, is what your lover has done. This is all down to you and your precious Nicholas. And if you don't start telling me what I want to know, then I promise you this, Isabella, you will end up just like your fiancé." Knox curled his top lip in distaste as he leaned down so they were cheek-to-cheek, and pointed at all the brain matter still making its way down the wall. "How is your lover going to stop me from killing you? If I have no use for you, that is what will happen. So, you better talk." Knox straightened his tall frame before drawing his gun and chambering a round. The metal mechanism rang out and reverberated around the room, filling him with a sense of satisfaction only that sound can give.

"You wouldn't dare… you won't shoot me, Lucas." Isabella looked Knox in the eyes with a mixture of contempt and disbelief.

"No? Do you really believe those words, Isabella? That I

won't kill someone who happily tried to kill me?" Knox replied as he pressed the muzzle of his gun down on Isabella's leg, purposely pushing into the fleshy muscle of her thigh. This was so he would miss the bone and she would have an entry as well as exit hole, if she called his bluff and he had to shoot. The point wasn't to kill her yet, because Knox still needed information.

"I am going to count to three and if you don't start telling me what Mac has planned, then you won't be wearing heels and a short skirt for some time," Knox threatened, giving her one last chance to cooperate.

"You can threaten me all you want, asshole, I know you don't have it in you," Isabella said, and just as a look of arrogance flashed across her face, Knox pulled the trigger.

"Knox!" Harris entered the room to investigate the gun fire and uncontrollable screams of pain coming from Isabella.

"Stay back, Harris, she is going to talk or she is going to die… *Painfully*," Knox replied in a calm, cold manner, not flinching at the act of shooting the woman he was once charged with protecting.

"I won't be asking you again, Isabella, talk," Knox said as he placed the still-smoking barrel of the gun on Isabella's other thigh. The heat of the muzzle silencing Isabella's screams.

"You fucking shot me! You shot me in the leg!" Isabella yelled in disbelief, frantically trying to break free from her bonds. But her every movement sent pain up and down her throbbing limb as it bled out from both the entry and exit wound.

"Yes, and I am going to do it again," Knox informed her as he applied downward pressure with the gun and moved his finger slowly to the trigger.

"STOP, STOP… Please just stop! I will talk, I will talk!

Please just don't shoot me again," Isabella pleaded as she began to sob almost uncontrollably.

"I am waiting, Isabella…" Knox coldly reminded her, doing so with not one ounce of pity as the faces of everyone that had died because of her flashed before him.

"Okay, so yes, I have been helping Nicholas."

"Tell me something I don't know, Isabella!" Knox snapped, once more adding pressure to her leg, fully prepared to give her a matching bullet hole.

"We became lovers shortly after we first met. He was my bodyguard at first, but then he became my bastard father's henchman. Nicholas impressed him in time, so much so that they eventually became partners. But Nicholas hated my father as much as I did and…" She paused, as if trying to find the right words.

"And!?" Knox snapped, prompting her to say more.

"And we planned to ruin him together, that's what! He wanted to help me avenge my mother, and in doing so, it meant getting revenge for his family too," Isabella said, spilling her guts through winces and the tears of pain that were streaming down her face.

Knox picked up a chair and sat backwards on it, no longer needing to keep the pressure of his gun on her leg as she had finally stopped resisting. Instead, he faced her, rested his arms on the back of the chair, and tapped the gun in front of Isabella to remind her that he was still a threat. Isabella's eyes widened at the sight of the gun's barrel, still with traces of her scorched blood on it.

"Avenge your mother and his family?" Knox's asked, knowing this was important information.

"You know nothing! Perez, my father, he is a tyrant. He funded the Greeks," Isabella told him, her words laced with malice and hatred, but her tone suddenly changed to one softer and bereaved as she continued. "He was close friends with General George Grivas, who led the Greek Cypriot National Guard and Greek Army. They are the ones who attacked the area around the village of Kokkina."

"Kokkina? That is on the island of…" Knox replied but was cut short.

"Cyprus, yes," Isabella said, deflated, and he soon discovered why. "My father took my mother from the spoils of war, she was from that village, the same village where Nicholas's family were all slaughtered." Isabella's head dropped at what was clearly a painful memory. It was a story told to her by her mother, one she could then relate to when hearing the one Mac had to tell.

"His name, his looks, he is Cypriot? His surname is McCarthy. He was US military, Delta force, for Christ sake," Knox questioned as he tried to put it all together.

"He was adopted, part of some UN aid," Isabella told him, her lips downturned, no doubt at all Mac had suffered at the hands of her father's money, as if she had been there herself experiencing it personally.

Knox shook off any reasoning Mac must have had for avenging his family because he knew it wasn't his true motivation. If it had been, Mac would have simply killed Perez. The likely truth was, Mac had gotten greedy and he wanted more than vengeance. Blood retribution wasn't his end game, Knox knew that for sure.

To slay the King wasn't enough, Mac wanted to take the King's place.

"Then why attack T.I.7? Why?" Knox was getting frustrated at trying to make sense of everything, but all Isabella could do was shake her head, her lips firmly closed.

"Keep talking, Isabella!" Knox said with purpose, his frustration turning back to anger.

"He will kill me! I can't betray him," squealed Isabella in fear, her emotions getting the better of her.

"You are already dead in his eyes, he left you to fend for yourself. You needed to kill me and you failed. Trust me, you are nothing to me either, so you better continue to give me a reason not to kill you," Knox told her, reminding her of the cold, hard facts.

"Fine! I downloaded data from the nest. He gave me something, I don't know how it works, he just told me to plug it in and how he would end up with all of T.I.7's computer files when it was done," Isabella said, her shoulders slumping, completely dejected knowing that she had sealed her fate.

She had betrayed Mac.

Harris, who had remained silent until now, left the room to go check and confirm Isabella's story.

Knox stood up and walked to the door, taking in just how big this all was. Mac now had countless amounts of data he could use and profit from. Worse yet, he had the names and contact details of everyone and anyone connected with British government agencies. Operations and mission details. Knox's mind almost hurt with the endless possibilities of how the shit was going to hit the fan as he rubbed his temple.

"Where are you going? You can't leave me, I'm fucking bleeding… Knox!" Isabella called, but her hopeless cries fell on deaf ears as Knox walked out of the room.

Harris and Rose came running over to him as soon as he left the small office space and entered the main part of the warehouse.

"She's telling the truth. They used Dani's hack device on us, the one that was left on the ship. Max has everything, Knox," Rose said in panic after catching her breath, one that was quickly stolen the second they all heard,

"Freeze…!" The order came from a large tactical team who

quickly flooded into the area. "Get down, get down on the ground, now!"

Knox tossed his firearm before slowly dropping down to the ground. Knowing the drill, he lay face down, holding his arms out to the sides to show his cooperation, just as Harris and Rose hesitantly did the same. The Major glanced to his side to find Rose looking scared and he acted on impulse as he stretched out his hand to place it on top of hers. He then mouthed the words, "Don't worry," and smiled, hoping this would give her enough reassurance that everything would be okay.

The echoes of boots around the cavernous warehouse soon faded as all the tactical team found their stations. Then they waited, their job done now that the space had been cleared.

Knox took note that from the few words that had been spoken, they were an American outfit, and just as he began to wonder exactly who they were, it soon became all too clear.

The sound of high heels snapped on the concrete as their owner walked into the area. It was a grating sound that grew louder with every step. Whoever the tactical team had been waiting for had arrived.

Her unmistakable trademark red-soled size five Louboutin's stopped right next to Knox's head.

"What the hell kind of a fuck up is this, Captain? Same question to you too, Major?" The caffeine-fuelled, sleep deprived, monotone voice of Patricia Miller rang out. The CIA agent wasn't impressed, irritation screaming from her body language and hard-faced expression.

"Get up, Harris, Knox, you are making this shit hole look even more of a mess than it already is," Miller said with a dullness that hailed from whatever boring, backwater town she had been recruited from.

Knox knew the type, patriots that wanted to serve their country. But most of all get out of the small town only seen on the map when passing through to some other exciting destination. You would be hard pushed to place her American accent.

Harris, Rose, and Knox got to their feet. For the second time today, Knox dusted himself down.

"Where is Carter?" questioned Miller.

"He took fire in the ambush, I have tended to him, but he needs air-lifting to a hospital," Harris replied as he stood to attention to report to Miller.

She clicked her fingers at a few of her CIA tactical team, who jumped into action when she then gestured for Harris to show them where Carter was. The Major couldn't help but first look to Rose before touching her on the arm, making sure that she was okay. Then he looked to Knox, conveying a silent message for him to look after Rose in his absence. Miller watched on and in response, rolled her eyes.

"Captain, report and make it quick, we need to clean up this cluster fuck of an operation," Miller said, her arms crossed over her chest. It was clear that her patience was wearing thin.

Knox got her up to speed fast, and Miller only made one comment when he was finally finished.

"Do you think Isabella has any more information?" Miller asked as she looked over to the room Isabella was still inside. Knox thought for a moment, racking his brains for some credible reason to give, because he knew where this was going, and it was going there fast. But he also couldn't get away with spinning Miller any bullshit here, so he told the truth.

"I don't think so, but that's not to say she has no value alive."

"How so? Is she of any use as leverage on McCarthy?"

Knox sighed, wishing he had something to give her. He may have been the one to shoot Isabella in the leg, but that wasn't to say he wanted to be the cause of her death. However, his reaction must have said it all because Miller raised a hand, stopping him from what she knew would only be an excuse at this point.

"Right, take care of her and let's move out of here. The cleaners are on their way," Miller ordered as she began to walk off. Then she stopped when Knox didn't move or respond to her command.

"Problem, Captain?" Miller asked over her shoulder, loathing lacing her tone at the fact Knox had not jumped to her demands.

"I don't answer to you and I am sure as hell not killing for you," Knox said folding his arms and holding moral ground.

Miller's scowl deepened and she drew her weapon, making Knox tense and draw his own in response. However, Miller, completely deadpan, walked straight into the room they had used for interrogation, ignoring Knox and his weapon.

He then closed his eyes because he knew what was coming next. Pleading cries from Isabella filled the space, cries which soon stopped at the sound of three shots reverberating in rapid succession. Flashes of light strobed from the doorway before Miller walked out and headed straight towards Knox. Once there she passed him and at the same time, she hilted her weapon and informed him,

"I can do my own fucking killing, Captain. Now get the fuck out of here."

THREE
BLIGHTY

The normally quiet, single terminal was full to bursting with the hustle and bustle of British holiday makers returning from their cheap, summer package holidays.

Knox passed through the busy passport control, strolling shoulder to shoulder with a large crowd of red-skinned, sunburned Brits. Most of which were still wearing flipflops and their holiday clothes, desperately trying to get as much wear out of them as possible.

Knox stretched out the aches from his legs and spine, one of the drawbacks of being tall and crammed into a budget airline seat for almost four hours. It was something that resembled more of a livestock trailer to him, and was a far cry from the early pioneer's future visions of transatlantic aviation and global travel. The RAF C-17 transports Knox once travelled in may not have been luxurious, but Christ, at least there was plenty of leg room.

Knox walked out of the glass fronted building and looked up to the grey-filled skies above him. It was a vast difference from the blue, cloudless skies of southern Spain he had recently been used to. He headed directly to the Taxi rank, opened the boot of the parked car at the front of the queue, and threw in his military-green duffle bag. Before the driver had time to get out, Knox had shut the boot, opened the front passenger door, and sat down.

"Where to?" said a flustered driver in a thick Somerset accent.

"Fowlers," Knox simply replied, to which the driver looked confused.

"Where's that, mate? I don't know of any Fowlers," the driver questioned. Knox looked over with a raised eyebrow.

"Twelve Bath Road, big Triumph bike dealer. Give me a prod when we get there, okay, pal?" Knox said, and with that he leaned his seat back and made himself comfy as he closed his eyes.

Knox wanted to catch up on some shut eye because he could never sleep on a flight, and taxi chitchat about the weather, where he had been, Bristol City or Town football club, was not something he was in the mood to indulge in.

Twenty-five minutes later, they pulled up outside the large, impressive dealership located in the centre of Bristol itself. Knox was out like a light as soon as the taxi pulled away from the airport, and the driver was hesitant about waking him. The driver opted to get out of the car instead, slamming the door before walking around to retrieve the luggage from the boot. The plan worked because Knox woke from his deep sleep.

Quick to orientate himself, Knox got out of the vehicle, taking hold of his bag from the attentive driver who was holding it out for him.

Slipping the driver his fare, plus fifty on top for good measure, Knox followed it up by saying, "You didn't drop me here if anyone ever comes asking. Are we clear, Brian?" Knox narrowed his gaze, his features set firm, making sure the driver knew that he wasn't to be messed with.

The driver looked shocked at hearing his name, but also impressed. Knox had simply taken notice of the driver's taxi ID and registration… obvious, but it still took the driver off guard.

"Er… yeah, sure thing… no problem. Hey if you need any more lifts, here's my card. Ring me anytime on or off the clock," Brian said as he held out his card, obviously not put off by Knox's subtle threat.

Knox took the card and smiled, leaving Brian with a gentle head tilt as he slung his bag over his shoulder and walked off towards the stylish dealership.

That classic motorcycle shop smell hit Knox as soon as he entered the building. Rubber, leather, oil and oddly, but in this dealership, wood. The whole showroom floor was fitted with solid golden oak flooring, with large, dark, squared areas where groups of motorcycles were tastefully positioned. Knox did not have time to look around and admire the machines, he knew what he wanted.

"Hello, Sir, if you need anything, please let me…." The voice came from a young, wet-behind-the-ears salesman who spoke out as Knox swiftly strolled past.

The lad was on his knees polishing a beautiful, deep-red Ducati 959 Panigale. To Knox's eye, one well-versed in all things motorcycle, it looked as though the Ducati was a high-level trade in. It probably belonged to some poor bastard whose aches and pains were too much for the aggressive riding position. Knox took one short look at the lad, sized him up in a second, then carried on his way, but not before giving the young salesman a knowing nod.

An older, more seasoned salesman was sitting, lording it up at a desk, most likely responsible for the young lad being on his knees polishing. A man who didn't do the work, wasn't a man worth his salt, in Knox's opinion.

"Good morning, Sir, my name's Brad, I am the head salesman here at Fowlers."

Knox was faced with the bright white teeth and mahogany skin tone of the over-tanned salesman. Obviously seeing that Knox was a man who knew what he wanted, he stood and made his way towards him with an extended hand. Knox held back his frustration of having his path blocked and shook the man's hand. After all, there was no reason to be rude… *yet.* He then quickly took note of Brad's overly bling Rolex watch and large sovereign ring.

"Hell of a grip you have there… please come take a seat and we can discuss what it is you are looking for," Brad said, trying to hide a wince as his right hand throbbed under the grip of Knox's shake.

"Can I get you a tea or coffee?" asked Brad as he pulled out a seat for Knox, before planting his own arse down behind his desk.

"A coffee would be good, but I am in a hurry and…" Knox began his reply, but did not get the chance to finish. Brad very enthusiastically interrupted him, and it was obvious he was more focused on clearing his sales figures from his desk before looking up with a fake smile.

"Coffee, did you say? Perfect. Hey, Alex, bring me two coffees!" Brad annoyingly shouted over to the young salesman, who was still polishing the Ducati.

"So, mister…?" Brad asked, waiting as Knox sat back in the chair and looked him over before turning his eye to the messy desk in front of him.

"Knox, the name's Knox," he replied in a dry, unimpressed tone. The longer Knox sat at the desk, the more his dislike of the salesman grew.

"Two coffees, I didn't know if you wanted milk, cream, or sugar so I brought everything over," a quiet voice said over Knox's shoulder. The salesman, Alex, tried to put a paper cup down in front of Knox but struggled to find a clear space.

"Just put it down, Alex, and stop dawdling," barked Brad, to which Knox stood up having seen enough of this arsehole.

"Alex, is it?" Knox said as he took the coffee from the young lad and took a sip, raising an eyebrow in acknowledgement that it didn't taste half bad.

"Yes…" Alex replied with a slightly confused expression.

"Tell me, Alex, how are your sales for this month, pal?" Knox asked, placing an arm around Alex's shoulder and began to walk him in the direction Knox originally was heading in.

"Er… not great, to be honest," replied the young lad.

"Well, I have a feeling they are about to go up. So let me tell you what I want…" Knox said before he reeled off a list of everything he wanted, the top of that list being a Triumph Tiger 1200 all-terrain adventure.

Riding at speed alongside hedgerow upon hedgerow, on roads that cut through the foothills of east Wales, Knox was struck by the rich greenness of the place. The landscape was managed, orderly, a beautiful countryside sculpted by countless generations of farmers and seemingly untouched by advertising and the modern world. Dotted here and there were small signs of civilisation, with overgrown stone walls leading to sleepy villages connected by the narrow lanes. Weathered stone and brick dwellings seemed as fitting to the environment as the livestock in the surrounding fields.

Knox's attention was momentarily distracted from behind the windshield of the top-spec Triumph thanks to his phone vibrating in his jacket. With a fist full of brake, he locked up the wheels as traction was lost on the loose, gravely, road's edge.

Pulling up in front of a roadside country pub, Knox removed his gloves, and took out his phone, only to be greeted by eleven missed calls. Each number was different, but Knox knew by the arrangement of key numbers that it was T.I.7.

"What do they want?" muttered Knox, looking up to the sky in a form of acceptance that they would be tracking his phone... a phone he foolishly believed T.I.7 knew nothing about.

"Rose girl, you are a devil," said Knox as he took the phone to bits and discarded the sim.

A quick glance at his watch focused his mind and, within moments, his gloves were back on, he was in first gear, and rapidly accelerating. Knox had been forced to take the longer, more scenic route, away from the possibility of prying eyes on the road networks, CCTV, and AMPR. He still had forty-five minutes of riding left until he reached his destination. He needed to get their before local shops closed, one store in particular.

4:35pm, one-point-five miles over the Welsh-England boarder on a clear open stretch of perfectly straight road. Knox spotted the sign, 'Welcome to Bishop's Castle, please drive carefully' and a large smirk crossed his face. Dropping a gear and holding the motorcycle's engine at just the right revs, Knox feathered the clutch, then popped the front wheel up into a controlled wheelie at speed past the sign.

Some guys never grew up, their toys just got bigger, Knox thought with a grin.

He took in the mighty roar of the exhaust note as the engine dropped in revs, the smile on his face made his cheeks ache.

Heading into the centre of the small southwest Shropshire market town, Knox parked up in front of a black and white

Tudor building. The ground floor had been converted into an art gallery. Entering the bright, clean, airy space, Knox in his crisp new black bike jacket, dark jeans, and shit kicker boots, couldn't have contrasted any more if he tried.

"Good afternoon, I am afraid we will be closing soon," said a stern, well-spoken female voice that travelled from somewhere at the back of the gallery.

"That's okay, lass, I don't plan to be here long, I am looking to settle an account," said Knox with a slight grin on his face.

"Be right with you, Sir," she called through, followed by a quickening tempo of her 4-inch heels as she made her way across the iron hard, uneven oak timber floor.

"Hillary Meyer, Manager of this gallery, pleasure to meet you and you are?" asked the plum-voiced woman with a striking full face of war paint and a smart, expensive pinstripe suit. Meyer was unable to hide her look of disapproval of Knox and his rough and ready attire, let alone the nerve to be dressed this way in her gallery.

"Ethan Connelly…" Knox replied, holding out his hand as he gave her the fake name, one she would know well.

Meyer's expression changed to fake welcoming and attentiveness. Ethan Connelly known only to her over phone calls and emails, but nevertheless, her biggest customer by a long mile.

"Mr Connelly… so nice you have come to visit." Meyer took Knox's hand before she rushed over to the street-front gallery door, locking it and turning the window sign to closed.

"So we are not disturbed and we can talk in private. What brings you to the gallery, Mr Connelly? If you had of called in advance I could have made arrangements," Meyer said, ramping up her charm qualities to the max. "Please come this way. Would you like a drink? Hot, soft, or maybe a little something more indulgent, perhaps?" As Meyer spoke, she ran her hand over Knox's shoulder and motioned for him to follow her to a perfectly unmarked white designer sofa.

Meyer's general demeanour pissed him off, she was irritating the hell out of him, but he was there to gain sensitive information. He wasn't about to lay into the target about her shitty attitude because she had information he wanted, so he played along.

Knox unzipped his jacket, and Meyer couldn't help but appreciate his muscular physique as it was revealed when slipping the leather from his shoulders. His torso was covered in a black, fitted, long-sleeve T-shirt that did little to hide the fact that he worked out.

"Please let me take that for you..." Meyer offered, almost falling over herself to take Knox's jacket from him. Then once in her hands, she took it into the back room of the gallery, heaven forbid that the jacket be left to make the gallery look untidy.

Returning from the back-room, Meyer had also removed her suit jacket and let her hair down. She sauntered towards him with her hips sashaying, showing her curves in a fitted white shirt tucked in tightly to a pencil skirt. She held two glass flutes and a chilled bottle of bubbly in her hand too, and Knox resisted the urge to roll his eyes.

"Champagne? Would you mind doing the honours, Mr..." Meyer handed the bottle to Knox, who interrupted her before she could finish saying his alias's name.

"Call me Ethan, Mr Connelly sounds so formal, and we don't want to be formal now, do we, Hilary?" Knox said with a smile, turning on the charm as he made short work of opening the bottle. The pop of the cork made Hilary jump and she giggled. The sound grated on him, but he kept up the charade anyway. He was a professional, after all. Knox served her the champagne first, making sure she had a larger glass full of liquid than himself.

"Forgive me, Ethan, but you said you wanted to settle your account? I am sure my records state you are fully up to date," Meyer said, before clinking her glass with Knox's and taking a sip.

"Yes, that's true, but this is more about a debt of respect," Knox said, then he took the smallest of sips, but he gave the impression of drinking more by holding the glass to his lips for just a little longer.

"Now I am intrigued, Ethan, please do explain," Meyer said in an amorous tone as her wet, red lips developed into a large smile.

"Well, as you know I have taken ownership of some fantastic pieces from one particular artist, and I have purchased all of them through you," Knox said, topping up Meyer's glass.

"Yes, I must say you are clearly her biggest follower. You have almost all of her work," Meyer said, trying to mask her personal views of the art in question, because let's just say that the subject matter wasn't to everyone's taste.

"Almost?" Knox said as he sat up a little. Inside, he was cursing the idea that he had missed a few of Dani's paintings and that they had been sold to someone else.

"Yes, there were two I had in the gallery which I was yet to advertise, when the artist herself came in and requested them back," Meyer replied with a tone of indifference, flicking her hair as she tried to make eye contact.

It was obvious to Knox that she only wanted to talk about herself, not the artist in question. Something proven to Knox when she placed a casual light hand on his knee before speaking.

"You know, if you like the subject matter of this artist, I

have a few other artists on my books that I think you would…." Knox was quick to interrupt her, his main focus being on Dani.

"They came in and collected the paintings themselves?" Knox questioned before catching himself in his eagerness. He was here to press for information, but he knew he wouldn't get it without first playing the part. Which is why the moment he saw Meyer's sour expression, he leaned in a little and softly began to run his hand over hers, looking back at her with a smile.

"I can't see why I wouldn't be interested in anything else you had to show me… here's to art, *in all its forms,*" Knox said, lying through his teeth because he had no interest in any other artists work, nor did he have any interest in the woman he was forcing himself to flirt with.

Meyer caught the inuendo that had been implied, her wide eyes and easy grin confirming to him that she was interested in more than just how big his wallet was.

"Well, Ethan, I will hold you to that. So how can I help with your 'debt of respect'?" she asked, her cheeks slightly flush after he continued to top up her drink.

"It is more of a self-inflicted obligation. You said the artist came in to collect her work. Would that have been an easy task for them?" Knox asked, again pretending to sip his own drink and prompting her to do the same.

"Ethan, where are you going with this? And are you trying to get me drunk?" Meyer asked with another giggle.

Knox leaned in closer and lowered his voice, locking eyes with her.

"Forgive me, I can't help but drag out the conversation when it's with someone so lovely, and would it be such a terrible thing for us to get a little drunk and relax?" he said, making a point of looking at Meyer's naked ring finger before continuing. "Is there a good reason not to enjoy ourselves?" He gave her what he hoped was his most devastating smile, and one full of sexual promise that he would never give her.

"No… I don't think there is," Meyer said with a small swallow and a nervous bite of her lip.

"What I would like is an address, so that I can send flowers and a card. You can give that to me, can't you? Sure, it's a small break of trust, but I am positive they wouldn't mind. I mean, who doesn't enjoy flowers, right? And you would have my gratitude." Knox laced his words with almost a velvet-like warmth that Meyer mentally wrapped herself up in.

She hung on every word Knox spoke as he placed a large, warm hand on her leg.

"I… I don't know…"

Her lack of immediate action to comply with his request was frustrating, but Knox turned it up a notch, taking her glass and placing it down on the coffee table in front of them. Then with utter confidence, he leaned in closer and started kissing her neck, making her draw in a quick breath.

"Oh, but I think you do… besides, it would just be between the two of us… *our little secret…*" he said, whispering these final three words just below her ear.

As much as the idea disgusted him, Knox knew that when she turned her head, he wouldn't be able to get what he wanted without sealing the deal. She made it clear she wanted him to kiss her. So, with his end game in mind, Knox did the deed, stopping far quicker than he usually would with someone he actually wanted to kiss. But he needed to leave her wanting more and took the time to remind her,

"So that address…"

Meyer released a breathy sigh, still in the midst of arousal and clearly not thinking of client confidentiality. A little unsteady in her feet, she stood before composing herself and she walked over to her desk. After flicking through an address book, she stopped on a page and wrote an address down on a post-it note. Knowing he had gotten what he came for, Knox stood up to meet her halfway and took the address from her before she could react. Her look of surprise that he was leaving almost made him feel bad.

"I could get in trouble for giving you this, you can't ever say you got it from me. I wouldn't want to lose her as a client," Meyer said, worry causing her brows to furrow a little.

Knox looked down at the note and put it swiftly into his pocket.

Simply put, the job was done. It was time to get out of there.

Knox stepped in closer and looked down at Meyer. The grin she gave him was full of hope and expectance, and because he wanted to fuck with her, Knox began to lean his head down. Then just as she closed her eyes and held her breath, he asked,

"Is my jacket back here?" He placed his hands-on Meyer's upper arms, holding her so she couldn't move in any closer.

Her eyes snapped open, and her flustered face was worthy of a picture. Without waiting for Meyer to regain her senses, Knox spotted the jacket and retrieved it himself.

"Thank you, Hilary, but I should go, the time has flown by. The drink was lovely," Knox said as he walked away from her dazed state, heading towards the door and quickly unlocking it.

"Wait! You're… you're leaving? But we haven't finished our drink and…" Meyer stammered, clearly puzzled at how quickly this had taken a turn.

"Yes, well, things to do, lass, and people to see. I can't drink anymore, I am riding. Thanks again!" Knox said, holding up the key fob to his bike and half waved as he was almost fully out the door by the time he finished speaking.

Meyer rushed over and she opened the door in time to

watch Knox throw his jacket on and fire up the mean straight-three twelve valve 1200cc engine.

"Call me, Ethan…" Meyer mouthed the words.

Pulling down his helmet, Knox gave Meyer a wink as he began to pull off with speed.

The fitted satnav system on the Triumph told him that the address he had also committed to memory was only a few miles away. With a pleased grin, Knox opened up the throttle, a mere eleven minutes from his destination, leaving the small market town in the same spirited manner in which he arrived.

Slowing to a snail's pace, Knox reached the area he had been guided to, and right on cue he saw a sign. 'Heron's Pool Mill' was carved into a slab of aged, weathered wood. It looked as old as the Shropshire sandstone walled entrance it was fixed to.

This was a place Knox thought he would never visit. Dani's home. She had always been so secretive and had made her residence very hard to find.

Due to the manner in which they parted ways, Knox felt a twinge of nervousness. It was a feeling that grew as he steered his motorcycle into the entrance and up the pine-needle covered driveway. His path was suddenly illuminated as the automatic halogen headlights switched on under the canopy of trees that momentarily blocked the sky.

A large clearing opened up in front of him as he passed the edge of the woodland and reached the old mill. It was clear to see the mill had been lovingly renovated and tastefully modernised. The thick, square, oak timbers used in the construction of the storm porch had weathered to a beautiful grey that sat well against the stone.

Knox parked in front of the main front door, dismounted, and retrieved his weapon from where it had been stored in his pannier. He decided against the holster it was stowed in and instead tucked it into the back of his jeans, being ready for anything. He then made his way to the property, feeling better now he was armed, something he hadn't wanted to do in the gallery. But then carrying a gun openly around in England was never a good idea. They weren't a regular occurrence or even legal for civilians, and he hadn't wanted to chance Meyer freaking out. After all, nothing spoiled the appearance of a rich art collector like the sight of a gun.

As Knox approached the door, he couldn't help but wonder how Dani would greet him. Would she send him packing? Would he at least get a chance to explain?

Well, there was only one way to find out…

FOUR
TAKE DOWN

Knox took a sideways step back after seeing that the Yale lock had been left on the catch. It instantly put him on edge, especially when the door opened an inch under the force of his knock. Instinct took over and he immediately reached for his weapon, thankful of his T.I.7 security clearance allowing him through the airport with no problems.

Holding his SIG handgun up close and looking directly down the barrel, he slowly pushed the door open with his foot, his adrenaline building with every movement. He leaned back as much as he could, taking cover from the hinged side of the door.

The long, dark, chunky slate floor running the length of the hallway was clear, no lights were on, and the only sound to be heard was Knox's own breathing. In moments like these, he had become accustomed to fighting his paranoia, knowing that his breathing wasn't loud enough that whoever else maybe in the building could hear it too. What Knox wasn't used to, was the fearful thoughts of Dani running through his mind. Was she alright? Had she been captured? Was he going to find her hurt inside or worse yet… *dead?*

Knox closed his eyes and shook his head. The feeling he had when first walking into the hotel room not so long ago in Spain, seeing Dani sleeping, came back full force to the front of his mind. He pushed the unease down and regained his focus.

Slowly inching his way forward, Knox scanned the hallway and moved to the side, pushing the door closed behind him. Walking alongside the half wood-panelled wall, Knox noticed the stench of stale air. No one had been there for a few weeks at least.

This was soon proven as he entered the open living-kitchen area. A large vase of withered lilies well past their best sat in stagnant water, dead stalks and dried up petals scattered around the base. The house was otherwise like walking onto a staged room for a glossy Country Living magazine shoot. It was stylish but homely, pristinely decorated in a farmhouse style. Dani had an artistic eye that was clear for Knox to see, and not just for the erotic.

He swept the house from top to bottom, finding it clear.
No Dani.

She had not been there recently and there were no signs of anything suspicious or even foul play. Knox had a deep gut feeling of worry. Where was Dani? Why hadn't she returned home from Spain? Could Mac have gone back on his warning and gotten to her after she had landed? All the questions quickly assaulted his mind one after the other.

The still quiet was broken when, outside the building Knox could hear the hum of a car's engine and the sound of tyres rolling on gravel. The vehicle came to a halt and the crunching stopped. However, it hadn't pulled up directly outside the house, making him wonder if the sight of his bike parked there was the reason.

He quickly tried to estimate its distance. It wasn't easy, but he put it at about twenty metres away from the house. He could feel his heart pumping hard in his chest as he strained to hear what was going on outside. The faintest click of a car door opening. Knox moved so his back was to the wall in a shadowed corner, giving him a view of the front door but also of the large French doors off the kitchen, leading to the patio. All entry ways were covered.

Forty-five seconds passed before a fleeting shadow crossed the blind obscured window. Twenty metres, forty-five seconds. It didn't add up. Nobody walked that slowly. Which meant whoever was out there was currently circling the building. They were checking for exits or in this case, entrances.

Knox's eyes were darting around the room, looking for something, anything he could use as a distraction. Sitting on a rustic wooden shelving unit to the left of him, a brown box with television remotes stood vertically inside the slots. Picking up the main remote, Knox took cover and waited for something to happen.

Ten more seconds passed, twenty, forty, then a creek made Knox hold his breath.

The noise of the front door eventually being pushed open echoed through the silence, sudden and sharp. The evening light flooded into the room like orange paint had been spilt around the shadow of a single figure at the front door. Knox could only assume it was from the same guy he'd seen circling the house. He then noted from the reflection cast on a glass ornament sitting on the shelf, that the figure was dressed all in black. A hunter's jacket, a cap, and a suppressed handgun. Knox couldn't see what type, but it was held at eye-level. One hand gripped the handle and caressed the trigger, the other surrounded it and kept it steady. This guy was a pro. Someone had turned up to get Dani.

Knox's gut wrenched at the thought of it.

Another second later, Knox realised something was wrong. *Just one guy?* Mac would have sent a four-man unit at the very least, unless he was doing the job himself. Was it Mac? Knox's eyes darted around the room as these thoughts ran through his mind. Time felt like it had slowed down as the dark figure walked into the living room area. The figure took in the space as they panned side to side, and Knox switched the television on to distract them, pressing down on the volume key and turning it up full whack.

The figure was startled by the flash of light and blaring sound, making the intruder turn before letting off two rounds in the screen's direction. The noise of the rounds exiting the gunman's weapon was like a fist thumping quickly on solid wood, followed by shattering glass and the television audio decay. Knox jumped from his cover, taking his moment with no hesitation.

Shoulder charging the gunman down to the floor, Knox clambered to the man's gun hand, grabbing his wrist, and keeping the weapon angled away. Knox swung his other hand up and just as he was about to bring the handle of his pistol down on the jaw of his opponent, he paused.

"Knox! It's me, Harris. Stand down for fuck's sake, stand down!" called out the harassed Major.

"Harris? Sir… what are you…?" Knox said as he leaned back and released Harris from his grip.

"Doing here? Well, if you let me get up, I will tell you," Harris replied, annoyed and brushing himself down after Knox offered him a hand.

"Christ, Knox, you don't hold back, do you? Last time I was hit like that was at the annual officer's vs squaddie rugby-sevens match at base."

"Ah come on, Major, it wasn't that hard. I'm sure your

granny hits harder." Knox half chuckled as he took the piss and brushed his coat down. Harris cut Knox a look that made him struggle not to laugh.

"I am here for Dani, and you. Clearly, I have found you, but you would have known all this if you would have answered your bloody phone!" the Major complained.

"About that… I…" Knox tried to explain but was cut off.

"Save it, Knox, we know all about it. But what you don't know is about Dani," Harris said, getting straight to the point like he knew Knox would appreciate.

"Dani? What about Dani?! Why are you here for her? What do you know? Tell me!" Knox said, almost in panic as he grabbed Harris.

Just as his friend was about to speak, they both turned their heads in the direction of the hallway and the front door. A metallic pitter-patter made its way across the floor as a cylindrical object bounced erratically over the slate tiles.

"Grenade!" yelled Knox, charging to meet it after pushing Harris back over the furniture for cover.

With a well-timed kick, Knox made just enough contact to deflect the cylinder casing off towards the kitchen. This was before flinging himself down, covering his ears and shutting his eyes tightly.

A disorientating flash of light followed by an explosion filled the room, hitting them like a boot to the chest. Knox knew the feeling and smell well from his days of training in Hereford. There was no fire or debris, being that it was a flash grenade. One designed to temporarily disorientate an enemy's senses.

In the smoke haze, Knox rolled onto his back and aimed in the direction of the hallway. A silhouette moved through the smoke and Knox, without mercy, fired off two rounds. The first bullet missed but the second entered the skull of the target and blood splattered up the hallway. At this close range it knocked the man back a few metres, before he tumbled to the ground.

"Harris! Cover right!" Knox called out as he got up and pressed his back against the wall closest to the hallway entrance.

The Major made his way to the kitchen as a second gunman came through the front door. He took two steps into the room and aimed his weapon at Harris.

"Harris, take cover!" Knox yelled as he put his gun to the back of the intruder's head and fired, and at that moment two more masked men smashed through the French doors into the kitchen.

Harris charged, grabbing them both after he launched himself into the air. The momentum meant that he took the two of them back out the shattered door frame and landed hard on the patio slabs. Three shots sounded, but with a slight muffling.

"Harris!" Knox shouted, making sure there was no more hostiles before he ran over to the three, still and lifeless, bodies on the ground.

Harris lay on top of one of the masked gunmen with the other to his side. Just as Knox was about to call out to his friend again, there was movement in the form of the Major slowly lifting himself up. This was before then rolling off to the side, revealing the catastrophic chest wound to the man he was lying on. Another dark red streak trickled down the path from a second bullet wound coming from the masked man's head.

"Harris, are you okay?" questioned Knox, looking around as a stillness began to fall on the area.

"Help me up, Captain."

"This is becoming a habit," Knox commented, making Harris groan.

"I'm getting too bloody old for this crap," he replied, once more taking Knox's offered hand with a look that silently spoke about how lucky they were to be alive.

"These are Mac's men," Knox said as he checked over one of the goons, his eye catching on the tattooed symbol on the dead man's neck. He couldn't place it, but it seemed familiar to Knox.

It was a dagger passing through a black sun, which was a circle with angular sun rays. Harris noticed it on the second man when checking him over, prompting him to pull out his phone and take a photo.

"I will get Rose to run this," said Harris, immediately sending the picture via an encrypted message.

"This is why you're here, isn't it?" asked Knox, turning to the Major and looking him square in the eye.

"Yes… so, come on, let's get out of here before these guys are missed," replied a jaded Harris as he walked back into the house.

"I am not going anywhere until you tell me where Dani is," said Knox, his tone becoming frustrated as he stood his ground.

"All in good time, Captain. I don't know about you, but I need a pint. You coming? I'm buying."

FIVE

LOCKUP

THE ANVIL INN, THIRTY OR SO MINUTES
LATER

I t was almost fully dark overhead, the Shropshire sky was indigo at the horizon, bordered by lights scattered over the hill sides. Harris's black T.I.7 Land Rover stood out against the stony gravel car park of the pub, the warm yellow streetlights giving the vehicle a menacing look.

Harris and Knox were a mere ten or so miles from Dani's house, and to Knox's mind's eye, things weren't looking good. Where was she, and was she safe? He needed answers… fast.

The pub was like any other, not really offering them a lot of privacy, but it was what they both needed to calm their adrenaline from the gun fight at Dani's house. Harris placed a pint glass down in front of Knox before pulling a stool in closer to the well-worn, aged table. Knox picked up the glass of dark amber ale for closer inspection before taking a large sip.

"It's Hobsons, Twisted Spire, I believe," said Harris as he took note of Knox's approving look before he, too, took a good, thirst-quenching sup.

"Yeah, lovely, now cut to it, Harris. What the fuck is going on? *Did you know Mac was sending that team?"* Knox at first shouted out before dropping his tone and volume down to an aggressive whisper.

This was after a look from Harris, who had started to notice that Knox was drawing attention from the local punters and bar maid. The only thing that was stopping Knox from flying off the handle, was the assumption that T.I.7 and whoever was responsible for the kill team had no idea where Dani was. If they did, then they wouldn't have been at her house looking for her like he had.

"Rein it in, Captain," Harris replied with a stern look.

Knox knew he was letting his emotions get the better of him. Dani affected Knox in a way he wasn't used to, let alone knew how to handle.

"We have had some intel, and the Brig sent me to find Dani," Harris admitted, after waiting for Knox to compose himself.

Knox nodded for the Major to go on.

"I don't know what that intel is, but it involves Dani, so that's why I am here. Tracking down her house was the only lead we had, and by the looks of it, the only lead you had too," Harris said sipping at his drink.

Knox wasn't sure whether to trust this information or not. It wasn't that he thought Harris was lying, but he did question where they had gotten her address from. Which was why he went on to question,

"Did you pay for this intel? Where did it come from?"

Harris smirked at this before answering.

"No, it came from a few sources in fragments. But it's believed to be good, otherwise I wouldn't have been there. Lucky for you, I was."

Knox couldn't argue with that as four on one would have been poor odds.

"You will need to be briefed by the Brig if you want to

know more because I don't have that info. Of course, Carter was going to send you, but we couldn't get hold of you." Harris gave Knox a disapproving look as he spoke.

"So, he survived then?" Knox asked, taking another sip.

"He did, and he's still dishing out orders from his hospital bed."

Knox laughed at that. "I'll be sure to send a fruit basket," Knox commented dryly.

"Or you could just fuck the fruit and get your arse back to work," Harris offered, making Knox sigh.

"Yeah, well after the shitstorm at the nest, I needed to get out and lay low. How is the Brig?" Knox asked.

"You know Carter, death wouldn't stop him turning up for work, so three bullet holes have no chance. As for work, if you're not coming in, I have to ask, what's your next move here, Knox?" Harris mocked.

"I have to find Dani, but honestly, I am out of ideas," Knox replied as he took a drink. Because, in reality, he didn't have the time nor the heart to worry too much about the Brig, he was old enough and ugly enough to look after himself. Now Dani, that was another matter.

"You two are close, right? I mean, you have been working together for some time? Well, that's what I have been led to believe," Harris said as probed Knox.

"Yeah, but we have both kept our distance and stayed professional," Knox said. But couldn't help the glint in his eye because he knew full well his imagination had pushed it far from professional. Damn, but the word obsession was closer to the mark.

"Did you know her address?" Harris asked, once again pushing Knox and trying to learn the full extent of his knowledge on Dani.

"Not exactly, no. Let's just say that I had an angle and it

played out. How did *you* get her address? You said you had a lead which helped you track where it was?" Knox said, his tone a little cagey.

"I followed you, Captain. What you need to ask yourself is if you had an angle on Dani, does that mean she would have an angle on you?" Harris asked, planting the seed and giving Knox food for thought. Something Harris continued to do when he leaned towards Knox before continuing. "Is there something about you that's not on file, something that she could use?"

Knox felt his jaw harden at this before gritting out, "What are you getting at, Harris? There is nothing. And how the hell did you follow me?" he asked, looking Harris in the eye, doing so with his best poker face. He knew full well there was something, but he would be damned if he was going to give it up to the Major or anyone else.

"Dani needs you to find her, how you do that is down to you, Captain. We need to get her safe, T.I.7 is now at a dead end," Harris replied before finishing off his pint, standing up, and giving Knox a knowing look. A look that said, 'I know you are keeping shit to yourself'.

Harris may have been old, but he wasn't stupid. He knew what former SAS types were like. Most of which suffered with high paranoia that led them to have very private and secretive lives. Harris could understand the reasons for it, with the types of missions and deployments they were assigned to do, and the type of enemies they made, most of which they didn't even know about.

"I have to head back to HQ. I will inform the Brig you are on the job and doing everything you can to track down Dani," Harris said with a nod as he began to turn away.

"Give my best to Rose, Major," Knox said with a wink, and Harris let a rare smile slip over his lips for a split second. Knox had made his point with just the mention of the cute tech, and it was clear what Dani was to Knox… Rose was to the Major.

"As always, it's been a pleasure. Find Dani and check in ASAP, Captain. Oh, and how did I follow you? Your Sat Nav," Harris replied with a smirk before walking away, saying thank you to the bar staff as he left.

Knox sat staring at his half pint of ale left, he thought about his next course of action and how he was going to track down a woman that was a master of not wanting to be found. At the very minimum, her skill-set meant she could set herself up with a new identity, bank account, driving licence, passport… the whole works. Meaning she could be on a plane, heading to a distant country in the time it would take most people to fill out a tax form.

The question Harris had left him with plagued on his mind too. Could the implication be right? Could Dani know more about him than he thought she could?

Knox racked his brain. He was sure that he had been watertight with his private affairs. She couldn't know about his biggest secret, could she? No, it would be impossible for her to find out. There wasn't a single thing linking him to it. Or was there? Knox downed his drink, he had to get on the road because this line of thinking was going to send him crazy.

Standing up and heading out of the public house, Knox made his way to his bike. The only way to stop the thoughts going around his head was to go and see for himself. But first, he needed to go to his lockup and for once, not to look at his collection of paintings by Dani. No, that would just be a bonus.

The lockup held much more than paintings, and Knox needed to pick up some kit and ditch the Bike. He may have only just purchased the machine, but there was a chance that he could be tracked by it by someone else. T.I.7 had already been able to, it would seem.

The last thing Knox needed was to find Dani, only to then lead the next kill team straight to her. Which meant that he needed a clean ride and he needed it ASAP. So, after pulling the antenna cable off the bike's sat nav, he fired the Triumph into life, knocking his foot down on the left peg and putting the Tiger into first gear. Knox then sped off out of the carpark and hit the road, back to being focused, ready, and determined. He had the smallest possible chance of tracking Dani down but it's all he had, and he was jumping on it with no time to waste.

HOCKLEY, OUTSKIRTS OF BIRMINGHAM CITY CENTRE

The burbling note exiting the Triumph's exhaust reverberated around Knox as he rode, passing arch after arch of Victorian brick railway line. All had been utilised and converted into businesses such as mechanics, fabricators, carpenters, even coffee shops and delis. Turning right, he rode beneath one of the arches that had been left open to allow a road to flow through. Knox blipped his throttle as he went under the tunnel, it was for no reason other than to enjoy the sound. He had enjoyed the Tiger, it had served him well in the brief time he had ridden it. He would have felt a slight twinge of sadness to be leaving it behind, if it wasn't for the fact he knew what fun awaited him.

On the other side of the tunnel to the left, set back a little off the road, was a set of formidable, tall metal gates, with a keycode pad in the centre. Knox pulled up as close as possible before dismounting and walking over to the lock. Then before entering the code, he looked up at the CCTV camera that was watching over the entrance, making sure to cover the code he used with his free hand. This habit also extended to turning his head and having a good look around to make sure no one was watching.

When all was clear, Knox hit the enter key and the gates opened on a motorised sliding system. It was a communal entrance for only a handful of people because this wasn't a big brand self-storage kind of set up. It was more lowkey. Being that it was run by a former 22nd man who understood first-hand the needs of his clients.

Pushing his Triumph through and clear of the gate's path, Knox waited for them to automatically close behind him, not moving until they had fully shut to be sure no one followed him in. On arriving outside lockup number zero-eight, under the bright artificial light, Knox pushed out the kick stand on the Tiger with his foot and set the bike on it. Taking off his helmet and gloves, he walked over to the single door which was set into a much larger door. These units had the easy single door access or the option to open a much larger door for storing large possessions such as furniture and vehicles.

Dialling in the correct combination on the hefty padlock, an echoing clunk and clang rang out as Knox took it off and pulled across the locking mechanism. There was a silence and stillness about the place. Every sound felt amplified, the hustle and bustle sounds of Hockley outside was deadened by the deep, thick brick walls. The silence was only broken by Knox's breathing and the high-pitch creek of the large metal-enforced hinges as he swung the hefty door open.

Knox flipped the light switches on, and the fluorescent tubes flickered as the starters kicked in and brought them to almost eye hurting radiance. The unit was around eighty feet deep, and just over two car widths with space between. Everything was covered in sheets, his possessions like motionless ghosts just waiting for his return.

Knox scanned the space then turned to walk back out. He

threw the keys to the Triumph only a few inches back behind him onto a large wooden crate, but as he started to walk back outside, he stopped dead in his tracks. The crate also had a sheet on it as usual, but something wasn't right. The sound he heard as the keys landed was not what he was expecting. Instead of a thud, they dropped inside, pulling the sheet inside with them.

Knox walked over to the large crate and ripped the sheet away. Frowning down at it the moment he saw the lid was missing. His eyes scanned around for it, finding the lid set behind the crate on its side. Knox thought for a second… did he really leave the lid off? He shook his head because that wouldn't be like him. He looked inside and counted the stacked bubble-wrapped packages. Eleven were perfectly intact, but the twelfth was not.

It had been opened.

Knox carefully lifted the open package and put it down on the crate, removing the bubble wrap that had only been placed on top. Then he looked over the oil painting with a keen eye. It was dark, moody, and sexy as sin. The portrait was of a woman blindfolded, bound in scarlet rope, naked in her bondage of intricate Shibari knots. Provocatively positioned, with a male hand running a thumb over her bright red lips. For a moment, Knox found himself lost in his thoughts of acting out this particular scene with Dani.

After all… *he was damn good with rope.*

Knox snapped out of his gaze as a heat rose from deep with in him. Arousal soon turned to anger. Who the fuck had opened this and who had been inside his sacred place?

Placing the painting down carefully, Knox looked around for any other signs that someone had been in the lockup. He began walking towards the rear of the unit, running his hand over the sheet that covered a vehicle. It may have been covered but its low stance and sleek line screamed high performance sports car. He paused for a second before pulling on the door handle. The door was locked, so he continued walking, his eyes darting to the sides as he moved, trying to take in as much as possible. He was looking for the slightest clue. He quickly made his way to the most important item in the lockup, with a lump in his throat at the thought of it being missing. He lifted a sheet that was draped over an antique Welsh dresser.

Knox knelt and opened the bottom cupboard, pulling out a black steel tactical security case. A smile crossed his face at it still being there. Placing his thumbs on the print reader, two red lights turned to green and audible clicks fired off. Knox opened the case, and inside was an array of passports, two or three for all the major countries. Driving licences to match each document, along with around two hundred grand in different currencies all divided up into clear sealed bags. Contact lenses, glasses, and a field medical kit all sat under a Browning High-Power handgun and two magazine clips unloaded with a box of 9mm ammo.

Knox closed his eyes for a second as he let out a sigh of relief, the case was still where he had left it. And just as he opened his eyes, he felt a hand touch his shoulder.

"Lucas…"

Knox jumped and instinctively gripped the hand, pulling it into a lock as he spun around and dragged the person down to the floor as he rolled onto them. A scream and a yelp followed, before a stream of obscenities.

"Lucas… for fuck's sake! Fuck, that hurts, you're going to break my wrist! Let go!" screamed a woman's voice.

Knox instantly let go at the recognition and realisation of whose voice it was. He lifted himself from the pinning position on top of her just as her lush scent filled his nostrils, triggering his memories of a hotel room. The light that his body was blocking now flooded down onto the woman as he stood up.

A single name and the only one that mattered escaped his lips on a whisper…

"Dani."

SIX

CONFESSIONS

Knox held out his hand to help Dani up from the cold, painted concrete floor and she reluctantly took it. Once on her feet, Dani cast a rather funny figure, a fact that made it difficult for Knox not to openly chuckle. She looked so cute in her colourful bobble hat, scarf, and woolly gloves. Plus, the big winter coat that seemed so padded out, she must have had three or four layers on underneath. To finish off her winter look were big Ugg boots with thick knitted socks pulled up to her knees, and a few layers of leggings. Knox looked Dani up and down, trying to keep a straight face. It was good to see her, but he wasn't expecting her new look. Then he considered that she looked like she had planned for cold nights on the streets, and the thought was a sobering one for Knox because this was something he would not have.

"Dani! It's you… er… it's really good to see you, lass," Knox said, stumbling at first for words in his shock. He also took a step forward to hug her but Dani took a step back, which halted Knox in his tracks. It pained him to see how she stared at the ground as if she couldn't bring herself to look at him.

"Dani, please look at me," Knox pleaded softly as he

reached out to her arm, intending to pull her closer. But she flinched at his touch before yanking her arm out of the way and turning her back on him.

"Dani… I Don't… I don't know what to say, but I… am Sorr…" Knox spoke, rubbing the back of his neck in frustration as he tried to get his words out and apologise. Admittedly, apologising was something that had never come easy to him which was, no doubt, the reason he was so bad at it.

Dani spun around quickly and punched Knox in the arm.

"You are sorry, Knox? For what? Sending me away? Hurting me? Breaking… *Breaking my heart?"* Dani at first shouted then broke down into a whisper, hitting her fists on Knox's chest before falling into him.

Knox instantly wrapped his arms around her, feeling her tense in his hold. She half shrugged him off before quickly giving in. Not wanting her to try and break away again, he held her tightly and took a deep breath in through his nose. Her sweet, calming scent filled his airways, taking him to a new level. He closed his eyes, rested his head on hers, and savoured the moment.

The realisation had hit Knox, especially when hearing the way she admitted how hard she had taken his rejection, how it had broken her heart. But he also knew that the fear of her being hurt, taken, or worse, killed, terrified him to his core. However, knowing that she was in just as much danger without him as she was with him, well now… *that changed everything.*

"Easy now, lass…" Knox hummed down at her, rubbing her arms as her crying slowly subsided. Then he gave her the apology he knew she deserved. "I am sorry, Dani. I was a fool. I shouldn't have said the things I did."

Dani moved backward and tilted her head to look up at him with her tear-filled blue eyes. "I don't understand… why… why did you?" she asked, her red nose wrinkling a little as she sniffed through her upset.

"I wanted to push you away, but only to protect you," Knox said as he held her tight, at which she started shaking her head.

"You are horrible, do you know that? Honestly, I'm so angry with you! But…" Dani said without the malice the words would suggest, and Knox could also see the relief in her eyes.

The word 'but' lingered in the air and Knox couldn't help but use it as an opportunity to ease the tense between them.

"But what, darlin'? My good looks and charisma stop you from staying mad at me, is that it?" A cheeky grin crossed Knox's face as he spoke.

"Honestly, Knox, you are intolerable." Dani gasped as she pushed Knox away from her and tried to cross her arms. The number of layers made the rigid movement uncomfortable, so she awkwardly moved her arms around, not knowing what to do with them.

Knox couldn't help but smile at her that time, to which she huffed and stomped her foot then pointed at him.

"None of this is funny! I am really fucking mad with you!" Dani shouted, pulling her gloves off and throwing them at Knox in frustration, before walking away and out of the unit.

"Dani, hold up! Come on now, you have to know how worried I have been about you," Knox called out as he caught up to her and took hold of her hand.

The instant their hands touched, they froze in their tracks, the contact affecting them both.

"Worried about me?" Dani asked softly, with a slight smile she hid from Knox by not looking back at him.

Knox knew she was going to milk this and saver it, and damn but did he want to give it to her. So, he would grovel if that's what it took. Because he knew that he deserved it. He should have kept her close, looked after her and kept her safe from the beginning. After all, he was the reason she was now in this mess and had a target on her back. Or at least, that's what he had assumed. It had always been obvious that Knox had a thing for Dani, which meant Mac must have known this. Knox hadn't figured out Mac's end game yet, but involving Dani was a low fucking blow.

"Of course I was worried about you! I came back from Spain to make amends but when I couldn't get in contact with you, and you weren't at your home, I..." Knox explained but Dani jumped in.

"At my home...? Wait, you went to my house?" she asked, the shock and confusion merging into one emotion, but before he had time to answer she quickly demanded, "How?"

Knox inwardly flinched at her question, but it also instantly put him on edge as another realisation hit him. Dani hadn't been the one to open the crate like he thought. She hadn't been in his unit at all, and therefore, she didn't know how he could have tracked her down.

"It's not important right now, what is important is the fact..." Knox tried to brush off the details but unsurprisingly, was swiftly interrupted.

"Lucas, how did you find my house?" Dani turned serious. In fact, it was a seriousness he hadn't seen before.

Knox cleared his throat and tried once more to fudge his way through the answers.

"Let's just say, I have my ways, even though I may be a dinosaur when it comes to technology. Sometimes the old ways are still the best," Knox said a little tongue in cheek, hoping for his Scottish charm to save him. Needless to say, *it did not.*

"Cut the shit, Lucas, I want to know. Actually, fuck wanting, *I need to know!"* Dani said with infuriation coating every word, but Knox knew that deep down there was more to it. There was a real fear behind the attitude.

With a sigh, Knox knew the best way forward from this point was to just come out with it and be honest, especially if they had a future together like he hoped. It was time to finally lay down the foundations for that to happen, and lies told tended to crack.

"I will show you," he told her, before walking back into the unit, relieved to see Dani followed. Then Knox walked over to the crate and after tearing off the loose bubble wrap, he lifted one canvas up and let her see for herself just how deep his obsession with her was rooted.

"Your paintings, Dani, your paintings led me to your house," Knox admitted, taking on an attitude of his own and one that said, 'You asked for this'.

"My painting… how, how the hell did you…?" Dani couldn't finish in her shock, words failed her at the same time her eyes darted. *"Why do you have one of my paintings? How the hell did it lead you to my house?"* Dani whispered, her mind trying to make sense of it all.

"No, Dani, not one painting. I own all of them," Knox replied calmly, watching as the full gravity of his confession sunk in.

"You… *you bought them…*? But why… why would you do that? You asked me about them… Was it some kind of game…? Taking pity on the little wannabe artist!" Dani shouted by the end, her anger building as her embarrassment took over.

She felt like a fool and was utterly mortified to discover that Knox had this personal insight to her hidden desires… A dark taboo and kink that she craved to experience for herself, having only ever fantasied about it and expressed this forbidden side of herself through her art. It was like sexual therapy of sorts, she never believed anyone would discover whose hand lay behind the sexual brush strokes.

As for Knox, the moment he heard this coming from Dani,

he gritted his teeth because it was like a kick to the gut. Did she really think he thought so little of her?

"No! Not in the slightest. I think you're very talented, extremely so, in fact," Knox said, not raising his voice even though it hurt him knowing that Dani thought he was playing games with her like this.

"But… they are…" Dani couldn't bring herself to say it. To say what they both knew her art represented.

"I can't do this!" Dani shouted, throwing her hands up as her feelings of awkwardness and embarrassment grew too much to control.

She turned on her heels and began to run. In her haste, she bumped into the door frame, knocking her a little off balance but enough to stop her.

It was a good job she had all the layers on otherwise it could have hurt, Knox thought, concerned not only for her feelings getting hurt. He released a deep sigh of frustration as he watched her, having no need to run after her. His long legs cut the distance between them easily due to the restricted way she moved. Admittedly, had the situation been any different and he didn't feel like a bastard, then he would have found the sight funny. How she was dressed, in all the layers, was making a normally graceful woman act like she was in a sumo suit.

"Dani, stop! Hold up," Knox pleaded, but it fell on deaf ears as Dani exited his storage unit.

The second she tried to break out into a faster pace, he too sped up and just as he got through the door and out of his unit, he saw Dani going into one directly across from his. This stopped him dead in his tracks for a second as he questioned why and what was Dani doing with a lockup unit across from his.

Determined to find out, and even more determined to stop her from walking away without hearing an explanation, Knox got to her unit door just before Dani could shut it in his face. He slammed a hand to the metal door and pushed his way in with ease. Dani's eyes grew wide when she realised it was a battle she would lose because she knew she was no match for his strength. Not when she still had the memory of all those perfectly sculpted muscles burned to her brain and had not long ago felt the strength in those arms wrapped around her. So, with a cry of frustration and anger, she stepped away from the door and turned her back on him just as he burst in.

"Get out, Lucas, go away and leave me alone!" Dani yelled, to which Knox swiftly took hold of her padded arm, yanked her around to face him, and pulled her close.

The sight of her walking away from him was like a switch being flipped. He couldn't stand it and instinct quickly took over. Just as he was about to lose his cool and scold her for running, she looked up at him with those blue eyes. Blue eyes that projected pure, raw emotion… the hurt and anger clouded by that of her fear.

In that moment, Knox lost all outside awareness as he locked onto those eyes, easily losing himself in the power of her lure. Before he could stop himself, his head dipped to her level, and his lips only had one destination in mind as he finally kissed the woman he loved.

SEVEN

EVASION

The second his lips touched hers, something stirred quickly within them both and when Dani parted her lips slightly, Knox took this as the only invitation he needed to deepen the kiss. Dani's reluctance clung to her, questioning his motives in kissing her and her doubts made her try to resist him. But as Knox wrapped his arms around her and held her more firmly against him, unwilling to let her go, she couldn't help but lose the fight within herself. She relaxed into his arms, and he happily took her weight as their embrace intensified.

Knox could have taken her there and then, his desperation to have her and finally make her his was almost too much temptation to resist. But he also knew there was still a lot left unsaid between them, and he didn't want Dani to have any regrets the first time he claimed her.

With this in Knox's mind, he slowly released his tight grip on her, giving Dani the time she needed to take back her balance. Slipping his hands up to her face he made the agonising decision to end the kiss, so he pulled back and his eyes opened.

When he first entered the room, he hadn't taken in his surroundings, but now his focus wasn't on Dani the view slapped him across the face. The passion of the kiss fed his fury at what he saw. There was a fold up camp bed, blankets, a small butane gas stove with a kettle, fast food packaging, chocolate wrappers, and lots of plastic bottles. Knox saw red.

"What the hell is this?!" Knox snapped as he pulled away and passed Dani, leaving her half pouting and half wondering where their passionate kiss had gone and how it had been replaced by his anger.

"Well, that was not what I was expecting," Dani muttered in annoyance, looking around and composing herself from the warm flush she was having. One that had started out as lust and had quickly been replaced by embarrassment.

"Dani, please tell me that you haven't been staying here? In this fucking place, in the cold, like this?!" Knox said, trying in vain to rein in his temper as he walked around the evidence of her living rough.

The idea that she had spent even a single night here grated on him enough that it cut to the core. His protective nature rode him hard, to the point where he just wanted to toss her up over his shoulder and take her back to his place where he would make sure she remained.

"Lucas, calm down, okay? I am a big girl and it's not like I don't know how to rough it. It's not like…" Dani's sarcastic tone was quickly interrupted by Knox, who made it clear he was not about to accept this, nor was he about to let her finish. He stepped into her, intimidating whatever else she was about to say straight from her lips.

"Why didn't you come to me? I would have kept you safe. Made sure you…" Knox shouted. He was finding it difficult to keep his cool, but this was where Dani had hit her limit.

"Made sure of what? Made sure to break my heart some

more?!" You sent me away, Lucas, remember?" Dani snapped back.

Her ire knocked some of the wind from Knox's angry sails, forcing him to realise that he had no right to be acting the way he was. Because he knew deep down that he had caused this. Pushing her away the way he did, how could he really expect her to then come to him for help? But even as he questioned this, he also knew that her being here was not a coincidence.

"Look, Dani…" Knox dropped his voice, but it was no good, she was too far gone in her own rage.

"Don't you, look, Dani, me, Knox!"

"Damn it, just let me explain!" he argued but once again, she was having none of it.

Fuck… at this rate he would kiss her again just as a way to shut her up long enough to let him explain!

"Oh, you want to explain? Like you did that day. What was it you said again…" Dani's tone was laced with venom and being that Knox was in no hurry to relive the regretful moment, he tried once more to calm the situation.

"Dani…"

She snapped up a hand at this and ignored his silent plea to stop, instead driving the knife in deeper with a memory he wished he could have forgotten.

"There can't and never will be… remember, Lucas?" Dani said, welling up.

The second Knox saw this he couldn't help but react, the guilt of knowing he had hurt the woman he loved was eating him up. Meaning nothing could have stopped him as he once more took a step into her before taking her in his arms. She began to cry, her face pushed into his chest, and he cupped the back of her head to hold her there.

As for Dani, she was torn, because as much as she wanted to be strong enough to walk away, she also hated how much she wanted to be in his arms. How much she needed to be close to him, despite the way he had hurt her.

"Hey now, come on, Dani, sweetheart. I am… fuck, baby, I am so so sorry," Knox said, and for the first time in his life, it came easy.

"You told me… *you didn't want me and never did*," Dani sobbed, letting out all her hurt and emotion.

Each sound tore a deeper wound in his heart, and he fucking hated himself for how much he had hurt her. If he could go back to that day and kick his own arse for thinking that was the only way to keep her safe, he would do it in a second.

"I know, I know. I thought I was protecting you. I was wrong, so wrong. Please, Dani, please forgive me? I was a fucking idiot," Knox said. He held her with one arm and stroked down her face with his free hand, trying his best to wipe away her tears and with them, the memory of why they were there.

"I promise you, Dani, I promise you that…" Knox started to say, but Dani shook her head, her blonde hair falling from the messy bun she had scrunched it all up into.

"Don't, Lucas… please don't make promises you can't keep," Dani asked as she looked up at him, her blue eyes glistening with a mixture of hope and pleading. Knox released a heavy sigh before trying to make her see the truth in his words.

"Dani… I promise, *I fucking promise you, I will never hurt you like that again."*

As Knox said the words, Dani looked down to hide her face. Her expression unknown to him, he softly lifted her chin, so their eyes could meet and, in them, he could read her thoughts of doubt.

"Forgive me, baby," Knox whispered, placing his forehead to hers, hoping the intimacy of this moment would forever be ingrained against his soul.

Dani felt it too, and she reached up to cup his cheek before pulling back enough to smile, even as fresh new tears fell from her eyes. This time, though, the tears were filled with hope and relief that this wasn't the end like she had feared it was. Deciding to be bold, she held his gaze as she pushed herself up on her tip toes to kiss him.

"Alright, Knox, but can I promise you something?" Dani said with a whisper over his lips and a knowing grin.

"I am all ears, lass," Knox replied after he sneaked another quick kiss.

"If you ever hurt me like that again, I swear I will… I will… oh I don't fucking know but I promise you, it won't be nice."

Knox couldn't contain himself as he threw his head back and laughed. He also knew that she didn't have a mean bone in her body because she was the polar opposite of him, but he hadn't been lying when he made the promise that he would never hurt her again. She was his weakness, and he could no longer deny his need for her. Which meant that when all of this was said and done and the threat had been neutralized, it was time for him to seriously consider a career change.

That or fucking retirement. It wasn't like he didn't have the funds to do it.

"Okay, okay, I get it. Now can you stop hitting me? You're stronger than you look." Knox smiled as he guarded his face like a boxer on the ropes.

"It's not my punches you need to worry about, Lucas, it's what I could do when you are sleeping you need to fear." Dani cracked a smile and giggled as they play fought, and the tears on her cheeks began to dry.

Knox returned the smile then cupped her face in his hands, rubbing the rest of her tears away with his thumbs.

"Come on, lass, let's make a brew and you can tell me about

how you got here," said Knox, before making his way over to the camp bed and beer crates.

He shook his head slightly as he knelt at the little camping stove, knowing this was the last fucking drink she would have in this makeshift home of hers.

Dani joined him and as he made her a brew, she told Knox how she felt that her and Rose were followed to the airport, even though she admitted that she didn't actually see anyone. When she landed in the UK, a few odd things happened that spooked her. Like the guy waiting for her at arrivals with her name on a card but it wasn't her name, it was the fake one she had booked the flight under.

At first, she thought maybe Knox or Rose had sent a driver to collect her and take her home, not knowing she had her car parked at the airport. But something told her the guy just didn't fit. So, she kept her head down and snuck passed him. Although when she had finally gotten to her car, she found that her tyres had been slashed. After that, she knew someone was after her because she noticed the same guy that waiting for her in the arrivals hall, was now searching for her from a distance in the car park. Her reaction to this was to duck down out of sight before she made her way around the cars on all fours just to get away unseen.

Dani went on to explain that after getting away from the guy at the airport, she booked a rental car under a new fake name—she usually had enough fake ID's on her just in case. She also knew that she couldn't just go home in case they had managed to discover where she lived just like Knox had, so she went to a hotel.

The hotel wasn't all it cracked up to be because Dani hadn't slept well that night and had a bitch of headache. So, knowing that it wasn't the type to just go away on its own, she decided to get up and do something about it. She had noticed a twenty-four-hour petrol station near the hotel on arrival, so she went out in the early hours to pick up some pain killers. However, when she was paying at the kiosk, she noticed a van pull up outside the front of the hotel and a group of men got out.

Knox tensed hearing this, especially when she confirmed, *"They were there to kidnap me."*

"How did you know it was a kidnap team?" Knox questioned with concern.

"Well, they weren't dressed like a bunch of guys just getting back from a stag do."

No, thought Knox, the only celebrating they would have done is after getting paid to do a snatch and grab job, and Dani had obviously been their target.

Dani went on to tell him that they looked like a kidnap team, with black rucksacks to match their black outfits, and the van… well, the sliding door they all filed out of screamed at her to run away. She wasn't about to wait around to find out which room they were headed to, so she walked away, with only the purse she carried, leaving the rest of her belongings at the hotel. The only way they could have tracked her to the hotel was by the ID she used when hiring the car and booking the room.

With that in mind, her next plan had been to find somewhere safe and go off grid. Using an internet café, she looked up the information she had on Knox, because she believed he must have had some kind of base in the UK. She told Knox that she discovered he had used a credit card for a one-off payment that stood out. When she investigated the lead, it led her to the storage unit.

She rented the only free unit left that just so happened to be the one directly opposite. After that, she had set up camp and explained that she had been there for only a few days, despite it feeling like a week.

The local leisure center was a good place to wash and get out of the dingy environment, and lucky for her, there was a big supermarket where she could pick up clothes, food, and basic camping equipment. Once she had all she needed, she ditched the car at a train station car park in hopes that anyone tracking her would think she had gotten on a train.

"Smart thinking," Knox praised.

Blushing, Dani looked down into her cup of tea before she went on to explain how she had waited for him, in hopes he would eventually show up. That wasn't her only plan, though, because she was a whizz with a laptop. Without one, she was blind, so she had decided to arm herself with what she knew would be her only weapon of defense. It would be the only way she could try and discover who was after her and get ahead of the game.

"I picked up a half decent laptop and thankfully I still had my purse on me with my bank and credit cards and other ID's. But even if they managed to track these, I knew I could create a new identity with the laptop. I also paid cash for the unit so it couldn't be traced… and well, this has been my new home for the last few days," Dani said with a shrug.

Knox suppressed the burning anger stewing in his gut as he looked around. By the far wall was a couple of beer crates being used as a table for her laptop.

"How long were you planning on staying here, Dani?" Knox asked, swallowing back the desire to lecture her. The thought of Dani living in this cold, dark unit didn't sit right with him.

"Well, I hadn't really got that far ahead. I have been too focused on trying to find out what's going on and discover who it is that's after me," Dani replied, making Knox wince.

"Dani, you don't need to worry about that, I am going to deal with this," Knox assured her, his jaw tense and his hand forming a fist as the thought of Mac's threat crossed his mind.

The picture of Dani left in the medical tent with a knife stabbed through her form had left a venomous impact on Knox. Now it was time for him to find Mac and eliminate the threat because the bastard had gone back on his word about leaving Dani out this.

"I know you're good, Knox, but just how are you going to do that when we don't even know who they are, let alone where they are coming from?" Dani asked with a shake of her head as she watched Knox rise from the beer crate he had been sitting on. It was clear to her that he was now a man on a mission.

"I know who it is, *and they are going to pay,*" Knox admitted with a growl under his breath, fucking furious after hearing her account of what had happened since landing back in the UK.

He couldn't help but think about what could have happened to her had she not been as street smart and resourceful as she was. *Thank fuck his woman was a borderline genius,* that's all he could say. And if he was being honest with himself, he thought of Dani as being his woman long before he kissed her and the protectiveness that came with that was evident considering how angry he was now just looking around the room.

Well at least he was here now, which meant he could take care of her and ensure her safety from here on out.

"Right, pack up everything you need, I'm taking you somewhere safe, and somewhere that's a lot more fucking comfortable than here," Knox said with a loud clap of his hands before rubbing them as the cold penetrated his bones. It may have only been September in the UK but that didn't mean it was decent weather. It was a far cry from the heat of Spain and being inside this storage unit, that was void of any natural light, made it even more fucking colder. Hence why Dani wore so many layers that she looked more like a stuffed toy. Too fucking cute at that.

"Wait, you know who they are?" a puzzled Dani said looking up at Knox.

"I will explain on the way but the sooner we get out of here, the better," Knox replied firmly, needing to get her out of here as soon as possible because the constant reminder of her living rough was fucking with his head.

"And where exactly are we going?" she asked, folding her arms across her chest... or at least trying to. The sight made Knox supress another grin.

"Somewhere no one knows about. You will be a lot safer there, trust me," Knox told her.

Trusting Knox wasn't going to be easy for Dani, not after how he treated her, but she wanted to try. Although she did widen her eyes a little at the information about somewhere safe to stay. It came as a surprise because she thought she knew everything about him.

"Okay, Lucas, well if you give me a few minutes I will be ready to go," Dani said, hinting that she wanted privacy.

Knox nodded before walking out of the unit, wishing that she trusted him enough to stay, but it would take time to rebuild the trust he had lost with Dani.

Knox walked back over to his own unit and unlocked the main large door before swinging it open. To his surprise, the padlock on the larger door was missing, which was an important fact he had overlooked when first arriving.

Knowing now that it wasn't Dani, he had to question who had been in his lockup, could it have been someone from T.I.7? If they had, then he would be bringing that shit up with Carter the next time he saw him.

Pushing the Triumph in and parking it to one side, Knox walked back over to the security case. Taking out a car key fob from the tactical box he clicked the remote, and a blip of the alarm and flashing glow from under the dust sheet followed.

He walked over to the low, sleek shape and ran his hand over it. Fond memories crossed through Knox's mind as he reached the bottom of the front end and took a fist full of the sheet covering it. Slowly pulling back the material, his eyes widened, knowing the only feeling better would be revealing the soft, smooth skin of Dani's naked curves.

Flowing body lines with sculpted contours and pronounced haunches were revealed as the unmistakable presence of a Jaguar. The flawless black-mirror finish of the F-Type looked as new as it had when coming off the production line.

This marquee car was a way of hiding the money Knox received from his tax-free, under the radar contract work.

The big cat it looked like it was traveling 100mph standing still, and Knox enjoyed admiring it as he walked around to the back. Knox popped the rear boot and unhooked the trickle charger before placing his security case inside—the one he had retrieved from the Welsh dresser, knowing that he and Dani may need it. Before he closed the boot, Knox walked over to the crate that had been opened. If there was only one thing in his lockup that could get him more excited than the Jaguar, it was Dani's paintings.

The thought that someone else had seen one of them, irked Knox to the point his knuckles cracked as he tensed his fist.

Damn it. He knew he should have set up surveillance inside. But in his arrogance, he had believed no one would ever find this place. Dani, he could understand. As his broker, she was the one who set up his hidden finances and well, she was one of the best hackers he had ever known.

He wrapped up the painting that had been disturbed and selected one of the others before placing them in the boot. Then after slamming it shut, he made his way around to the driver's side and slipped in behind the wheel. Sitting in the F-Type, Knox soaked up the aroma of leather and suede, every aspect of its plush interior had him itching to share the luxury with Dani.

Taking his right hand off the three-spoke steering wheel, he pushed the start button and was rewarded with an eruption of orchestral machine movements as the exhaust thunder boomed into life. The rich sound enveloped everything around the lockup. A smile swept over Knox as he selected first gear and eased off the brake pedal. The Jaguar rolled forward in an almost poised elegance, ready at the plunge of his right foot to rocket off like an Exocet missile.

Knox left the beast running and got out of the car just as Dani walked out of her own lockup. The sight, for the second time today, had Knox sucking in a quick breath. He was near struck down with lust. Dani was wearing figure-hugging jeans that accentuated her curves, a tan cashmere sweater, and a long, dark jacket down to her knee-high boots. Her bouncy, long blonde hair was freed from the bobble hat and looked a touch wild. It made Knox want to tame it back with his fist before kissing her breathless, his hand keeping her locked to his lips.

Knox couldn't help but stand there and admire her natural beauty. Something Dani would have been a fool not to notice because he watched every move she made, like he was stalking prey.

To hide her embarrassment, she called out, "Hey, are you

just going to stand there or are you going to be a gentleman and help me?" She grinned, holding up her laptop bag and a near overflowing backpack. Her gaze then caught on the rumbling Jag next to him. Knox smirked at her sassy demand and shook his head lightly before walking over to her. Dani swallowed hard at the sight of Knox leaning in, he made her feel tiny compared to his towering, muscular frame.

"Looking like that, you make it hard to be a gentleman..." Knox paused so he could whisper seductively in her ear, "... *especially with all the sinful thoughts I have when it comes to you.*"

Dani inhaled sharply as the sexual intent struck a chord within her deepest desires. In fact, she even closed her eyes as if at the ready for him to finalise this confession with a kiss. She was left disappointed when he took her bags with nothing but a chuckle as he walked away.

"Come on, lass, time to get that beautiful arse of yours in the car," he said once he had put her bags inside and opened up the passenger door for her.

Her sassiness returned as she said, "Well, it's a step up from the Fiat 500 I hired."

Knox laughed at that, but the sound quickly died in his throat the second he saw her bend over to look inside the vehicle.

"Although not much room in here." Then she winked at him in a flirtatious way before sliding down into the bucket seat.

He was left shaking his head and willing his cock to go down or it was going to be an uncomfortable drive. *Damn, he couldn't wait to get her home.* But first, he locked up his unit, using a spare padlock he was thankful he had among his possessions. The mystery of who had been in his lockup was still playing on his mind, but there was nothing he could do right now. His priority was to keep Dani safe. The lockup investigation could come later.

"Why? What did you have in mind, lass?" he asked when slipping in beside her and becoming instantly aware of how close they were.

Dani gave him a coy look before saying, "Well, twister is out of the question."

Knox laughed, enjoying the easy banter between them both and unable to stop himself from saying, "Now's that's a shame, you looked damn good bent over before getting in the car."

She blushed at that and smacked him on the arm, warning playfully, "You just keep your mind off my arse and on the road, mister."

"Not possible, but I will happily lie to you and say, I'll try."

Dani giggled as he pulled away from the units, stopping only to key in the code so they could get out of the main gates.

"Now let's get going, I have somewhere special to show you," Knox said as he suddenly accelerated hard, knocking her back into the seat.

"Whoa! You in a rush?"

Knox granted her a look as if to say, *what do you think?*

"So, this somewhere special, what did you have in mind? 'Cause, it's a bit late for a Michelin star restaurant, Lucas," Dani teased, unable to help herself from looking over the interior of the expensive car.

"No, something a little more personal, but hey, if you're hungry there's a drive thru not far," Knox replied, followed with a devastatingly handsome grin that Dani wanted to kiss. Not that she was ready to admit this.

"Oh how you know how to woo a girl, Lucas. Saying that, I could murder a Big Mac, but you have a problem," Dani said, biting her lip.

"A problem? How so?" Knox asked with a questioning frown.

"Well, this boy toy of yours, for all its power and sexy looks, has a flaw," Dani said, her grinning face at the ready for the punchline she was about to deliver.

"Go on…" Knox said dryly, looking at Dani and waiting for the ridiculous complaint.

"Cup holders, there are a serious lack of cup holders!" Dani said as she giggled, to which Knox smiled as he shook his head.

"Come on, lass, let's get you to my house," Knox said, planting his foot to the floor and once more sending Dani back into her seat, the roar of the exhaust echoing off the buildings around them.

"Wait… your house? But you don't have a house," Dani yelped as she gripped the door handle and seat bolster for dear life.

Knox just granted her a smug look and replied, "Don't I?"

NINE

BEN JOHNSON

NEW JOHN ST WEST, HEADING TOWARDS BIRMINGHAM CENTRE.

Dani could be forgiven for thinking she was traveling down a country bypass. A thick tree line canopy flanked both sides of the dual track carriageway out of Hockley. The roads were dead this time of night and without the security lights that had lit up their meeting back at the lockup, there were only the brief flashes of streetlights that illuminated Dani's face. Knox noted that she was fidgeting nervously with the hem of her sweater, and he wished there was a way to ease her clearly busy mind.

For the most part, Knox knew that Dani's sassiness was a mask worn to hide her true nature, one he could tell she struggled with sexually. He could see it in her paintings. The shy, submissive girl hidden behind the bravado she displayed. But ever since she had heard where it was that Knox was taking her, he could see that brave mask begin to slip with each mile they travelled. The dark, stillness of the city did not help to ease her anxiety, and the only clue they were still in the city was thanks to the 1960's, square high-rise flats looming over the tree line.

The F-Type's exhaust rumbled as Knox made his way through the gears enjoying the clear road in front of him. The green verges and matured manmade parks interlinked between the tons of concrete. This gave way to the grey, rundown, industrial tones of Birmingham, a city that was quickly re-developing as time passed.

Sleeping construction sites seemed to be everywhere, development plots sandwiched between gloriously designed Victorian and Georgian buildings. The skilled craftsmanship fought against the hideous post-war concrete-dominated structures, the polar opposites stood lined next to each other. There was a nickname Birmingham was desperately trying to shake off, 'The concrete Jungle', and Knox wondered if it would ever happen.

Not for the first time, Knox also wondered what Dani was thinking. She had quickly become the main event in his own mind, and he hoped she was feeling the same, despite their situation.

"Not far now," Knox said, cutting through the silence and making her jerk a little.

She hadn't said much since leaving the drive-through, and she hadn't been kidding about being hungry. As they veered off Newtown Middleway slip road, onto and around the Dartmouth Circus ring road, she yelped when he sped up.

"Hey, steady on, are you trying to get this diet coke in my lap?" Dani playfully shrieked, the straw still in between her lips as the sideways force pushed her towards the door. She gripped the centre console handrail as it was the only thing stopping her from being pressed against the door.

"As if I would try and get you all wet and sticky," Knox replied with a wink after his eyes momentarily crossed over to Dani's lap.

Thoughts of peeling her out of wet denim flooded his mind, and he knew that simple act was worth the cost of the car valet. Dani cut Knox a feigned sarcastic smile, one even Knox knew didn't hold any weight because he hadn't missed her breathy sigh.

Dani stared at the many road lights before being plunged into a brightly lit tunnel. The exhaust made her jump when it popped as Knox sped through, making the roar of the engine echo louder than ever before.

After this ride, there were two things Dani was certain of; one, Knox obviously loved this car and the second, the man could most definitely drive. Although with the way he kept looking at her, practically undressing her with his eyes, then maybe there were three things… the third being, *Knox was speeding for a reason.*

As the road elevated out of the tunnel and then up above street level, Knox pulled off down another slip road. Dani watched as the express way rose above them and the bright light faded into darkness. They passed red door after red door of the central fire station building on their right.

Dani's expressive eyes told Knox she might have had a thing for firemen, making him comment, "Don't get too excited, it's been closed for ten years, and there are plans to turn it into student apartments." Knox smirked.

"Oh, that is a shame…" Dani faux-sighed with a giggle.

Student apartments definitely weren't as sexy as the image of firemen all at the ready to jump into action. Maybe Knox would throw her over his shoulder as soon as they got to his place and then throw her to his bed. *Well, a girl could dream,* Dani thought, despite knowing how nervous she was just thinking about what was going to happen between them.

"Like you will soon see, most of the old buildings in this

city are not as they first seem," Knox said cryptically, continuing to drive around Lancaster Circus ring road, which had the Aston expressway snake over the top of them. Seconds later, Knox did a complete 360 and headed back in the direction they came from.

"Here we are," he said with a grin.

"What, we are here? You have lost me, Lucas. All I can see is the Birmingham council building and an old boarded up abandoned pub," Dani replied as she glanced out the window, looking around the dimly-lit streets.

"All will become clear, lass," Knox replied with a smirk as he drove around the back of the city council building to the entrance of an underground car park.

Pulling up to the barrier, he waited as he eyed Dani with a knowing grin, enjoying her confused expression. It made her look cute as fuck, especially when she mouthed the words, 'Where the hell are we?' to herself.

The number plate recognition took note of Knox's vehicle and the barrier raised. They drove down two levels under the building and then pulled into a private parking bay.

"Right, we are here," Knox said as he got out of the Jag.

Dani sat for a moment, looking around and wondering what the hell was going on.

"Lucas… we are under the local council building. I don't get it, do you have an office here or something?" Dani questioned as she unfolded herself out of the low sports car.

By this time, Knox had her backpack over his shoulder and handed over her laptop bag. Then he took out his tactical case and purposely left the painting in the boot, knowing now was not the time to remind her of the true depths of his obsession with her.

"Follow me, lass, I think you're gonna like this," Knox said.

He started walking away from the Jaguar that bleeped as the alarm activated.

Dani quickly caught up with him because she didn't fancy the idea of being left behind in a dark, underground carpark on her own. The lights in each area illuminated automatically as they passed, with the same lights then dying behind them once the timer had run down. After fifty or so meters, they reached a black reinforced steel door, making Dani eye it warily. Knox entered in a key code which was followed by a loud clunk and a click came from the door as it unlocked. The sound made Dani jump.

"This tunnel leads under the road above. Before the council building was built there was a Victorian network of tunnels between all the buildings in this area," Knox explained as he swung the door open and switched on the lights.

The strip lighting ran down the right-hand edge of the rising tunnel floor, the incline effectively lighting up the old brick tunnel and giving a rich, visual texture to the aging walls.

"Hell no! I am not going in there, is it even safe, Lucas?" Dani hissed, shaking her head and shrieking the second they heard the rumble of a large lorry driving overhead.

"There is nothing to worry about, lass, I wouldn't put you in any danger. It has been here over a hundred years, so I don't think it's going to collapse now. Plus, it is not far, I promise," Knox said, understanding how daunting it may look because even he had to admit that it wasn't the most inviting of places.

"That doesn't exactly fill me with confidence, Lucas," Dani grumbled as he held out his free hand for Dani to take.

Hesitantly, she took his offered palm before following, unable to help casting a quick glance over her shoulder just as the last of the lights went out. She released a sigh, accepting the fact there was no going back now. That didn't stop her jumping, yet again, when the impenetrable door bellowed closed behind them.

"Easy, lass, nothing bad is gonna to happen to yer," Knox assured her, his Scottish accent coming out deeper and somewhat comforting to Dani's nerves.

As they walked down the tunnel the only sound was their feet crunching on the fine gravel beneath them. The air was dry and, surprisingly, the smell of damp Dani had expected wasn't there. She wondered what stories these walls of history would tell if they could speak, they looked worn and were clearly very old.

"Here we are…" Knox said as they reached a second reinforced door, and he couldn't help his smile when he heard her relieved sigh.

Dani thought she could smell hammerite paint, admittedly, not something she had smelled in years and, stranger still, it reminded her of her childhood.

Again, Knox entered in a pin code and the door mechanism sounded, only this time the door swung open towards them, making Dani jerk back because she hadn't been expecting it.

"Jesus Christ, Lucas, I thought someone was coming through from the other side!" Dani exclaimed, gasping for breath as she held her hand on her chest.

Knox laughed and opened the door fully before walking inside.

"Welcome to my private oasis. Come on, don't be scared, it's only me and the rats here," Knox called back with a chuckle laced in his words.

When Dani's eyes adjusted to what little light there was, she saw a well-used, stone staircase and she was hit by another smell, this time the faint smell of stale beer.

"Lucas! Wait up, did you say rats? Lucas!" Dani called out as she made her way slowly up the staircase, holding one hand up in case there were any cobwebs in her path, and the other gripped on tighter to the strap of her laptop case.

Dani finally reached the top of the stairs and found herself in almost complete darkness. Only a tiny amount of light came from the tunnel at the bottom of the steps she just climbed up… Well, that was until the door slammed shut.

"Lucas…?" Dani spoke out into the silent darkness, quickly getting scared now without Knox by her side.

The sound of one loud click after the next signalled that Knox was flicking switches. Her racing heart began to even out and she took a deep, fortifying breath as one after the other, lights came on along with the hum of electrical panels.

Dani looked around to find that she was in a large cellar, with peeling white paint on all the walls. From the cold metal pipe work, she guessed they were standing in the cellar of the old boarded up pub she had seen from the street. This was obvious despite there being no barrels, bottles, or even empty crates to speak of.

"Over here, sweetheart." Knox's calming voice soothed her frayed nerves as it came down from the far end of the cellar near a wooden staircase.

Dani wasted no time joining him, following him up the stairs. Knox's long legs meant he was up them and out of sight before she had even made it halfway. When Dani reached the top, she tentatively poked her head out beyond the door frame, again, not knowing what to expect. She was greeted by the sight of Knox leaning on the old original bar, a smirk playing on his lips as he waited for her.

"Come on in, it's perfectly safe," said Knox as he waved Dani inside.

The lights were on, but seeing as most of the bulbs were missing, it gave the old pub an ominous feel. Adding to this gloomy vibe, was how abandoned the place looked, confusing Dani even more and she asked herself if he really lived here.

The pub was bare, practically stripped back to its bare bones. There were no tables or seats, even the walls had been stripped of all pictures and decoration. What was there, in its place, was graffiti… and lots of it. This once vibrant, social place had been defaced to what she imagined was an unrecognisable state to those old enough to remember its heyday. Yet despite its decay, there was a feeling of lingering history about the place, as if the many souls that had patronised here had each left a piece of themselves behind.

Dani looked around, opened mouthed, and tried to take in the size and heritage. Something didn't seem quite right, though, and she couldn't put her finger on it. The place looked like vandals had broken in and squatters had once called it home. But the place smelled and looked clean. There was no dust, no cobwebs, no staleness, nor did it even have that old beer smell like the cellar had.

As they walked through the building, areas were lit up with a multitude of colours from the old stain-glass windows. The colours reflected from the wall and ceiling lights, bouncing back into the room. The windows had clearly been protected from vandals because they were fully boarded up from outside.

As Dani continued to take it all in, she noticed even the ornate stone masonry surrounding the windows had thick Perspex to stop damage or entry. What rubbish there was inside the building was in a corner next to a large piece of cardboard on the floor with a sleeping bag on. Closer inspection showed it didn't look used. In fact, the whole thing kind of looked staged, but what was this all for?

"Don't worry, that's not going to be where you're sleeping, lass." Knox chuckled as he walked past Dani and headed into a different area of the pub. She followed him by what would have been a seating area, with panelling divides and tiffany lead-lined stained-glass decorative inserts.

"Lucas, what the hell? Why have you brought me to a derelict pub?" Dani asked incredulously.

"This used to be one busy pub back in its day, it was known as the Ben Johnson, but was really called the King Edward Inn," Knox said as he pointed to a weather-worn, hand-painted sign resting against one wall. A sign that would have originally been hung outside the building.

Dani looked to see for herself. What was left of it depicted a gold crown and the screen printing in gold leaf.

"Here, there used to be a large open staircase up to the first floor, but someone used it for firewood to keep warm when they squatted here," Knox explained, finding the idea funny as he looked up to a large hole in the celling where the sweeping staircase would have been. It was now boarded over with no signs of being able to get up to the first floor.

"So, you can't get upstairs then? Lucas, this is all very odd. I don't understand why we are here. Please tell me you don't actually live in this mess?" Dani asked, completely confused as to why he had brought her here.

"Well, that's kind of the point. That's what I want people to think," Knox replied as he stood by an oak panelled wall and looked back at Dani with a smirk.

"Honestly, Knox, I really can't work you out, how is this place safe and not only that… you said it was more comfortable than the lockup but so far all I have seen is…" She stopped talking the moment he stepped up to her and used his thumb and finger to grip her chin.

He lifted her face up to look at him and away from all the mess, as she had called it.

"Dani, don't you trust me?" he asked, the soft depth of his

voice luring her in along with the knowing glint in his dark brown eyes.

"I do, kinda, it's just…"

With a tutting sound, Knox stopped her from continuing before taking her hand and pulling her back towards the oak panelled wall. Then without looking at her, Knox pressed on a small panel, causing a much larger part of the wall to pop open, revealing a secret room. Dani's eyes widened at the space beyond before looking back up to Knox.

"You see? I told you not everything is as it seems," Knox said as he stepped inside, pulling a shocked Dani in with him.

Knowing there was no going back now, Dani let herself be led inside as the panel closed behind them. She couldn't help but question what she would find next because so far, this was nothing like she would have ever expected from Knox, despite knowing how secretive the man was. This… well, this was taking it to the next level. And speaking of next levels, what she saw next, she was not expecting.

What looked like a brand new, flawless, stainless-steel elevator met them both. It wasn't big by any means and could most likely only hold four people at a squeeze, but it was perfectly fine for just the two of them. Knox used a key he retrieved from his pocket to unlock a panel that revealed yet another keypad. I think it was safe to say that Knox was big on security. He punched in the code and soon got the elevator moving upwards. It looked like they were going to the first floor, after all.

"Hey, don't worry…" Knox said as he glanced over at Dani and saw the trepidation on her face the second there was a loud clunk as it stopped.

"Yeah, okay, nothing to worry about," Dani muttered dryly. She followed Knox once more as he stepped out into the new space, and she wondered what she would find this time.

However, everything she had seen so far hadn't prepared her for this. She found herself doing a double take for a whole different reason.

"What do you think… do you like it…? Will it do?" Knox asked in a self-assured tone. He knew what he had, and he was proud of the space, so he stood back, letting Dani take it all in for herself. And what awarded her this time was essentially… *The secret home of Lucas Knox.*

TEN
BIG BED

A shimmer of light crossed over them both for a fleeting second and Dani's eyes were instantly drawn up to the rafters above. The hundred-plus-year-old timber roof frame had been exposed, and a third of the roof had been replaced with glass. The light came from a large vehicle passing on the expressway. The road's rising elevation was almost the same height as the roof of the Victorian building.

Knox flicked a switch and light flooded down from the lofty ceiling, making the whole place feel warm and inviting. All the outer windows on this level hadn't been boarded up like the ones below, but instead filled in by reclaimed brick to match the exposed walls. This created arched alcoves which were brightened by up-lighters. Knox had designed it this way with a mind to one day display his growing collection of Dani's paintings. Not that she knew this yet, having only just discovering who her mystery buyer was.

Awe filled Dani as she took in the place. It felt like a New York loft apartment that had been dropped into an English turn of the century building. She walked over the original hardwood floorboards that had been sanded, smoothed, and stained. Some areas of the boards were painted in large square sections that marked out each zone.

The first zone was a no-nonsense, modern kitchen. It was void of any personal touch that would suggest a woman had ever set foot in it. This made Dani smile. The island was the focal point with a five-gas ring stainless-steel hob and extraction, all offset with a solid granite work surface. Dani couldn't help but picture Knox shirtless and bare foot in just a pair of worn jeans, standing there in the mornings making himself a brew. She nearly sighed at the thought, questioning if she would get to witness such a sight now that she was there?

As for the rest of the vast, open space, most of the walls were exposed brick. There was just one that had the original plaster, it had been sanded back to give a smooth, aged look.

Clean, polished copper pipes with brass fittings were made into a feature, and they snaked around the walls connected to big, chunky column radiators. The fixtures looked as old as the building itself, with their elaborate decorative castings and tarnished colour finish. In the centre of the space was a U-shaped, low sitting sofa that focused on the slick, flat screen TV mounted to the brick wall.

All this was overlooked by a dominating steel framework that supported a mezzanine floor above. To connect the floors, a metal staircase swept up in a spiral.

Dani would soon find that the top featured Knox's bedroom, along with a Victorian roll top bath. And those lucky enough to experience its masculine opulence could sit in it, looking up at the stars at the peak of night. Or there was the option to look down from the vaulted twenty-five-foot-high vantage point at the living area below.

"Lucas… this is… well, it's stunning," Dani said, turning to look at Knox with an expression of shock and amazement, one he couldn't help but smirk at.

"Thanks, lass, but I wish I could take credit for it all," Knox said with an unapologetic shrug of his shoulders.

"Designer?" Dani guessed, making him nod.

"Well, I would say that she was worth every penny then," Dani added.

Knox grinned. He was proud of the place he called home, and knowing that Dani liked it too was the icing on top of the cake. The place was striking and grand in its own industrially raw way. It also had had a lot of effort, time, and money invested in it.

"You didn't do any of the work yourself? I don't believe that, not with you being so handy and all," Dani asked with an inquisitive look and a little wink, something he chuckled at.

"Someone has kept me busy enough to be able to pay for it," he replied, making her blush.

"Well in that case, you're welcome," she smirked, loving their banter together.

Dani had momentarily enjoyed the fantasy of Knox getting all sweaty and dirty, wearing nothing but overalls tied at the waist and work boots. While she admired the fact that he had a designer do the work, she was a little disappointed.

Although thankfully, Knox was quick to bring back the fantasy.

"The contractors did most of it, but I at least managed to get my hands dirty and do a few jobs, demolition being one of them," Knox said, adding a wink at the end and making Dani's smirk turn into a full-on grin

"But of course," she muttered.

They stared at each other for a few moments, stuck in a battle of wills. Neither wanting to be the first to break and give in to the temptation they were both clearly feeling. Dani watched as Knox was first to move, taking off his jacket... and she tried not to focus on the way his T-shirt stretched over his muscles as he tossed it over one of the carved wooden bar stools situated on the other side of the kitchen island.

Then he walked closer to Dani and said, "Here, let me give you the tour, but first…" He paused, placing his hands at her shoulders before he rid her of her jacket, and his touch made a shiver race down her spine.

Dani refused to look up at him, she didn't want to see the knowing grin she knew she would find because try as she might, she couldn't help her response to Knox. Being here in his private space now, well, her nerves were all over the place.

Knox knew not to push her too quickly to a place he admittedly was eager to get her… *in his bed.* So instead, he simply took her jacket and folded it over the back of the sofa she was standing beside.

Then the tour ensued. He walked her around the space, explaining that the roof took the most amount of work and was the biggest problem the contractors faced when Knox took on the project. This was because the roof was previously beyond repair.

In fact, that had been one of the main reasons for him choosing the property. He wanted a place that had no windows, so from the outside no one would have any idea what was on the inside, let alone it was being lived in. The removal of the roof and having the large glass skylight was perfect for getting around the whole not having windows thing.

"Lucas, that's not a skylight, that's a whole roof of glass," Dani said, smirking after he told her all of this.

"Well, skylight or not, I think it turned out well. You can enjoy it while you're having a bath and looking up at the stars," Knox said with a glint in his eye. At the same time he was undressing Dani in his mind… and not for the first time tonight.

"Sounds lovely," Dani replied quietly as she fidgeted on the spot, thinking about Knox being in that bath with her.

Needless to say, the sexual tension around them was building, even as Knox continued to point out details and told stories of how design ideas came about. Their movements were slow and their steps lingered as Dani politely smiled and listened, feeling every single touch Knox gave her. Those small gestures were building to something much bigger and to the point, Dani was finding it hard to concentrate on what Knox was saying, let alone the space that surrounded him.

In truth, her mind was awash in its own thoughts of them being there, in total privacy... *together*... *alone.* It was something she hoped for but after Spain and the last time they spoke, it was only in her dreams.

If they got close again, would he break her heart once more? Because Dani was in love with the man in front of her, which meant she knew deep down that, no matter how big the real risk of rejection was, she would put herself in the firing line time and time again.

Knox noticed Dani's quietness and knew she was distracted in her own thoughts. She may have been smiling, nodding, and giving all the right answers here and there but he knew what was really on her mind. He knew because he himself was playing out his own internal monologue. The fact he was talking so much about the renovation was a mask for what he really wanted to talk about.

Acting this way for the first time, told him all he needed to know. *He was actually nervous. Because* he didn't want to fuck this up with Dani again.

"Come on, let me show you the mezzanine level," Knox said abruptly, making Dani jerk a little as the statement brought her fully out of her thoughts and back to the realisation that she was going to step foot into Lucas's bedroom.

Yes, they had been in his apartment in Spain. But back then

they hadn't exactly been alone, and the hotel room had been a neutral battle ground.

This place however was his own personal space, somewhere Dani knew that Knox didn't bring anyone. The thought alone was as intimidating as Knox himself.

Knox motioned his arm for her to go first as they reached the foot of the stairs. Dani felt the hairs on her neck stand on end as his hand gently touched her shoulder. Slowly, she moved to take the first step, and he let his hand slip down to the small of her back as his hand guided Dani up the stairs.

Knox was unable to keep his eyes off her shapely arse as she walked up, and he couldn't wait to see it in all its naked glory. In fact, he was so invested with the erotic sight, that he didn't even notice Dani as she nervously looked back and caught Knox checking her out. It made her feel good, and she couldn't help accentuating her movement, making Knox's eyes widen with the extra sway of her hips.

Fuck! He loved a woman with curves…

They reached the top of the stairs and Dani took it all in. To the right of them was the glorious bathtub, standing in the centre of a vaulted area with the glass roof being its ceiling. To the far wall was a tiled shower room that was big enough for four people, at least, and had two wall-mounted square rain heads. It also had several jets all set behind a sheet of toughened glass which separated the shower from the rest of the space.

To the left was the bedroom area, transitioning from the bathroom's hard wet-proof floor to a thick, high-pile carpet dominated by the large seven-foot by seven-foot Emperor bed. Different gradients of greys, blacks, and whites made up the masculine décor with its minimalist yet stylish, calm vibe.

"Wow, this is just wow…" Dani said, and as she looked at Knox and was about to speak again, she stopped herself.

Of course, Knox didn't miss it.

"What were you going to say?" he pressed, finding her shyness sweet and endearing. It only added to how much he craved to make her his.

"Well, er… There is no loo, and where do you keep all your clothes?" Dani asked quietly, feeling almost shy for asking, even though it was a perfectly valid question.

Knox laughed and guided her to the wall behind the bed.

"It is around here out of the way. It was the designer's idea," Knox replied as they walked around the side of the wall the head of the bed was pushed up against.

Access was from both sides of the bed and took them to a dressing room area with row after row of cupboards. There was also a large floor-to-ceiling mirror in the centre that faced an ox-blood-red chesterfield sofa. Beyond the dressing room was a door that led to a separate toilet.

"There is another bathroom downstairs too," Knox told her after showing her around and leading her back to where his bed dominated the space.

"So, do you think you will be comfortable here?" Knox asked, wanting to cut the sexual tension that had still continued to grow. Something that wasn't helped by being in the presence of his bed.

"Frankly, Lucas, I am speechless, it's lovely… really lovely. But there is one thing," Dani replied, feeling as if she needed to ask about the sleeping elephant in the room. Especially seeing as, so far, she had only been shown one bedroom. But then she gathered Knox wasn't the type of guy to have many house guests, so she couldn't say she was surprised.

"Go on, ask, sweetheart," Knox prompted softly.

"It's a big bed," she said, giving Knox cause to grin.

"Aye that it is, Lass," he replied, knowing exactly where this was headed and smirking because of it.

"It really is big, huge in fact… a very big bed," she muttered, and he couldn't help but take a step closer to her.

She was just too fucking cute, Knox thought, especially when she was being all shy and unsure.

"Very big," Knox commented as he took another step, this time one that put him close enough to reach her. Then he grumbled her name while simultaneously taking her chin and forcing her to look up at him. *"Dani."*

"Mm?" This sound came out breathy and Knox once again had to fight the urge to chuckle.

"Is there something you wanted to ask me about my bed, sweetheart?" he asked, his voice a soft timber she was quickly getting lost in.

"Your bed, will I um… be sleeping in it?" Dani braved to ask.

Tugging her to him was his first answer, and it ignited a breathy sound of surprise from her before he told her firmly, "Yes, Dani… you will be sleeping in my bed… *With me.*"

ELEVEN
CITRUS SOAP

The hard swallow from the top of Dani's throat to the bottom, was clear for Knox to see being this close to her. Her face flushed a little, and he wanted her to know his intentions so she had the time to process it.

Instead of kissing her raw like he wanted to, he forced himself to step away, heading to the bath and turned on the taps. One kiss would be all it took before he threw her onto the bed that had been such an interest to her. But Knox wanted to be sure that this was what she wanted because he knew there was no going back from this point. Not after he'd finally had her.

He wouldn't let her go again.

"What…what are you doing?" she asked when she came out of the sexual daze Knox had put her in with his promise of what was to come.

Knox looked back over his shoulder at this and winked at her.

"Is this your way of telling me I smell or something?" she asked in a teasing tone, making him scoff.

"No, this is my way of helping you relax…" Knox said, letting the sentence linger when straightening from where he had been hunched over the bath, making sure to get the temperature right. Then he walked back over to her and paused his steps long enough to tell her… *"…Before I wear you out."*

Knox left her to 'relax', although admittedly that part of his plan was easier said than done. Especially knowing she was currently naked in his amazing bathtub while being very aware he was just downstairs.

The simple task of washing herself was more difficult than it should have been, her nerves almost getting the better of her, but thankfully she found a bar of soap and sponge in a cabinet next to the bath.

It didn't exactly smell of him, so Dani knew his amazing scent was most likely down to whatever aftershave he wore. This being said, it wasn't like it was a girly scent either, having more citrus notes than flowery ones that she couldn't ever image Knox indulging in. No, he was too manly for that. The thought that had her squirming at just the idea of him downstairs and coming up there to find her still in the bath.

Better yet, what if she made it happen? Dani dared to form a plan in her mind, because she knew that Knox was giving her time to settle her nerves. He wasn't an idiot, the man missed nothing.

So, what if she was to make the first move?

"Oh, fuck it," she mumbled to herself before deciding to take matters into her own hands. It wasn't like she had played this first-time fantasy between them in her head a million times before.

Well, now was her chance.

"Erm… Knox?" she called before she could talk herself out of it. She didn't have to wait long before he called back to her.

"What do you need, Dani girl?" he asked, giving her this new nickname that admittedly only made her want him more.

"Could you bring up my bag, please?" she asked, holding her breath as she waited for his reply. It didn't come instantly, it was as if he was trying to read between the lines and asking himself if it was what he hoped it was… *an invitation.*

"Sure," he shouted back, after first clearing his throat.

She waited, listening out for every sound he made, jumping slightly when she heard him making his way up the staircase because she knew just what he would find when he finally made it up there… *her naked, wet, and waiting for him.*

Of course, facing the staircase, she had a full view of his reaction the second he saw her, and let's just say that Knox wasn't the type of man to have bubble bath stocked in his bathroom cabinets. This meant that only a fine film of soap suds floated on the surface, making the parts of her body appear as skin-coloured islands surrounded by the breaking of the white water.

As for Knox, his eyes drank in the sight of her, stopping dead in his tracks the moment he saw what awaited him. In fact, he dropped the bag, making it the only sound to echo in the vast space as his heated gaze swept each milky line of her skin. He had never seen a sight more beautifully erotic and because of it, he couldn't have stopped his feet from taking him closer even if he had tried.

Dani's wide-eyed doe look only heightened the experience for Knox, and he was quick to take control of the situation. Thanks to her artwork, he was sure he knew the type of submission Dani craved. And she wasn't a fool because she also had a fair idea what type of man Knox would be in the bedroom.

This invitation upstairs was as good as the word green being uttered from her lips. However, Knox still needed to hear it from her directly, just to be assured she knew what she was getting into here.

For Knox, sleeping with a woman was more often than not, just sex. But when it came to Dani, the woman he loved… well, for him the need to dominate her in the bedroom was a craving he felt rooted to his soul. If he discovered he had been completely off the mark about her sexual desires, then he would take all she was willing to give him. Either way, he was going to find out soon.

"Could… could you hand me a towel please?" she stammered, making him smirk as he walked with purpose, bringing him so close to the bath that she had to look directly up at him.

"You're not finished," he stated firmly, and again he drank in her nervous reaction like the finest ale.

"I'm not?" she asked, and he shook his head.

"No, you're not."

She watched as he crossed over his arms and gripped the hem of his shirt before pulling it up over his head. The sight instantly made Dani's mouth go dry as she took in every perfectly sculptured hard line that Knox possessed. Even the stitches, a testament to Dani's careful handiwork, along with the fading bruises and scrapes, only seemed to enhance the raw, rugged beauty of the man before her.

His heated gaze held promises that she knew his muscles would come in handy for later.

She wasn't the only one taking the time to memorize every inch of the other because Knox couldn't take his damn eyes off her.

He tossed his T-shirt off to one side, landing on the floor and he knew it would soon be joined by his jeans. But first, there was something he had in mind. It was time to show her that he could be gentle with her before introducing her to a firmer hand.

Dropping to his knees he said only a single word, not trust himself to say more in that moment from fear of scaring her.

"Soap," he demanded, making her swallow hard before she quickly started fumbling in the bath water, knowing she had dropped it at some point.

"Here, let me help you with that," Knox offered, his lips twitching in a knowing grin. He dipped his hand beneath the water, followed by his strong forearm, making her jump as he came into contact with her naked body. She felt his large hand skim along the outside of her thigh, running the length of her leg in a slow, measured movement.

"Are you even looking for it?" Dani dared to ask, teasing him and making him grin.

"What can I say? It must be well hidden," he replied, making her giggle, a sound that died in her throat the moment he dipped in between her legs. His quest of discovery took him to a more forbidden place... or at least it had been for Dani, because it had been a while since any man had touched her there.

After tonight, Knox knew that he would come to know every inch of her, something he took great pleasure in as he made the slow, sensual journey along the curves of her body. *Fuck*, he couldn't wait until she was spread out on his bed so he could see just as much as he could now feel. He knew she would be a fucking feast for his eyes as well as his tongue.

The moment he skimmed the back of his fingers along her pussy, she jolted in the water, making him barely hold back his smile, and as she let her head fall back on the rim, she couldn't hold back her sassy retort, even if it came out breathless.

"I don't think it's up there."

"I do like to be thorough," he growled.

"Good to… *know,*" she replied, this last word coming out even more breathless as he ran a knuckle between her folds, purposely grazing her clit.

The moment he saw how responsive she was to him, he was in two minds on whether or not to just slip his fingers inside and bring her to orgasm right here in the bath. But then he knew once he saw that, there would be no stopping him, and for what he wanted to do to her, she would first need to be out of the bath. So, despite it paining him to do so, he left her silky folds and looked for the soap in earnest this time.

Like he had said, he wanted her nice and relaxed, ready for what he had planned for her. So, with this in his mind, he took the sponge and lathered it up, wishing he had foreseen this moment and bought a more feminine scented soap for her. Hell, he would have bought every fucking luxury he could have gotten his hands on if he had known. But then one look at the lust on her face as he began to soap up her body, running the sud-soaked sponge across her skin… he didn't think she would have noticed any of it. His home could have been burning to ash around them and she wouldn't have looked at anywhere but him.

The feel of what Knox was doing felt amazing but when he added his spare hand to the mix, it had her near panting. He followed the bubbled road up her torso, spreading the soap over her belly before moving up to her heaving breast, and it was little wonder why she gasped the second he got there. The texture of the sponge caught on her erect nipples, before his fingers stopped there in order to pay special attention to them. A deep and lustful moan escaped her as her head fell back once more.

"Lucas."

At the sound of her whispering his name, Knox couldn't help but close his own eyes in anticipation of hearing it over and over again as he finally got to slide his cock into her sweet pussy. The heavy weight pressed uncomfortably against the denim of his jeans and he swore the sound had made all the blood rush to his cock.

It was like sweet torture for both of them as he took his time memorizing the map of her body with every glide of his hand as she arched and writhed, practically willing him to spend more time on the most erotic parts of her. In fact, it was when he started to move his hand away from in between her legs before she could come, that she suddenly gripped his wrist, holding him there and begging him with her eyes.

It was the perfect opportunity for Knox to teach Dani her first lesson, and a brief insight as to how this evening was going to go.

"Tut tut, you wouldn't be topping from the bottom now, would you, Dani girl?" Knox asked, his voice not showing even a hint of teasing, making her swallow hard at the authoritative tone.

She shook her head at this, but the narrowing of his eyes told her that wasn't good enough.

"I asked you a question and I expect to be answered properly… now do I need to ask again?"

Dani's eyes widened as she shook her head again. The mistake in doing so was quickly learned as he gripped the inside of her thigh hard enough to create a sting.

"No! No, Si…" she stopped herself before finishing the title, making him nod his head and encourage her after easing the pressure on her thigh.

"Go on, girl, you know what I want," he prompted, easing her through the submissive steps.

"No, Sir," she whispered in an unsure tone, making him grin.

"Good girl," he praised. Again, he watched the hard lump in her throat make its way down her slender neck.

"Now before we continue, I need to hear you say that you understand where this is going and that you want this as much as I do," Knox asked her, and just hearing this broke down a few of Dani's walls. Knowing he didn't want to cross any lines with this was also already one of the hottest things she'd ever experienced.

"I understand, Lucas, and… I want this... *I want you to be yourself.*" Dani's reply made Knox close his eyes for a moment as he sighed in relief.

His assumptions about her desires were right and he couldn't have been more fucking happy to hear that. Which was why the next words out of his mouth were to ensure her continued trust in him with this.

"In that case, Green is go. Amber, we slow it down and Red, everything stops, do you understand?" Knox asked.

Dani nodded, but that wasn't good enough for him. He needed her words.

"I need to hear you say it, lass," he said in a gentle tone this time. It wasn't reprimanding in any way, telling her how important this was to Knox.

"I understand," Dani said softly, her shy smile telling him that she was thankful for the care he showed in this.

"Good, now which is it?" he asked, his voice once more taking on that more demanding demeanor, which was like flipping a switch for both of them.

Dani couldn't help but get even more turned on by it, the deep timbre of his dom voice sending sparks straight between her legs, which was why she quickly answered, "Green… definitely green."

He grinned at that, her quick reply infectious and causing him to grin.

"Now time to get out of the bath," he ordered after he rose back to his feet, enjoying the sight of her looking vulnerable and shy.

The sight mixed with her blown pupils full of lust fed his sexual dominate nature. But knowing this was her first time dripping her toes into a dark world of kink, one she had obviously fantasied about, he decided to go easy on her. He did this by offering her his hand instead of reprimanding her for making him wait.

She looked relieved and Knox knew he had done the right thing when she trusted him enough to put her hand in his. And his own reward was the glorious, sexy as sin sight as she rose from the soapy water like a goddamn water goddess! The water dripped down her naked body, the soap suds remaining as if teasing her skin, and they too trickled down the path he wanted to follow with his tongue.

"Damn, girl, all the things I want to do to you..." Knox rumbled as he actually licked his lips like a hungry predator ready to pounce. And pounce he did, giving Dani a taste of what was to come.

He suddenly bent into her, and at the same time lifted her up over his shoulder, smacking her arse when she cried out in shock. This was one of many fantasies she'd had about Knox, so it was a great start.

"Quiet, girl!" he ordered, making her yelp at the sting before arousal flooded her core.

He then walked with purpose before her wet body slid easily from his shoulder as he threw her down onto the bed. Her naked body was spread out and on show, every inch of her no longer hidden by the soapy water.

And as for Knox, he didn't miss a thing. He drank in every piece of her as he stood at the end of the bed enjoying the sight.

Then he told her, "Fuck me, Dani girl… *I can't wait to make you scream for me.*"

TWELVE
FAR FROM DONE

The moment Knox spoke, Dani couldn't help but shiver. Especially when he started to lower himself down over her, the heavy indent of his knee pressing down on the mattress a startling reminder of what was about to happen.

Knox moved slowly, angling himself in such a way so his weight remained off her… *for now.* Then he started to draw his fingertips up her naked wet body, stroking his way up her soft belly and in between her heaving breasts as her nerves returned with a vengeance. This slow, sensual journey continued until he made his way up to her cheek, then her hair. Taking a soft hold of the back of Dani's head, threading his fingers through her hair, Knox angled her to give him access to what he wanted; her velvet-soft, full lips.

Their eyes were transfixed, and Dani held her breath as Knox lowered his lips to hers, but there was a split second of hesitation as they hovered a paper-width apart.

Goddamn it, Knox wanted this woman so badly, every cell in his body compelled him to kiss her and take her as his own.

Why was he not kissing her yet? He screamed this to himself over and over.

Dani's hands slipped up over the sides of his torso, and she kneaded her fingers into his skin, finding hard, tensed muscle there. It was difficult for her to hold out for much longer, even knowing that Knox had tried to slow himself down for her sake. It was a selfless gesture she obliterated in an instant by lifting her head the rest of the way for their lips to meet.

The delicious taste of her exploded on his tongue and he actually made a sound like a fucking growl. A sound she responded to and her hands found their way to his hair as she moaned into his mouth. Knox knew that if he carried on kissing her, then nothing would stop him from burying his cock deep inside her. Not that there was anything wrong with this plan, but the primal side of him wanted to give her the type of experience he knew she had always dreamed of.

He wanted to dominate over all other sexual encounters she may have had in the past, the thought of which quickly uncoiled the snake of jealously in the pit of his stomach. The anger at knowing someone else had seen and touched her exquisite body had him momentarily tense the hand he had fisted in her hair, granting her that slight bite of pain he knew she craved. He was quick to ease his grip though, because he knew how damaging bringing emotions into this situation could be.

The growing emotion was why Knox pulled back from kissing her, trying to slow this down and with it, trying to rein back some control. Dani's eyes flashed a look of disappointment before she then tried to continue the kiss. In response, Knox moved his head back further, releasing the hold he had of Dani's hair completely.

He skimmed the backs of his fingers down her cheek, stopping at her mouth. Then he rested his thumb over her lips, caressing them as he began to tease the seam.

Dani got the hint and kissed his thumb before opening her mouth a little, all the while looking at Knox with a hunger as she let out the breathy sigh. He slipped his thumb inside her willing mouth and she closed her eyes as she sucked it in deep. The saltiness of his skin played on her senses as she imagined the next part of him she was hoping she would soon taste.

After this erotic, sexy as fuck sight, Knox was done with waiting. He had to taste her again. So, he took a hold of her jaw and with no gentleness or subtlety, he pulled her closer where his lips met hers hard and hungrily. Knox sucked Dani's bottom lip into his mouth and scraped his teeth along it, sending delicious shocks across the sensitive nerves and making her blue eyes widen. When he licked at the seam of her mouth, she opened for him as he knew she would, and their tongues met with zealous force. Knox groaned as Dani pulled at his hair, wanting him closer.

Once again, Knox took control and dominated a responsive Dani, despite it pleasing him to see just how eager Dani was. With slow, measured movements he directed Dani, putting her exactly where he wanted her… starting with restraining her.

Dropping his weight to his, his hands were free to snake up her arms where she still clutched onto his hair. She got the hint quickly when he disengaged her hold on him by taking her wrists with both hands. Then, once gripping them tightly, he pulled them from his head before pushing them forcefully into the bed, pinning them above her.

Dani's eyes widened at the sudden and forceful action, watching as Knox's lips turned up into a devilish grin. A grin that she soon felt against her skin as he dipped his head down to her neck, the pressure on her wrists only adding to the dominating position.

But it wasn't enough, Dani wanted more.

Arching her back she began to push her hips up to meet his.

The hard length of his cock pressed against his jeans and told her that she wasn't the only one who wanted more. However, her impatience didn't bring her the outcome she was hoping for because he bit down on the skin between her neck and shoulder, making her cry out.

"Now are you going to be good for me?" He pulled back enough to ask, after first soothing the sting with his tongue. She could only nod her head a little, making him warn, "Now what did I say about answering me?"

The way he spoke to her made her mouth drop a little, her mind whirling back to only minutes ago. She found the memory a lot quicker when he narrowed his eyes down at her before starting to dip his head to her neck once more. Just as he opened his mouth to bite her again, she suddenly remembered.

"Yes, Sir!" she shouted, giving him what he wanted, and she felt his grin against her skin before he kissed her there.

"Good girl… now, keep your arms above you and spread your legs," he told her, making her gasp at the firm order given.

This time, all he needed to do was give her a stern look before she complied and let her legs fall open. However, when he shifted back, her nerves got the better of her and she began to close her legs in shame. Knox's eyes darkened and he took matters into his own hands by suddenly gripping her legs and forcing them apart.

"This body is mine, understood?" he warned.

Dani nodded up at him, stopping when he raised an expectant brow.

"Yes Sir."

This time, he didn't praise her but simply grinned before lowering himself over her spread legs. Then once his face was only an inch away from her pussy, one she knew he would already find soaked, he inhaled deeply.

"Mm… fuck, you smell delicious, girl," Knox rumbled before dipping closer and indulging in his first taste.

Dani pushed her head back into the sheets as he pressed his lips hard against her pussy before licking up the seam. A tongue that Dani knew should have come with a warning sign began to stimulate the bundle of nerves hidden between her glistening folds of pink flesh.

"Fuck!" Dani swore, the breathy and laboured sound hissed through her teeth.

The reaction had Knox grinning against her inner thigh before biting down and making her squeal before squirming away from him. With a low growl, he grabbed her arse cheek and yanked her back to him with a forceful tug. Knox then used his fingers on one hand to spread her apart, giving his tongue the freedom to dart from side to side before then licking up the length of her from entrance to her clit.

Dani bit back another shriek at his exploring all around her most intimate parts, now building into a rhythm that was sweet torture. Her legs began to tremble slightly from the tension he had evoked within her. Finally, when Dani thought she couldn't take any more of his teasing, he flicked his tongue right over her honeyed clit and kept it there. The release she screamed out felt like it had been ripped from her and her legs shook from the sensations.

Knox continued with featherlight strokes of his tongue in a tempo that made Dani pant as he prolonged her release.

It became too much for her, too sensitive, so she clamped his head with her thighs as he stretched out her pleasure.

"Please… oh God, Lucas, please… I can't…" Dani whimpered, and Knox wouldn't lie… he fucking loved hearing her beg.

He also knew how addicted he could become to this woman… shit, he was already there! Everything from her taste to her sweet cries as he fucked her with his tongue were utter perfection. And this was all before he had even felt his cock inside her. But he also knew that his little submissive still had a lot to learn, and it was a lesson that made him as hard as a fucking rock, knowing he was about to give her…

Because she needed to know that, in the bedroom, she wasn't the one who got to make the demands. She didn't call the shots.

She simply had to obey.

And it was time to put that obedience to the test. Starting with Knox forcing himself to leave her beautiful glistening cunt. His stubble was wet from her recent release, and he looked up at her as she continued to tremble. Her eyes were still shut, with her face turned to the side, and he knew now was the time to re-establish his dominance over her.

Knox placed a single finger beneath Dani's chin and turned her head to face him, her eyes still shut tightly as she gulped down hard.

"Look at me, Dani girl," Knox ordered, trying to keep his lustful thoughts from making his voice too harsh. His reward was her doing as he asked, her striking blue eyes now staring at him in a way that made him feel he had the power to hang the moon.

"You are so beautiful, I just want to test every inch of your skin." The depth of his words sent a new thrill thrumming through her core.

"You mean taste?" Dani asked nervously, before adding, "'Cause I think you just did that."

Knox was in half a mind to tease her back, but he knew that would defeat the object here because part of the pleasure gained through this Sub/Dom dynamic meant keeping a tight control on any play in the bedroom. Of course, Knox wasn't a bastard. He could see himself enjoying Dani in all manner of ways.

Fooling around, teasing one another, and playfully fucking were things he actually looked forward to. But that wasn't what this was, not right now.

This was her first test, one Knox knew she craved just as much as he did. Which was why he corrected her in a level, calm tone.

"Test, Dani. Now present yourself to me," Knox demanded, nodding down to her beautiful breasts, making her question him with a shocked expression.

"I… er, well I don't think…"

Knox interrupted her, releasing a rumbled sound of disapproval before lowering himself closer to her and saying more sternly, *"Offer me your tits, girl."*

Dani released a shuddered breath as the crude order shot straight to her pussy. Unable to disobey him and wanting to please him, she cupped her breasts and lifted them up to his face, licking her dry lips as she waited for what he would do next. The praise he gave her once again affected her in a way that had her questioning her sanity. *Fuck*, she was more turned on than she had ever been in her entire life!

Knox took his time to look at them, lowering his lips to barely whisper his breath across her nipples, enticing another shudder from her.

"Mm, light pink," Knox said with a grin, and he made her feel like a new project of his he was currently studying. "I've been wondering what colour your nipples would be. They look fucking tasty."

Dani squirmed at his words, squeezing her thighs together as he took one of her breasts from her in his large hand and squeezed. Knox's thumb began to play over the nipple in a way that stirred a deeper hunger inside her. He then pinched it hard enough to make Dani draw in a sharp breath before he took her nipple into his mouth, soothing it before sucking hard. Knox's other hand stroked up her inner thigh, which made her clit throb once more, aching for more of him. In a moment of bravery Dani spoke again.

"They're so sensitive, I love them being… *played with ohh… you could make me… come from this,"* Dani softly whispered over heavy breaths.

Knox smiled as he put a finger to her lips, telling her silently to be quiet. Dani knew she should have been offended at Knox telling her not to speak, but she couldn't deny how she felt at being told what to do. How much it affected her and made her crave his masterful dominance even more. Which was when she decided to push it.

"Yes… oh yes, just like that… ouch, fuck!" This ended with a squeal of pain, and he bit down around her nipple in warning.

"You are not doing as you're told, girl," Knox chastised as he ran his other hand up Dani's body, around to her neck, and straight into her hair.

"Lucas, I…" Dani spoke out but before she could finish, Knox took a firm grip of her hair and tugged.

She yelped in shock and from the slight pain, although she knew Knox was also not hurting her as much as he could, had he wanted to. She knew that when he gripped the top of her arm and helped her into the position he wanted her in.

A position that put her over his knee.

Her heart started to hammer in her chest as she was held down by her neck into the bed. Her arse was arched over his denim-covered knees, his thick erection trying to escape against the tops of her thighs.

"Now I want you to be quiet. You should be following my commands, Dani," Knox stated calmly, showing her that he wasn't doing this through anger because he didn't want to frighten her. The slight stroking of his thumb against the back of her neck was to help prove as much.

"Lucas, this… I… please," Dani begged sweetly, squirming in his hold.

With the way she purposely wiggled against his cock, Knox knew that she was just playing the part of the unsure little submissive about to experience her first spanking.

"And still, you don't listen," Knox said with a deeper timber to his voice, despite his joy in now having the perfect excuse. *The excuse to punish…*

A sharp crack sounded as it cut through the air around them, and Dani became paralysed as silence fell on the room. She glared back at Knox in shock, despite knowing that this was going to continue as his hand continued to rub circles over her warming arse.

Knox looked her in the eyes and waited, watching…

Dani's mouth opened and as she began to speak… Slap! This time his hand fell on the other cheek… *hard and forceful.* It shocked Dani at first, but as the sting turned to a fuzzy warmth, she found herself closing her eyes as she whimpered.

It wasn't a string of curses or yelling for him to stop, because she didn't want him to stop. Not with the way it made her body feel, the way her mind summersaulted into a deliciously dark place she had only ever dreamed about venturing in to.

The masterful grip on her neck held her pinned over his knees, and the way his hand alternated between a soothing caress and harsh reprimand… Christ, it was already driving her closer to what she knew would be a blinding release. Somehow, the spanks and that feeling of what he was doing to her amplified her pain and turned it to building pleasure.

"Now, are you a fast or a slow learner?" Knox asked as he repeatedly spanked her.

The sight of her pale white skin turning flush with a glowing redness fed Knox's own pleasure. Her skin rippled from the force of his hand, the feeling on both ends excited them equally. Dani took the spanks with a few moans, but desperately tried to be a good sub. Knox was as surprised as much as he wasn't. Dani had wanted this for so long, and Knox could see it written across her face. It was time to reward such good behaviour.

"A fast learner, good girl." Knox's words of praise consumed Dani's thoughts, and she knew she could get addicted to being called a good girl by Knox... *her fantasy Dom.*

"Good girls get rewarded," Knox continued as he pushed her thighs apart, his fingers parting Dani's folds.

He gently pushed a teasingly slow thumb inside her wet silkiness, and the feeling of him entering was heavenly, causing Dani to react by lifting and pushing herself back onto him. Knox adored this reaction and he hooked his long, thick thumb inside her, touching something that made Dani cry out in untamed hunger.

"You like that, do you, lass?" Knox teased, knowing full well she did.

Dani nodded and whimpered when he pressed against it harder. This time he let her get away without answering him, because he knew for her first time, he would allow a few misdemeanours on her part.

The way he pressed the pad of his thumb against that spot inside her was like playing with his own personal fuck toy. It made Knox feel almost primal with the way he made her buck with pleasure. This all only added to the pressure building in his own cock. Christ, he needed to fuck her! But first, he wanted to make sure to get her off one more time before he did.

Knox continued to build her up to a point where he was not being gentle anymore, fucking her with his thumb in earnest. Dani started to feel overwhelmed by the sensation, and as if she was afraid it would make her come apart by the seams, she tried to move away.

"Oh no you don't, you're not going anywhere. Now stay," Knox demanded firmly as his other arm banded around her waist to hold her in place, keeping her exactly where he wanted her.

Dani opened her eyes and found Knox looking right back at her, reading her face and movements. There was such a hunger in Knox's harsh gaze that it made her want to hide, but she couldn't. There was nothing she could do but lay there, trapped in his arms, over his lap as he toyed with her body. He kept on pressing and building around that spot, then he added another sensation; his first finger pushed over her clit.

Dani began to pant in his arms, and she found she couldn't look away from him, trapped in his shameless gaze, a gaze that held an intensity she had never experienced before. Then without control or choice, Dani's release crashed over her. It was the most all-consuming pleasure descending all around her body. She had no awareness other than his hands controlling her body. No idea of the wetness that ran down her thighs, nor the way her muscles shuddered as aftershocks played sweet havoc on her body.

A body he now wanted even more of.

He ran a soothing hand down her spine, bringing her back to reality. A reality he currently controlled every aspect of, and he pulled his thumb from her dripping core before bending over her enough to bring it to her lips.

"Suck it clean, my girl," he ordered, and in between her still heaving breaths, she opened up and obeyed.

The taste of herself burst over her tongue and the power switched, if only for a moment, as Knox moaned at the feel of her tongue lapping up her own cum. As soon as it was clean and Knox could take no more of her gentle teasing, he pulled his thumb free from her lips. She then watched in fascination as he raised it to his own mouth so he could do the same, keeping eye contact the whole time and drinking in her response.

"Mmm addictive," he hummed to himself, before reaching down and whispering over her, *"And I am far from done with you yet."*

THIRTEEN
PERFECTION INTERRUPTED

Knox's eyes snapped open as he was jolted awake from the deepest sleep he had experienced in years. His heart raced as he reached out for Dani, but he only felt empty sheets beside him. Panic rose in his chest and he sat up, scanning the room, until relief flooded through him at the sound of movement downstairs in the kitchen. The comforting scent of freshly brewed coffee drifted up to the mezzanine floor, calming his nerves.

With a rueful smile, Knox swung his legs off the bed and pulled on a pair of jeans before making his way over to the glass balustrades. He leaned over and caught sight of Dani in just his T-shirt, pottering around the kitchen searching for coffee mugs. A wave of possessiveness washed over him and he couldn't help but imagine waking up to this every morning. The only way to improve it would have been waking up to the feel of her curvy body nestled into his. Just like he had spent most of the night sleeping with her in his arms.

It was obvious that he had worn her out, because after taking his cock for a second time that night, in too many positions to count, he had then made her come one more time.

Needless to say, she was exhausted and Knox found her practically passed out when he had come back from the bathroom after ridding himself of the condom.

Naturally, he grinned at the memory.

"Top right cupboard, lass," he said as he took in the sight of her going up on tiptoes to reach the mugs, awarding him with the most teasing view. Her tousled golden hair cascaded down her back and the delicious hint of flushed-crimson bum cheeks peeked from under his T-shirt. The evidence of her spanking had him hard in seconds as he remembered fucking her from behind last night. Her moans of rapture sounded like she was begging for more every time my palm met her smooth skin. Not once did Dani say Red or even Amber, and it was clear that stopping was the very last thing on her mind.

He was fucking elated.

Dani jumped at the sound of his voice, but her face lit up when she looked up and saw Knox.

"I hope you like your coffee black," she said before pointing out, "Because you have no milk or cream. But I did find sugar." Her voice floated up the stairs like a soothing melody. Knox followed the sound down into the kitchen to find her pulling two mugs from the cupboard.

She smiled back at him and Knox couldn't resist wrapping his arms around her from behind, pulling her close for a hug and planting a kiss on her neck. Her skin was warm and sweet against his lips.

"You're all the sweetness I need," he whispered, feeling content and at peace in this moment, asking himself when the last time was he had felt this way... *if ever.*

Dani snuggled into him, enjoying the warmth of his embrace.

"Such a charmer... mmm," she teased, a comment that

ended with a moan when his hands snuck under the T-shirt she was wearing and made contact with her skin.

The sensation took her back to the night before, when Knox had kissed, sucked, and bitten every inch of her last night. It had to be said, Knox had been insatiable in his need for her, dominating every piece of her one moment, then making her feel like a worshipped goddess the next. The rough with the smooth had always kept her guessing and made her head spin in the best way possible. He had fucked her hard and fast, making her come powerfully enough to see stars. Then in the next instance, he had also showed her slow and sensual, making her feel adored in a way she never had before.

And now here he was, bringing all these glorious memories back with just his teasing, gentle touch. However, when she felt him run his finger along the four-inch scar on the right side of her belly just above her knicker line, Dani flinched.

"How did you get this?" Knox asked softly, feeling her sigh as she leaned into him. He hated bringing it up, but ever since spotting it the night before, the question had prodded at him. His protective instinct over Dani flared, and he hoped with every fibre of his being that no one had hurt her. If they had, he knew he wouldn't rest until he hunted them down, with deadly intent.

"Oh, that was my twenty-first birthday present," Dani replied awkwardly.

"How?" Knox was tense and the singular word barely escaped through his gritted teeth.

It was clear that she understood by his tone where his dark mind had gone to, so she quickly reassured him.

"I was on holiday at my family's cabin and my appendix burst, I didn't even get to have cake," she said, turning enough so he could see her pout. Instantly she felt him relax behind her before he once again stroked the length of the scar in a sweet gesture.

"That sounds painful," he commented, unable to help himself as his other hand snaked up her body and cupped her breast, making her head fall back against him.

"Mmm hmm… I didn't even get the chance to blow out my candles and let's just say, I didn't get my wish."

Knox had to grin at that, especially when his hand dipped lower, slipping inside the waist band of her knickers where he swiped a finger along her wet folds. The action soon had her moaning.

"Wish, you say…? I'm sure I can help with that," Knox rumbled as his finger travelled lower, before he was cupping her pussy in his large hand.

Just before he could bend her over and claim her once more, he heard her stomach rumble and as much as it pained him, he left the warmth of her dripping sex.

"I think it's time to feed my girl," he told her.

The pout she gave him in response had nothing to do with missing cake. Knox however, ignored her sassiness and raised his fingers to his mouth, sucking them clean.

"Mmm, like I said, all the sweetness I need."

This made Dani blush before reaching up on tiptoes and telling him, "Didn't anyone tell you, *it's rude not to share.*"

This whispered part made Knox even harder, and her sexual teasing was already taking their relationship to the next level, one he fucking adored. She sucked on his fingers before they led her to his mouth, and the kiss was dirty and erotic.

In fact, had her stomach not rumbled once more, then he would have said screw the food and fucked her there and then.

"Behave, woman," he growled playfully, nipping at her lips.

Her response was to pat him on the butt and say, "With you

standing there all shirtless and looking all manly and stuff… er hello? I'm a girl with needs."

He laughed at that and told her, "I think you had many of those needs met last night, lass, and last time I checked, food is also a need."

She giggled at his quick-witted response and replied, "Well, I better go and see what I can whip up for us then." She flashed him a warm smile before heading to the freezer, eager to take care of her man and plan their first breakfast together.

Knox was more than happy to oblige, enjoying the view of her bending slightly as she peered into the bottom part of the freezer. Damn, he would need to get some actual fresh food at some point. But before that, he knew he had something to get out of the way first. Something that included Dani as much as it didn't.

"I will be back in a minute, lass," Knox told her.

She looked back at him over her shoulder, tossing her hair out of the way.

"Where are you going?" she asked, and he was happy to hear the slight neediness in her tone.

Good, he wanted her as addicted to him as he was to her.

"I should go inform T.I.7 that I found you and you're safe," he said, immediately snapping back into work mode.

Dani gave him a quizzical look from behind the freezer door, pausing her rummaging through its contents.

"Why?" she asked, her voice slightly strained.

"I promised Harris that I would let him know when I found you," he explained as he opened a drawer next to him, revealing a burner phone in pieces with the SIM card and battery removed.

Knox quickly reassembled the phone, sliding in the card and snapping the battery into place. He pressed the power button, and the screen flickered to life. The moment the phone connected to the network, Knox dialed Harris's number, which was etched into his memory thanks to all of his missed calls yesterday.

"Harris here."

"Harris, it's Knox, I found her," Knox replied.

The Major released a relieved sigh. "Good, that's good."

Something about Harris's tone instantly put Knox on edge. "What's going on, Major?" he asked looking over to Dani to find her still rummaging in the freezer. As for Harris, his tone quickly shifted from relief to urgency.

"Listen, Knox, we need you back at new HQ immediately. We've got a lead on Mac. He's in Germany, and we believe he's heading to Werl Prison."

Knox's grip tightened on the phone and just the mention of his old back-stabbing comrade.

"Werl Prison? What's his angle here?" Knox asked with a frown, still watching Dani and questioning whether he saw her flinch. He could tell she was trying not to make it obvious that she was listening in to their conversation. One he saw no need to hide from her seeing as she was a part of this now.

"We're still piecing it together," Harris replied, and Knox didn't like the sound of this.

Something was off… why the prison?

As if hearing his thoughts, Harris added, "But if Mac's there, it's for something big. We need to get ahead of him. Get back here as fast as you can. We're mobilizing a team."

Knox looked at Dani once more and this time, their eyes met for a split second. She continued to act oblivious to the conversation, humming softly as she prepared their breakfast. He hated the idea of leaving her again, but he knew what was at stake should Mac continue with whatever plan he had in mind.

So, the choice was simple, find Mac, kill him, then the threat to Dani goes away. Besides, now she was here, he knew she would be safe.

"I'm on my way. Send a location to this phone," Knox said, his voice filled with steely resolve. *Finally, an opportunity to get the fucker!*

"No need, we are very close, go spend a penny at The River. Say hi to the floozie. And Knox… be careful," Harris said cryptically.

The line went dead after that and Knox slowly lowered the phone, his mind racing. He couldn't shake the feeling that things were about to get even more complicated. But at least he understood what Harris meant. However, he had to ask himself how much of a coincidence it was that the new T.I.7 HQ was so close.

Knox stood by the kitchen counter, the phone still warm in his hand after the call as his gaze settled on Dani. She seemed lost in her task of trying to find something to eat, completely unaware of the turmoil brewing inside him. The morning light streamed through the large roof skylight, casting a glow over her, making the scene almost surreal. He hated that he had to shatter this moment, but there was no other choice.

"Dani," he started, his voice soft but firm, catching her attention.

She turned to him, a look in her eyes he couldn't fully decipher but if he had to guess, he would have called it worry. Did she know what he was going to say next?

"What's wrong?" she asked, getting the question out first, concern etching lines on her forehead.

He jerked his head, telling her to come closer, and the moment she was within reach he framed her hips.

"I need to head into T.I.7 HQ," he said, his tone laced with regret. "There's been a development, and they need me at a briefing."

Dani's eyes searched his, trying to grasp the gravity of the situation.

"Is it Mac?" she asked, her voice barely above a worried whisper.

Knox nodded, his jaw tightening. "Yeah, they've got a lead on him. He's in Germany, which means I have to go, Dani. I have to stop him."

She closed her eyes at this as a shiver ran through her at the mention of his name. A name that was quickly starting to haunt her dreams. She suddenly gripped onto Knox's bare arms, trying to steady herself.

"Okay… okay… But this… we… What happens now?" she asked, her voice trembling slightly as if she was struggling with what was happening.

He hadn't realised just how frightened she must be and Knox gently pulled her closer, wrapping his arms around her, feeling the warmth of her body against his. He rested his chin on the top of her head, taking in the scent of her hair, trying to memorize every detail of this moment.

"It will be okay, Dani, do you hear me? You stay here and you will be safe," he told her with a gentle firmness to his voice to reassure her. He felt her nod her head against his chest but when she didn't say anything, he told her once again, "I promise you, this place is safe, Dani. No one knows about it, not even T.I.7. But you can't leave, okay? And you have to avoid using any tech—no phones, no computers. I can't risk them tracking you."

At this she released a shuddered sigh. Then she pulled back slightly, looking up at him with wide, anxious eyes.

"But what if something happens? What if you…" Knox silenced her with a soft kiss, his lips lingering on hers, trying to convey everything he couldn't put into words. When he finally pulled away, he cupped her face in his hands, his thumbs gently brushing away the tears that began to fall.

"I won't rest until I've got him, Dani. Until I know you're safe from him, I can't let this go. But you have to trust me, okay? Stay here, stay hidden, and let me handle this… Can you do this for me?" Knox asked in a serious tone, and he couldn't help but hold his breath until she answered.

Her answer first came in the form of her nodding again, her hands gripping his arms even tighter, as if she could hold onto him forever.

"I trust you, Knox. I just… I hate that you have to go. We've only just…"

Knox cut her off by placing his forehead to hers, whispering back in regret, *"I know."* Then after this bittersweet moment shared, he pulled back enough to explain, "But this is what I do, Dani. I swear to you, I'll come back. I'll come back to you and we'll have every morning like this, I promise."

"Without the phone calls," Dani muttered sniffing back her upset.

Knox chuckled a little before agreeing, "Yes, sweetheart, without the phone calls."

Leaning into him, she pressed her forehead against his chest, listening to the steady beat of his heart.

"Just stay safe, Lucas," she whispered.

He held her tighter, feeling the weight of her words… and the weight of the promise he was about to make.

"I will."

But even as he made this vow, he knew he had no right to do so. Not in his line of work. This made him realise that maybe it was time to seriously think about a career change. It was a thought he couldn't yet give much consideration to, not when he first had someone to kill.

With a firm mission in mind, and a massive fucking incentive to do it, he kissed the top of her head one last time. Then he reluctantly stepped back, breaking their embrace before he made his way upstairs to get ready to leave.

For the first time in forever… He fucking hated this job.

As soon as Knox was ready to leave, he grabbed a jacket from the back of a chair, and as he slipped it on, looking at Dani one more time. The image of her in his home like she belonged was one he engraved into his memory. Although her face etched in worry was a look he knew would play on his mind, and not in a good way.

He had placed a food order to be delivered with enough groceries to last her a week at least, but he hoped it wouldn't come to him being away that long. He'd left instructions with the Uber eats driver to leave the food outside of the council building next door. Then once the app had alerted him on yet another burner phone that the delivery driver had arrived, he had retrieved the bags.

Dani immediately began unpacking the bags in the kitchen, and it was as though she was simply going through the motions. The idea of Knox putting himself in so much danger didn't sit well with her. So deep in thought, she jumped a little when she heard his voice.

"Remember, no leaving, no technology. Stay safe for me, Dani."

She released a heavy sigh before nodding. But Knox knew when she bit her bottom lip that she was fighting to keep control of her emotions. There was a slight wobble to her chin and it surprised him a little just how worried she seemed to be for his safety.

"I will. Just… *be careful, okay?"*

Knox gave her a small, reassuring smile, but his eyes were filled with determination.

"I will, Dani girl," he said, making a point of calling her this new nickname he had given her.

With a heavy heart, Knox turned and walked toward the elevator, leaving Dani standing there, her arms wrapped tightly around herself as if to hold onto the warmth he left behind.

But as the distance between them grew, she couldn't bear it. In a burst of emotion, Dani ran after him, wrapping her arms around his waist from behind. Knox stopped, turning to face her, and they shared one last, lingering kiss, filled with everything they couldn't say. Finally, Knox gently pulled away, and stepped into the elevator. As the doors began to close, he gave her a small, reassuring nod as their eyes locked until the very last moment.

***

The air was crisp, signifying the end of summer, and a chill seeped through Knox's jacket as he approached 'The River,'. The large water fountain stood proudly directly in front of Birmingham Town Hall. The sound of cascading water filled the square, mingling with the distant hum of city life. Knox scanned the area, his eyes narrowing as they darted to each person in the surrounding area, searching for any sign of Harris.

The cryptic clue over the phone had been classic Major Harris—deliberately vague, yet crystal clear to anyone who knew the city well. Knox, during his time stationed at the base in Hereford, had spent his rare downtime with the lads from the 22nd, hitting Birmingham's Broad Street for nights of drinking, picking up lasses, and inevitably, getting into the occasional fight. It was through these nights that Knox came to understand the city's charm and what Harris had been referring to. It was also why Knox had fallen in love with Birmingham and decided to make it his home. His investment in the pub was already proving profitable. Once a powerhouse of industry, the city was now transforming into a hub of cool, with trendy wine bars, microbreweries, and Michelin-starred restaurants drawing in a wave of the hip and fashionable.

He moved closer to the fountain, the spray of water misting his face. As he reached out to touch the cool stone, a familiar voice broke through the sound of the rushing water.

"Knox, you actually worked it out, we had bets on if you would," Major Harris called out. A grin spread across his weathered face as he emerged from the crowd, looking as if he had been there all along, hidden in plain sight.

Knox turned, his expression softening slightly at the sight of his friend.

"I'm surprised you didn't have me on a wild goose chase first. I take it you had your money on me?" Knox replied dryly.

Harris chuckled, clapping a hand on Knox's shoulder.

"Wouldn't have been the first time, would it? Although, I doubt anything could top that little dance we had at Dani's place. Four men down, and neither of us even broke a sweat."

Knox smirked and was quick to remind him, "If I recall, I was the one helping you up off the last two guys because I was pretty sure your arse was on the floor."

"Help me up? I don't remember that," Harris shot back, his eyes lighting up with amusement.

They shared a brief laugh, a moment of levity in the midst

of the tension that clung to them like a shadow. But the humour quickly faded as Harris's expression grew serious.

"Come on, we've got work to do," he said, nodding for Knox to follow.

Without another word, Knox fell into step beside Harris as they walked away from the bustling square, the sound of the fountain gradually fading behind them. They weaved through the narrow streets, Harris leading the way with a familiarity.

After a few minutes, they turned down a deserted side street behind the Town Hall, and the noise of the city reduced to a distant murmur. Harris stopped in front of an unassuming steel door, its surface scratched and worn. It looked like nothing more than a fire exit, but Knox knew better.

They stood in silence for a moment, the cold metal of the door reflecting the dim light of the streetlamp overhead. Knox glanced up, catching the faint glimmer of a CCTV camera nestled in the shadows above them. The lens swivelled slightly, confirming their presence.

"Still a fan of the dramatic entrances," Knox muttered under his breath. Harris chuckled softly.

"Gotta keep things interesting, Captain."

A heavy click sounded from the door, followed by the low grind of gears. Slowly, the reinforced steel door creaked open, revealing a narrow, dimly-lit hallway beyond. Harris stepped inside first, and Knox followed close behind, then the door shut with a resounding thud as soon as they were through.

The hallway was stark, and the concrete walls were bare except for a few industrial lights spaced evenly along the ceiling. Their footsteps echoed off the walls as they made their way deeper into the building. Knox's senses were on high alert, every sound and movement analysing for potential threats. But Harris seemed relaxed, his pace steady and confident.

"Welcome to the back door of HQ," Harris said, glancing

over his shoulder with a sly grin and adding, "Not exactly glamorous, but it does the job."

Knox nodded, his mind already shifting to the mission ahead, mentally calculating how long this shit would take and when he could get back to Dani. Fuck, he was addicted and the problem with that was, he needed to get his head back in the fucking game.

"So, what's the plan, Major? You mentioned something about Werl Prison."

Harris's expression hardened as they reached the end of the hallway, stopping in front of another steel door, this one with a keypad next to it and looking a lot more technical to open.

"All in good time, Knox," he replied, punching in a code.

The bullshit answer made Knox wonder why he wanted to get him inside first before actually telling him anything.

"First, let's get you briefed. There's a lot we need to cover, and we're on a tight schedule," Harris told him.

Knox wondered why all this cloak and dagger shit was necessary with such a tight schedule. He didn't understand why Harris wouldn't begin explaining things as they made their way inside. Naturally, Knox was impatient but refrained from saying anything because he didn't want to give away the reason why he was so eager to get this done. Although Harris wasn't stupid. Harris most likely already knew what was truly going on between Knox and Dani. Just like Knox knew the major was in love with Rose and would no doubt be feeling the same way if their roles were reversed.

The door slid open, revealing a large room filled with monitors, maps, and a handful of operatives already at work. Knox stepped inside, his eyes sweeping the room, taking in the familiar sights of a command centre. It was much like the Nest in Spain but a lot neater; the cables were hidden away with a more permeant feel to the setup. Unlike a makeshift Nest that could have been anywhere in the world.

But this was Birmingham, and the mission ahead was more personal than most. He could feel a sense of urgency in the air that thrummed through the room like an electric current.

Harris led him towards a central table covered in documents and photos, causing Knox to push all other thoughts from his mind. There was only one thing that mattered now: finding Mac and stopping him, preferably with a bullet to the brain.

As his eyes adjusted to the dim light, he noticed a figure standing by the central table, his posture straight and commanding, despite the bandages peeking out from under his uniform and one arm in a small sling.

"Knox, good to see you on your feet," the man greeted, his voice cultured and polished, each word articulated with precision.

It could only be the Brigadier Carter or 'the Brig,' as Harris and now Knox called him. Knox always felt he was the kind of officer who seemed to have walked straight out of a war movie: old school, refined, and as tough as they came.

"Brig," Knox nodded respectfully, taking in the man's injuries.

Though the Brigadier's face remained stoic, there was no hiding the stiffness in his movements or the bruising visible at the edge of his collar.

"Looks like you've had a rough go of it," Knox commented.

The Brig scoffed. "Nothing that can't be patched up with a stiff drink and a good cigar," Brig replied with a wry smile, downplaying the seriousness of his injuries as always.

"But I appreciate your concern, Knox. We've all had our share of scrapes, haven't we?"

Ha, scrapes… more like bullet wounds and knife attacks. Yeah, those type of scrapes.

Before Knox could respond, the sound of something clattering to the floor interrupted them. A petite blonde woman, her glasses askew, was hastily picking up a tablet she had dropped, her cheeks flushing pink as she fumbled with the device.

"Ah, Rose," Brig said with a touch of fondness in his voice. "You're just in time."

Rose adjusted her glasses, pushing a strand of hair behind her ear as she approached the table. Their tech specialist, a genius with anything that had a circuit board, had arrived. Her awkwardness was part of her charm, and the others had long since gotten used to her occasional clumsiness. Knox, however, was growing to like it also, but Harris liked it more.

"Sorry, Sir," Rose mumbled, avoiding eye contact as she focused on the tablet in her hands.

Harris stepped closer to her, his gaze softening for just a fraction of a second, and the look didn't go unnoticed by Knox… but it seemed to be totally ignored by the Brig.

"No need to apologise, Rose," Harris said, his tone uncharacteristically gentle. Her eyes rose to the handsome black man, who seemed to affect her just as much as she affected him.

"You're doing great work." Harris's words made Rose's face turn an even deeper shade of pink.

She managed a small smile as she started tapping away at the screen, mumbling a shy, *"Thanks."*

"Alright, everyone, gather round," Brigadier Carter instructed, motioning for Knox and Harris to join them at the table. "Rose has some critical intel for us," he added, giving Rose the floor.

Knox moved to stand beside the Major, his focus fully on the briefing. Rose took a deep breath, steadying herself before speaking.

"A few hours ago, our facial recognition software picked up

a match on Nicolas McCarthy, 'Mac', in Germany," Rose began, her voice gaining confidence as she spoke about her field of expertise. "He was spotted at the border, and we believe he's on route to Werl Prison. We believe he's after something… or rather, someone inside."

Knox frowned, his mind taking it all in while asking himself the questions before the answers came. The Brig took over, his voice grave.

"McCarthy has the data he stole from the Nest. But he can't use it, not yet anyway. The encryption on that data is some of the most advanced in the world. Our only saving grace. It's going to take a top-tier hacker to crack it."

Knox tensed instantly, thinking about his own little genius hacker he had locked away in his home. However, what Rose said next managed to put him at ease.

"And there are only three people in the world who can do it," Rose added, pulling up a display on the central monitor. Three profiles appeared on the screen.

"The first is, well… *me.*"

Knox didn't miss Harris tensing beside him when hearing this, and he glanced down to see his dark hands clench into fists. Oh yeah, he had it bad for the cute tech. Knox then glanced at Rose, who shrugged modestly.

"But I'm obviously not going to help him," she added with a nervous little chuckle that ended with a slight snort.

"The second is a ghost," The Brig interjected, his expression grim. "Someone who's been off the grid for years. No one's ever managed to track them down, and frankly, we don't even know if they're still alive."

"And the third?" Knox asked, gathering this was where their intel had led them.

"The third is Mark Thomas, known online as StealthScribe.

He's currently serving time in Werl Prison," Rose continued, her fingers flying over the tablet.

"And let me guess, Mac plans to break him out?" Knox said, easily piecing it together.

"Exactly," Harris confirmed, crossing his arms over his chest.

"And if Mac gets his hands on Thomas, it's game over. That data contains the identities of thousands of government assets around the world. If it's decrypted and leaked, it'll be a bloodbath," Brig said, the crease in his brow deepening because this was as real-life worst-case scenario shit as you could get.

Knox nodded, his mind already racing through the logistics of the mission. "So, we need to get to Thomas before Mac does," he surmised.

"Correct," Brig said, his tone decisive. "We've got a tactical helicopter prepped and ready. It'll take you straight to Werl Prison. Your mission is simple: secure Thomas and bring him back here. If Mac shows up, take him down and if you must take out Thomas, then so be it. Mac can't get his hands on him. The German government has been made aware by the home office and the prison warden is expecting you. This is our operation, gentlemen. There can be no mistakes."

Knox nodded before replying with a firm, "Understood."

Rose looked up from her tablet, her eyes meeting Knox's for the first time since the briefing started.

"I've uploaded everything you need to the secure servers," she said, her voice softening slightly as she warned, "Be careful out there." She first looked at Knox, then Harris, holding onto the major's gaze that little bit longer. Harris gave Rose a small nod, his expression unreadable.

"Good work, Rose. We couldn't do this without you." Rose ducked her head, a small smile tugging at her lips as she returned to her station, leaving the men to their preparations.

"Alright, you heard the man," Knox said, his voice steady as he turned to Harris.

"Let's gear up and get this shit done," Harris agreed, nodding his head before making his way towards the exit.

Knox followed, his mind focused on the mission ahead. There was no room for error. Mac had to be stopped, and they were the only ones who could do it. Then, and only then, could he be assured of Dani's safety.

As they left the room, The Brig watched them go, a steely determination in his eyes.

"Happy hunting, gentlemen," he murmured to himself, before turning back to the screens, already planning the next move and the back-up should they fail.

The back-up plan being the single face now on his screen…

It was Dani's.

FIFTEEN
WARDEN

The roar of blades whipped through the night air as the tactical chopper circled above Werl Prison, its searchlight cutting through the darkness. Knox peered out to the side, his eyes scanning the ground below for a suitable landing spot. The prison loomed beneath them. It was a hulking mass of concrete and steel surrounded by high walls and barbed wire. The embodiment of a fortress meant to keep its inhabitants inside and the rest of the world out.

"Over there, just beyond the west tower," the pilot's voice crackled through their headsets, and he pointed to a small clearing within the prison's perimeter. The space was tight, but it would have to do.

"Good enough," Knox muttered, giving the pilot a curt nod.

The helicopter tilted sharply as the pilot manoeuvred towards the clearing, its descent rapid and controlled. The moment the skids touched down, Knox and Harris unstrapped themselves and jumped out, their boots sinking into the soft earth. The downdraft from the rotors whipped dirt and debris into the air, forcing them to shield their eyes as they were immediately met by a pair of prison guards.

"Come," one of the guards shouted over the deafening noise, gesturing sharply for them to follow. Without another word, they were led away from the chopper, its turbines still whining as it powered down.

The guards were stern and stone-faced, along with being dressed in heavy, dark uniforms that matched the grim exterior of the prison. Knox noticed the way their eyes flicked over Harris with a hint of disdain as they walked, the subtle tightening of their lips betraying their discomfort. Harris, however, remained unfazed, his broad shoulders squared and his expression as unreadable as ever. Years in the Royal Marines had hardened him against this kind of subtle hostility, and he wasn't about to let it show.

They were quickly ushered through a side entrance, the heavy steel door clanging shut behind them with a finality that sent a shiver down Knox's spine. He was on edge and rightly so. The corridor beyond was narrow and dimly lit, the air thick with the scent of disinfectant and something else, something stale and metallic that made the hairs on the back of Knox's neck stand on end. The walls, a sickly pale green, were lined with worn posters outlining prison regulations in a blocky German font.

The guards marched ahead without a word, their boots echoing ominously off the concrete floor. Knox exchanged a brief glance with Harris, who offered a slight shrug. The situation was tense, and the cold reception from the prison staff wasn't helping.

After what felt like an eternity, they arrived at a thick wooden door marked "Direktor," the German word for warden. One of the guards knocked sharply before pushing it open and gesturing for them to enter.

Knox couldn't exactly put his finger on it, but his gut was telling him that something was off, and he didn't fucking like it.

In his line of work, he had always gone with this type of intuition but right now he was no longer a gun for hire. He had orders to follow… but that didn't mean he wouldn't stay alert.

Inside, the office was sparsely decorated, with utilitarian furniture arranged in an almost painfully orderly fashion. The air was stifling, the kind of warmth that felt more like oppression than comfort. Behind a large, imposing desk sat a man in his mid-fifties, his grey hair meticulously combed back, his uniform starched to perfection. His eyes, a cold, steely blue, narrowed as they landed on Knox and Harris. As though weighing their worth in an instant and finding it wanting.

"Guten Abend," the warden greeted them, his voice clipped and devoid of any type of welcoming. "I am Warden Hans Vogler. You are here to discuss your… *visit.*" The word 'visit' dripped with sarcasm, as though it was something distasteful he was being forced to endure.

Vogler's gaze lingered on Harris for a beat longer than what was comfortable, the disdain in his eyes barely concealed. He stood, gesturing stiffly for them to take the chairs in front of his desk, though he didn't sit back down himself.

Knox, taking the lead, stepped forward, ignoring the warden's icy demeanour.

"I'm Captain Knox, and this is Major Harris," he introduced them, his tone measured but firm. "We appreciate you making time for us."

The lie flowed freely off Knox's tongue despite feeling like he was close to spitting bile. Knox instantly disliked the warden, and this type of distain usually ended with Knox's boot pressed against their throat.

"Time," Vogler repeated in a mocking tone, as though the very concept was a foreign imposition.

"I was not informed of this visit until an hour ago. We run a tight operation here, Captain. Sudden visits from foreign agents are… how do you say…? *Disruptive,"* Vogler said with a curl of his lips.

Knox found himself holding back from grabbing the man's throat and asking just how disruptive he would find a fucking break in. However, he supressed the urge to strangle the haughty little prick.

"Disruption is the least of your concerns, Warden," Knox told him.

Harris followed suit, cutting in, his voice deep, authoritative, and to the point. "We're here on a matter of international security. Your prisoner, Mark Thomas, is a target. If he's compromised, the lives of countless people could be at risk."

Vogler's thin lips pressed together into a hard line, his eyes narrowing further as he sized up Harris.

"I don't know of the prisons you have in *your England,* but this is a German prison, Major. It is built to contain the most dangerous individuals. I assure you, we are more than capable of securing one hacker," Vogler said, letting them know exactly what he thought of the English.

Knox's knuckles cracked as the urge to correct him with a fist to the face was riding him hard. He was fucking Scottish!

Harris gave Knox a subtle shake of his head as he could obviously feel the tension thickening in the room, but he kept his expression neutral.

"With respect, Warden, the man after Thomas isn't just any criminal. He's highly trained, well-funded, and he won't hesitate to kill anyone in his way. We're not questioning your ability to run this facility, but we're here to ensure we get Thomas out so he's not your problem," Harris said, no doubt repeating their reasons for being there and hoping this would be the last time. As for Vogler, his expression remained stony.

"What is it you require?" Vogler finally gritted out, as if his superior had been a presence in the room, staring him down and forcing his hand of compliance.

Harris leaned forward, his presence commanding.

"We need immediate access to Mark Thomas. We'll interrogate him, then we'll take him into protective custody. And, Warden, I suggest you cooperate fully, because if someone gets to Thomas before we do, the consequences would be catastrophic."

Vogler's jaw clenched, the muscles in his face twitching as he considered Harris's words. The room fell silent, the only sound the faint hum of the building's ventilation system. Finally, after what felt like an eternity, the warden nodded curtly.

"Very well," Vogler conceded, though his tone made it clear that he was far from pleased.

"You will be escorted by guards to his holding cell, where you can speak to him before leaving. But…" the warden said before pausing.

"But what, Warden?" Harris barked, his annoyance at the Warden's attitude showing its first crack.

"You leave your weapons here, I can't have them in my prison down in the cells blocks. If you won't comply, then you have come a long way for nothing, gentlemen." Vogler smirked, trying to take back some control.

Knox clenched his jaw and looked at Harris. They both new they had no choice and as much as their guts screamed at them not to agree, both men disarmed and placed their guns on the desk.

"I will be coming back for this, Warden," Knox said as he stared Vogler in the eyes, wanting to boot the smirk off his face with his size elevens.

The warden's eyes dropped before he turned to the door, calling for the guards outside to come in. As they re-entered the room, Vogler addressed them in rapid German, his voice as sharp and precise as his demeanour.

"You will take Captain Knox and Major Harris to the prisoner," he ordered, his tone brokering no argument.

The guards nodded, their expressions unreadable as they turned to lead Knox and Harris back into the cold, sterile corridors of the prison.

As they exited the office, Knox couldn't help but notice the lingering gaze Vogler directed at Harris, a look that was equal parts resentment and wariness. But Harris, as always, remained unflappable, his cool restored and focus solely on the mission ahead.

"Ready?" Harris asked quietly as they walked, signalling he knew shit could go south rapidly.

"Aye, always," Knox replied, his voice steady despite that gut feeling of his getting worse. Especially as the guards led them deeper into the bowels of the prison.

The walls closed in around them as the cold, unfriendly atmosphere of the place seeped into their bones. They were getting closer to Mark Thomas… closer to their target.

The hallway leading to the cell block was dimly lit, a stark contrast to the sterile brightness of the prison area they just came from. The air was thick with the scent of sweat and something more pungent… fear, perhaps, or desperation. Harris and Knox walked side by side, the sound of their boots echoing off the walls as the guards led them towards the holding cells.

As they approached a heavily fortified security point, a sudden shrill ring pierced through the silence. One of the guards picked up the phone, spoke briefly in rapid German, then handed the receiver to Harris.

"It's for you," the guard grunted.

Harris raised an eyebrow in question but took the phone.

"Harris," he barked into the receiver.

On the other end, Rose's voice crackled to life, making his whole body tense. Ever since she had named herself as one of the potential targets, being one of the only three hackers, then he had struggled with himself. Struggled with taking orders and making his own. Because ever since what happened to the NEST in Spain, Harris wanted Rose somewhere safe and unknown. He was too aware that something could have happened to her that day and fuck, just the thought was putting the Major on edge, despite his calm exterior.

"Harris, we've just intercepted some chatter. It's bad…" Rose paused for a second, the worry in her tone making her breath hitch.

"Rose?" Harris said her name with urgency.

"Mac's already there."

"Come again?" Harris asked in response to Rose's recent intel.

"Mac's already in the area, and he's not alone. You need to move fast, get to Thomas. But that's not all."

Harris's eyes narrowed, tension tightening his features.

"Copy that," he said tersely, before glancing at Knox. "Mac's in the area, meaning time's critical. You go ahead. I'll catch up," Harris ordered.

Knox nodded in understanding. He then turned to face the cell block door, his expression hardening as the guard opened the heavy steel gate. Its mechanical motion felt like it was taking an age but once it opened, he wordlessly stepped in to the cell block. The guard told him to wait until the gate shut behind him before he continued. Again, it felt like a small forever until a resounding clang of finality slammed behind him, telling him to move.

Knox walked down the hallway that was on a second floor and glanced over the balcony railings to see the common area below. The cells on the left side of the narrow passage were filled with prisoners, some with their faces pressing against the bars, others were watching from their bunks. A mixture of curiosity and malice gleamed through each set of eyes before they began shouting and chanting in German, their voices rising to a cacophonous roar as Knox passed. The words were harsh, almost feral, but Knox knew enough to recognise the level of intimidation.

The guard pointed silently to a cell halfway down the hall in the middle of all the others. He glanced at Harris who he could see through the bars still on the prison phone, his expression one of frustration as he, no doubt, continued gaining intel from Rose. Knox then looked directly ahead of him and saw the same gated security door opposite, this one minus any guards.

Knox's senses were on high alert, every muscle in his body coiled and ready for action as he approached the cell. His eyes quickly scanned the other cells, noting the frenzied energy of the inmates, their eyes gleaming with predatory excitement. It was as if they were anticipating something…*waiting for blood.*

Knox finally reached the cell the guard had indicated. The cell door opened, and Knox looked down to the gate where the guard was and nodded. But when Knox looked inside the cell, he saw a lifeless figure on the bottom bunk. His heart rate spiked as he realised it might be Thomas, lying there in a pool of shadows and blood.

"Thomas!" Knox called out, his voice low and commanding.

But there was no response. Knox's gut twisted with the possibility that they were too late. Without hesitation, he rushed inside. The figure on the bunk was facedown, and Knox crouched quickly, reaching out to feel the man's pulse. As he did, he caught a glimpse of a tattoo on the man's neck. It was a marking that didn't match any of the information he had on Thomas. Because Knox had read the file, he knew everything about the man that Rose had been able to dig up.

Knox's instincts screamed at him, but it was too late. A heavy thud sounded behind him as a massive figure dropped down from the top bunk, blocking the cell's exit. Knox spun around, his muscles tensing as he took in the sight before him.

The man was a fucking behemoth! His enormous bulk nearly filled the narrow doorway. He towered over Knox's six-foot-four height, the giant's head nearly brushing the low seven-foot ceiling. The light from the hallway cast deep shadows across his face, but the cold, malicious gleam in his eyes was unmistakable. His lips curled into a sneer as he spoke, his voice low and menacing.

"Mac sends his best wishes," the man growled in a strong German accent, his thick, scarred fingers tightening around the hilt of a makeshift shank.

Knox's eyes flicked to the crude weapon. It was a sharpened piece of metal with a handle made from duct tape, one that glinted dangerously in the dim light. He had no time to think, no time to plan. The only thing that mattered was survival.

The giant lunged at him with surprising speed, the shank slicing through the air with lethal intent. Knox sidestepped just in time, feeling the rush of air as the blade barely missed his torso. The man was relentless, swinging the shank in wide arcs, each blow aimed to kill. The sheer bulk of the man made it easier for Knox to see where the next attack was coming from, meaning he could better prepare his own form of attack.

Knox ducked and weaved, his training kicking in as he deflected the man's advances with calculated precision. The confined space of the cell worked in Knox's favour, limiting his opponent's movements and forcing him to fight up close. The brute's size gave him problems because he hit the bunks, the walls, and the celling as he swung out to hit Knox, his knuckles splitting and busted from finding everything but Knox's head.

An opening presented itself and with a sharp hit into the inside elbow of his attacker, the shank was dropped.

With a savage roar, the giant grabbed Knox by the shoulders and slammed him into the wall, the impact rattling his teeth. Knox grunted in pain but didn't hesitate. Using the momentum, he drove his elbow into the man's ribs, hard enough to hear a crack which made him grunt and stumble back a step.

The giant was far from finished, though, because this gave him time to pick up the shank, leading to a boot to the face from Knox's size elevens. The force of the kick sent the inmate practically flying backwards into the cell wall, where he wiped the blood from his mouth on his sleeve as he stared at Knox. With a renewed determination, the man surged forward again, his eyes burning with a murderous rage. He swung the shank downward in a brutal stabbing motion, aiming for Knox's chest.

Knox caught the man's wrist just in time, the muscles in his arms straining as he struggled to keep the blade from plunging into his flesh. The two men grappled, locked in a deadly struggle, the air thick with the scent of sweat and blood.

With a sudden burst of strength, Knox twisted the man's wrist, forcing the shank downwards. At the same time Knox jumped as he head-butted up into the giant, catching him square on the nose. The man roared in pain as the blade sliced into his own thigh, the sharp metal biting deep into flesh. Knox pushed down on it as he dropped to the floor from his jump, seizing the moment by first twisting the blade and causing greater damage to muscle and tissue, hopefully slicing through arteries. To finish the movements, Knox then drove his knee into the man's groin with enough force to make him double over.

The giant staggered back, blood pouring from the wound in his leg. His face twisted in agony, but he still wasn't finished. He raised the shank, freeing it from his own leg, his grip shaky but determined.

This would prove to be a big mistake because Knox knew the man would only bleed out faster now there was nothing to slow the pumping blood.

Knox didn't hesitate, and with a swift and precise movement, he kicked the shank up and out of the man's hand. He caught it by its crude handle and drove the blade hard, plunging it into the man's chest, right between the ribs as his free hand struck the throat of his opponent.

The giant's eyes went wide with shock and pain as he gasped for breath, blood spitting from his mouth with every reach for air. Knox twisted the blade, levering it up and down as it rocked on the rib bone until the man's body went slack and crumpled to the floor. There'd be no coming back from that.

Knox stood over the fallen man, his breath coming in ragged gasps as he looked down at the massive body, blood pooling around it, the shank still protruding from his chest. The fight had been brutal, primal, and Knox's hands were trembling with the adrenaline still coursing through his veins.

But there was no time to rest. He needed to find the real Thomas, that was if the man was even still alive. As he wiped the blood from his face, he heard a voice that froze him in his tracks. It was a voice he knew all too well, one that sent a chill down his spine despite the heat of the battle.

"Oh Knox!" the voice called, low and mocking, echoing down the hallway.

Knox turned towards the door and clenched his fists, close to grinding his jaw in anger. Bending down, he ripped the shank from the giant's chest because he knew exactly who he would find out there. Then he stalked out of the cell with a grit of his teeth and blood dripping from his hand.

Knox's heart was pounding in his chest, and there at the far end of the hallway behind a gate, stood Mac. The man who had once been his closest friend, had now become his deadliest enemy.

Mac's silhouette was dark against the dim light, his posture relaxed, almost casual, as if he had all the time in the world. He had a gun in his hand that Knox knew he could have used the second his head made it past the cell door.

Which was why he questioned with a nod at Mac's weapon, "You going to use that at some point?"

Mac looked down at his Glock, a sadistic grin playing at his lips.

"You wound me, old friend," he mocked before saying, "Despite what you think of me, there is still honour between comrades, but you continue to get in my way, despite my warning."

"Fuck you and your honour. If you had any, you would toss that gun and fight me instead of standing there like a fucking coward," Knox goaded, knowing this was his only chance in getting the bastard close enough to kill.

Mac didn't bite like he had hoped, not having the same motivation to kill that Knox did and instead, he only laughed, nodding down to the prison grade weapon in his bloody fist.

"Think of me any way you want, Knox, but we both know who would win in a fight and I don't need this fucking gun to prove that. I have shit to do and unlike you, I have what I came here for," Mac said, shrugging his shoulders.

In response, Knox snarled, "Then you're a fucking idiot for not killing me when you had the chance, I won't stop until I put a bullet in your fucking head!"

"Oh, you're going to die, I just won't be pulling the trigger. Doesn't mean you will live to see another day… or your precious Dani for that matter."

"You leave her out of this!"

"Oh, she is very much in this, Knox. But then, I guess you

haven't figured that out yet. As for you, I should have known that it would take more than one man to take you down," Mac said, his voice thick with amusement and Knox felt his jaw harden.

"So, let's increase my odds, should we?" Mac, with a twisted smile, reached for the switch that opened all the cell doors at once. After which he then gave Knox a mocking wave before stepping back into the shadows, disappearing like a phantom.

Leaving Knox to face a gang of inmates… *alone.*

SEVENTEEN

STEALTHSCRIBE WERL

Knox's pulse quickened, his instincts kicking into overdrive. The situation was spiralling fast. He knew what was coming before he even heard the sound.

CLANG!

The sudden screech of metal echoed through the hallway when the cell doors all opened as one, and the heavy grating of steel against steel reverberated through the narrow space like a death toll. The roar was deafening, a guttural cry from prisoners desperate for a taste of freedom after God knows how many years behind bars. In their eyes, only one man stood between them and escape. The shouts and jeers from the prisoners still locked in their cells soon merged into a primal chant, a symphony of chaos unleashed.

And at the heart of it all stood Knox.

Looking from one side to the other, Knox focused on the broken phone the other side of the security door where Harris had last been seen.

"Harris!" Knox bellowed, his voice barely cutting through the madness.

There was no response, meaning Harris clearly had his own problems to deal with. Knox seriously hoped he had better odds than the Major did, because it looked like Mac had gotten his wish after all. Knox glanced down at the small weapon in his hand, hardly worthy of being called a weapon at all, as the first of the inmates appeared.

He knew the odds were stacked against him and things looked bleak, but if he was going down, it sure as hell wouldn't be without a fight. Rolling his shoulders and tightening his fists, Knox smirked and muttered, "Alright, then. Let's get this over with."

The first prisoner took in his new situation and instantly found Knox, seeing him as the enemy. The inmate charged at Knox, adrenaline driving his wild, reckless movements. He was too caught up in the moment to notice the shank in Knox's hand or the blood already staining his knuckles, proof that this wouldn't be Knox's first kill today. As soon as the prisoner was close enough, Knox took him out quickly, with rapid strikes to his torso's fleshy weak points. Finishing with a terminal strike to the man's neck, Knox snapped the shank with the force and blood strayed from the pressure of his carotid artery bleeding out.

So much for having a weapon.

Knox glanced at the useless duct-taped stump in his hand before tossing it aside, spinning quickly, ready to face the next threat behind him. But it wasn't the two men charging toward him that had his attention, it was the third.

The man was nearly as massive as the behemoth Knox had already killed in the cell. A lifer, no doubt. His shaved head, covered in tattoos and scars, tilted to the side as he cracked his neck, the sound as unsettling as his presence. His prison jumpsuit had the sleeves ripped off, revealing inked biceps nearly as big as Knox's head. He had at least five inches on Knox, with hands the size of spades.

He was by far one of the meanest mother fuckers Knox had ever seen, and if he didn't think his odds were good before, then now he knew he was a dead man walking.

The two inmates in front of him moved like a pack of wolves, eyes gleaming with hatred and hunger, as if smelling blood in the air. Knox braced himself, his body taut and ready for the onslaught, not taking his eyes off the inmate three cells down from where he stood. Others behind the giant followed but with the narrowness of the walkway, there was no chance of them getting past him.

The first prisoner lunged and Knox instantly sidestepped, dodging him with ease and gripping his wrist, then Knox was grabbed from behind and the second prisoner got in a cheap shot, punching Knox in the ribs.

Knox took the hit, his body tensing in anticipation, expelling little more than a grunt. The pain only fuelled the surge of adrenaline rushing through him. In seconds, his mind flipped through years of training, commanding his body to react. But just as he prepared to break free from the hold, his eyes widened.

The hulking inmate grabbed the first guy in his way and, with terrifying ease, hurled him over the banister. The brief scream was followed by a sickening thud, and Knox knew his prior thoughts about this guy were right. He was a lifer, no chance of parole, and no hesitation to kill.

Clearly, Knox was to be his next victim. The way the huge guy dealt with the first inmate had Knox wondering if this was another foot solider recruited by Mac. The thought quickly fled him as he took another hit from the second guy, only… it was to be his last. And as much as Knox would have liked to have been the cause, shockingly, he wasn't.

It was the giant.

The inmate's large hand landed on the second guy's shoulder, his fingers clenching hard enough to make his victim bellow in pain. Next he spun him round and punched him in the face, making his nose explode. The injured inmate had no time to recover as the crazed big bastard grabbed his head, framing nearly its entirety with his large hands. Then he used his thumbs and pressed them into the man's eyes, rendering him blind in seconds. The man's screams echoed around the cell block, sending the onlooking prisoners wild, like howling, fucked up monkeys in cages.

Meanwhile, another inmate had run at Knox, wrapping his arm around his throat from behind, but Knox took two forceful steps back, pushing the man holding him off balance enough he had no choice but to move. The inmate's hold stayed firm, still attempting to choke Knox, even as Knox quickly spun around to face the other way.

Yet another man caught his eye, and Knox knew what was coming. Calling on his training, he predicted and planned, knowing he'd have to get it just right to avoid the intended shank coming at him in his gut.

A wiry man with wild eyes rushed forward, holding a weapon made from a toothbrush and what looked like a sharpened piece of tin can. The convict lunged forward as Knox sharply twisted around once more. The shank embedded in his grappler's back, making him bawl in pain as he backed away but before he could fall to his knees, Knox turned and grabbed the screaming inmate. He then threw him into the wiry man, causing them to both fall to the ground. The shank dug deeper into the inmate's back thanks to landing on top of his assailant.

Another attack came from behind Knox, this time by someone far bigger, and he turned quickly ready for the next fight. However, what he wasn't ready for was meeting someone on his side.

The giant inmate twisted the head of the prisoner he had been torturing, the bloody, now hallow sockets of his eyes a sickening sight..

For a split second, Knox thought his time was up but after the big guy made no advance towards him, Knox wondered why. It was a look that must have shown on his face because the inmate told him, "He killed my bird," in a heavy Bavarian accent.

Knox had no idea what to say to this and merely shrugged his shoulders as he muttered, "Okay then." The threat against him was far from over so there was no time to say more.

What did surprise Knox was when the big bastard turned and faced the inmates coming at him from behind and, somehow, he had acquired an ally.

Of course, Knox didn't really have a choice when it came to trust whether or not the big bastard would at some point just turn on him. Not when the wiry fuck who had failed to stab him, was now trying to disentangle himself from under the dying inmate. So, before he could get too far in accomplishing this, Knox delivered a brutal kick to the prisoner's head, followed up with an even more brutal stomp to his neck. A move that ended up crushing his oesophagus and leaving him to die from asphyxiation, gasping for air he would never get.

Knox had no time to take a pause as another inmate saw this and suddenly rushed him. The inmate swung his fists around with murderous intent and Knox ducked, his muscles moving instinctively as he drove his shoulder into the man's midsection. The momentum pushed him forward and slammed him into the cell bars with bone-crushing force. The man crumpled, knocked out cold from the sheer force of the back of his head against the hard metal.

The narrow corridor quickly became a bloody battleground, and Knox glanced back towards his unlikely comrade to see him also making his way through the throng of prisoners. Men who all seemed to want a piece of the goliath. Yet despite being clearly outnumbered and pinned right in the middle of it all, this wasn't the first time he'd fought impossible odds. Scanning the corridor, Knox noted every potential weapon, every threat.

Another prisoner soon stepped up to the challenge, his eyes wild with rage, swinging a piece of broken metal pipe that reverberated against the metal bars behind Knox as he ducked. The pipe missed his head by only a few inches. However, the second swing made contact, because despite lifting his arms up and tucking them to the side of his head to protect it, his arm ended up receiving the brunt of the swing.

It stung to hell but thankfully didn't break a bone or he would have been in real shit. Knox ignored the throbbing pain and sidestepped when the third swing came in. But this time, he was ready for it, using the momentum of his attacker to grab him by the collar and slamming him headfirst into the wall. Blood spattered across the cold concrete before the man slid to the floor… another one unconscious.

Knox followed the attacker to the floor and picked up his metal pipe as the inmates just kept coming. One prisoner tried to grab Knox from behind as he stood watching what he thought was his next assailant coming at him. They wrapped their arms around his neck in a chokehold. Knox dropped his weight and drove the pipe into the man's sternum, hard enough to feel something crack. The hold on him loosened just enough for Knox to flip him over his shoulder, sending him crashing onto the hard floor. Then he brought down the pipe into the man's eye socket, the force killing him instantly as it penetrated deep into his skull.

A flash of movement caught Knox's eye as another man

rushed towards him, armed with a shard of glass, half wrapped in tape. Knox rolled and spun to the side, driving his arm into the back of the man's knee and taking him down with a sickening crunch. The glass shard slipped from the inmate's grasp as the back of his head hit hard on the grated flooring, leaving him dazed and bleeding. Knox picked up the glass and wasted no time in stabbing his jugular.

At this point, adrenaline was the only thing keeping Knox going because his muscles screamed in protest, his breath coming out in ragged gasps. There were too many of them, and they were relentless, driven by the taste of freedom and the promise of violence.

But finally, just as another wave of prisoners surged forward, a deafening bang echoed through the corridor, freezing them in their tracks.

"Knox, you still alive in there?!" Harris's voice boomed, and Knox could have laughed with relief.

Harris stood at the entrance of the corridor with a 9mm Parabellum pistol in hand, clearly taken from the guards. Its smoking barrel was a silent promise of more to come. Harris's face was a mask of barely contained rage, his dark brown eyes scanning the carnage with cold efficiency.

"About time," Knox grunted, wiping the sweat from his brow.

"Right, you bastards, who wants a fucking bullet?!" Harris barked, as he stepped into the corridor once the security gate had been opened.

The prisoners hesitated for a moment, sizing up the new threat, eyeing the gun like candy to a sugar addict.

"You don't want any of this," Harris muttered under his breath as he took aim. But just as Harris prepared to fire, a voice cut through the chaos, freezing Knox in place.

"Knox!" It was Mac, his voice echoing from a speaker in the corridor.

Knox turned, his breath catching in his throat.

"I see you're still alive… it seems as I just might have to kill you myself after all, but until then, say bye bye to your wings."

Seconds later, a boom suddenly thundered throughout the whole prison and Knox just knew that was T.I.7's helicopter exploding. The act stoked the bravery of the few inmates left and they charged at Harris, the only thing standing in their way of freedom.

Shot after shot rang out, Harris methodically firing at the oncoming prisoners. Shoulder, chest, and head shots. They fell like dominos, one by one, until he was out of ammo. The last two men finally reached him. The first of which received a brutal taste from the butt of the pistol, and the shattering of his jaw echoed through the hallway.

The second man saw his chance and tackled Harris to the ground. They tussled, rolling on the cold grate floor in a flurry of fists and elbows. Harris grunted as the inmate scrambled for an advantage, his hands going for Harris's throat. But before the man could press his attack, his body was ripped off Harris as if yanked by an invisible force.

The prisoner flew through the air, slamming into one of the cell doors with a nauseating thud, landing upside down in a crumpled heap. Knox stood over Harris and helped him up.

As Harris got to his feet, the man Knox had thrown, groaned from the floor, barely conscious. Knox and Harris exchanged a glance, both knowing exactly what was coming next. Without a word, and in perfect unison, they stepped forward and delivered simultaneous kicks to either side of the groaning man's head.

There was a final, pitiful grunt, and the inmate slumped into silence.

Harris exhaled sharply, then glanced at Knox with a smirk.

"Thanks for the assist. Thought I was going to have to break a sweat there for a second."

Knox grinned back, rolling his shoulders, and stretching out his aching arms.

"You know you could have broke into a sweat a bit sooner, can't let us have all the fun," Knox said… and speaking of fun, he glanced over towards his unlikely ally to find him finishing off the last of the inmates he was dealing with.

The carnage left in his wake scattered around him like something from a horror movie set. Blood spattered bodies lay crumbled on the floor in different states, depending on how much of a fight they had put up to begin with. Only a few were still breathing, and not for the first time, Knox wondered why the giant had helped him at all.

In the end, he didn't need to ask.

"I too have good woman at home." The giant gave Knox an approving nod before he walked calmly back into his cell.

"Making new friends, I see," Harris commented as Knox turned towards the security gate.

"Yeah, but it's the old ones I want to kill. Speaking of which, I think it's time we pay our friend the Warden a little visit," Knox gritted the words out and Harris grinned.

Cracking his knuckles Harris said, "Now you're talking."

Knox reached down and grabbed the metal pipe, swinging it into his hand and said, "Yeah, and soon, *he will be too.*"

EIGHTEEN

BLOOD TIES

Knox and Harris didn't waste a second. They tore through the hallways of Werl Prison, their boots pounding against the cold concrete as they made a beeline for Warden Hans Vogler's office. The roar of the prisoners echoing behind them faded as their singular focus sharpened on the man responsible for their ambush.

Knox's mind churned with fury. This whole thing stank. The false cell, the ambush, the diversion, the timing. Mac had planned it all, using the warden as his pawn. Now, they needed answers, and they needed them fast. Mac was back in the fucking wind and getting away with Thomas.

Knox and Harris quickly came across the same two guards that had escorted them to the cell block. Both of which were bloodied, beaten and dead on the floor.

"Your handy work, I take it?" Knox asked with a smirk, making Harris cock his head a little in acknowledgement.

Of course, he didn't need to say a fucking word because it had Harris written all over the situation. These assholes had obviously been foolish enough to think they could have gotten

Harris out of the way while leaving Knox to die in that cell block.

For the two guards, assumption was the mother of all deadly fuck ups. And speaking of fuck ups, the warden was about to learn what his own had been, and they soon reached the heavy wooden door of his office. Word that the plan had fucked up hadn't reached Vogler yet because the idiot was still sitting behind his desk and hadn't even bothered to lock his fucking door.

Vogler shot up in alarm as the two operatives kicked open the door, his steely blue eyes wide with fear. The air inside the room was suffocating, the oppressive warmth feeling like a weight pressing against Knox's chest, but he pushed through it, fists clenched at his sides.

"You set us up," Knox growled, his voice low and dangerous, like a predator ready to pounce.

The warden started shaking his head quickly and, in his panic, was fumbling around with a button on his desk that no doubt would send guards coming.

Knox couldn't have that.

Storming around to the warden's side he raised his metal pipe up and hammered it down on his hand without missing a beat. The warden screamed out like a fucking banshee as Knox broke all his fingers, making him clutch his shaking hand to his chest.

"Y-y-yoouu… broke… hand… y-y-you…" The warden stammered out.

Knox pushed him back against the wall where he still sat in his desk chair, the jarring movement making the warden scream out in agony once more.

"Trust me, I will break a lot fucking more than that if you don't tell us what we want to know! Now, where is Mark Thomas's cell?!"

Vogler's hands trembled as he raised his only good one in defence.

"I, I don't know what you're talking about," he stammered, his voice tight with fear.

Harris was on him next, grabbing the front of Vogler's pristine uniform, yanking him out of the chair and slamming him against the wall. The warden's breath hitched, his eyes wide with terror.

"You knew exactly what was happening!" Harris snarled, his face inches from Vogler's. "Mac didn't get in here without help. You gave him access!"

At this accusation, Vogler's face paled, his lips quivering as he tried to form a response. But Harris wasn't interested in listening. He shoved the man harder into the wall, rattling the framed certificates hanging behind him and making them fall, smashing on the ground. The sound of breaking glass mingled with the cries of pain.

"Talk!" Knox barked, stepping in closer. His presence was a coiled spring of violence, ready to explode. "Mac's gang knew exactly where we'd be and when. You fed us to them. Why?!"

Vogler's resolve shattered as fast as the frames on the floor. His body went limp as the weight of the situation pressed down on him.

"Please," he whispered, his voice barely audible. "I didn't have a choice."

Harris's grip tightened, and he yanked Vogler forward into his knee before slamming him back against the wall, making the older man bellow in pain.

"Wrong answer, Warden," Harris said warning him about making that same mistake twice.

"I swear to you, I don't know who Mac is!" Vogler gasped, his breath coming in short, panicked bursts. "It was the Stier. It was him! He threatened my family…he has men watching them. If I didn't help, he'd… *he'd kill them!"*

Knox's eyes narrowed, his anger simmering just below the surface. He knew Stier in German meant *Bull.*

"So you sold us out?!" shouted Knox.

"I had no choice!" Vogler cried, desperation creeping into his voice.

"He had his men threaten mine and my guards' families too. We couldn't fight him… we… we had to cooperate."

Harris let go of Vogler at that, but only so Knox could step in. Knox grabbed the man by the collar, pulling him close, his eyes boring into the warden's.

"Where's the real cell, Vogler? Where the hell is Mark Thomas's cell?" Knox asked, despite already knowing that Mac already had Thomas.

There was no way he would have left without getting what he came here for. No, killing Knox had only been a bonus in Mac's mind. But whether Thomas was gone or not, he knew that there may be some clues left behind as to where Mac was planning on taking him. He may have reached out to Thomas and for all Knox knew, Mac and Thomas could be in this together. Getting him out of here could only be the first part of the plan.

The warden's breath came in ragged gasps as he raised a trembling hand to point at a map of the prison on the wall.

"Cell block C," he croaked. "Third level… last cell on the right."

Knox shoved him back into his chair, his gaze cold and unforgiving.

"If you're lying, I'll make sure the '*Stier*' won't get the chance to hurt your family. Because I'll do it first," Knox warned, the threat empty as he would never hurt innocent people but then, Vogler didn't know this.

The threat worked because Vogler flinched, but Knox wasn't done. He stepped in close again, towering over the broken warden, his voice low and menacing.

"You just sent us into the middle of a bloodbath, Vogler. The mess we just made? *That's on you.*"

Harris leaned in next, his voice a growl. "We lost a chopper, had to fight our way through a pack of rabid inmates, and took out your guards. You think that's going to go unnoticed?"

Vogler's face paled further, the reality sinking in as he realised the full extent of the situation. Knox grabbed him by the front of his shirt one last time, pulling him close.

"You've got a lot of explaining to do, Warden. The mess in your prison is your problem now. But make no mistake, there will be consequences. You'll be hearing from our government as well as your own. Now if I were you, I'd make sure your men don't get in our way again." With that, Knox released him.

The warden collapsed into his chair, a shell of a man, and without another word, Knox and Harris took back their guns and stormed out of the office. Knox didn't bother to look back, there was nothing left for him in that office, Vogler would have to face the aftermath of his decisions alone.

Like the rest of the prison, this next block felt like a tomb as Knox and Harris made their way toward the last cell on the far end. The air was almost suffocating, as if the prison itself was alive, breathing down their necks. The flickering lights cast shadows that clung to the walls like specters, shifting and twisting with each step they took. Every footfall that echoed was a reminder of how deep into the belly of the fortress they had ventured and despite neither one saying it, they had to wonder what this cell block held for them.

Knox's eyes locked onto the last door, one he had opened himself, knowing this time it was Mark Thomas's true holding place. His mind raced, connecting fragmented pieces, but something still felt off. They had been played, led around like puppets while Mac advanced his plan. Knox clenched his fists and raised his gun because unlike last time, he was going inside armed. His jaw was held tight as he approached the cell door, knowing they were running out of time.

The cell door creaked as it opened, the heavy metal groaning under its own weight. Inside, the room was just as cold and empty as the rest of the prison. A barren cell, a small bed sagging against one wall, a worn metal sink and toilet in the corner. The air was stale, thick with mildew and something far more personal… *an eerie stillness.* As if the cell held onto the ghosts of those it had consumed before its current inmate. Well, the most recent one anyway because the cell was now empty.

Knox's eyes scanned the room, his senses on high alert. His gaze fell on a narrow shelf above the bed, where a few personal belongings sat, untouched by time. There wasn't much, just a battered paperback novel, pages yellowed and dog-eared, a toothbrush, bristles worn from years of use, and a single photograph, standing out like an artifact from a forgotten life.

He reached for the photo, his fingers brushing the worn edges, and as he lifted it from the shelf, Knox's breath caught in his throat. The photo was faded, the colors muted by time, but the faces were unmistakable. Mark Thomas stood beside a young woman, her arm around his shoulders, both smiling at the camera. The girl looked so familiar, her long golden hair cascading over her shoulders, her smile full of life.

Knox froze.

His heart lurched as he stared at the young woman in the photo, recognition crashing over him like a wave. He knew that face. The curve of her smile. The way her eyes sparkled with mischief. The girl in the photo wasn't just anyone.

It was Dani.

Dani, the woman he had just spent the night with. The

woman he'd left at his place to keep safe. The woman it felt like he had long ago fallen for. *She was Mark Thomas's daughter.*

Knox's mind reeled, his pulse pounding in his ears as the realisation hit him like a freight train. He flipped the photo over, his hands trembling slightly as he read the inscription scrawled on the back in delicate handwriting:

21st birthday at Lake Walchensee.

The pieces slammed into place. Dani wasn't just some woman he'd met by chance. *She was tied to everything.* And more importantly, Mark Thomas wasn't just a target to protect. *He was Dani's father.* And Mac knew. Mac always knew.

"This is it," Knox muttered, his voice thick with the weight of what he'd uncovered. He held up the photo for Harris to see, though his mind was already racing ahead.

Harris looked at the photo, then at Knox.

"Fuck, is that Dani?"

Knox nodded grimly at Harris, his throat tight.

"Yeah. She's… she must be his daughter… Fuck, Harris, she's at my place!"

Harris's eyes widened slightly, the shock registering before his face hardened with a renewed sense of urgency.

"If Mac knows who she is, it wasn't because of her links to you she became a target but because of her father. You know what this means, don't you?" Harris said, his mind going to the exact same place of dread that Knox's was going to.

"He'll come for her again," Knox finished off with a grit of his teeth.

His grip on the photo tightened and his jaw clenched with the weight of what this all meant. Dani was now in a whole new level of danger, and he had left her alone, *unprotected.*

Mac's reach was far greater than what he had first given

him credit for, the bruises and torn skin on his knuckles testament to that. Knox knew that when Mac connected the dots and found her, then Dani would become enough leverage not only on Thomas but on Knox as well.

"FUCK!" Knox bellowed as he kicked up into the rickety bed, breaking it away from the wall then picking it up and tossing it in rage.

The mission wasn't just about Thomas anymore. It was personal now… *too fucking personal.* But Knox wouldn't let Mac take Dani. Not while he still had breath in his fucking body.

"We need to get back to her," Knox said, his voice sharp, fueled by a new determination. "We need to move… *now!* T.I.7 need to get us a new ride and a fucking fast one!"

Thankfully, Harris didn't argue. He understood the stakes and Knox's loss of control. They exchanged a look, a silent conversation passing between them.

The mission had changed, and Dani *was everything.*

NINETEEN
SHATTERED SANCTUARY

The high-speed helicopter cut through the sky like a knife, slicing through the three-hundred and sixty-eight nautical miles between Werl Prison Germany and Birmingham, England. The rotors whirled with a relentless urgency, mirroring the tension mounting inside the cabin.

Knox sat in silence, his mind racing, his eyes cold and focused. Harris sat opposite him, his face set in grim determination, thinking over everything Knox had told him about his home. They had managed to extract themselves from the ambush, and now they were rushing back to Birmingham to protect someone far more important... *Dani.*

Knox's Dani.

They had to get there before Mac's men. Knox held on to the hope that Mac didn't know where Dani was but with every minute in the air, that hope was fading. He didn't know how Mac could know where he lived but he wasn't taking the chance.

Knox's home was no longer just a safe house, it was now the epicenter with a dangerous storm heading its way. He felt it in his gut. Mac was playing a bigger game, and Dani was an even bigger part of it. It was most likely the reason Knox was hired by Malcom and Isabella's father. They needed Knox to flush out Dani.

The helicopter began its descent, the city lights of Birmingham glittering below as the sleek machine landed smoothly. It touched down behind the government-owned building in the empty car park that led to the underground one where Knox's Jag was left.

Without wasting a second, Knox and Harris disembarked, their boots hitting the wet tarmac with purpose. They moved fast, cutting across the empty spaces into the underground car park, navigating down to the tunnel system that led to Knox's secret home. They reached the familiar steel door and Knox quickly entered the code. The door clanked open with a heavy thud, and they rushed down the Victorian tunnel that felt far more foreboding than before.

It felt fucking endless!

Something was wrong. The silence was too heavy, too still, but Knox put it down to his mind playing tricks on him. This was him losing his edge. An edge he had spent years homing, now being blunted by feeling actual emotions, love being the main one.

Knox's heart pounded as he reached the final reinforced door, the one that led to the cellar. He punched in the code, and the lock disengaged with its familiar mechanical sound. They burst inside, weapons drawn.

The place was eerily quiet, save for the hum of the electricity running through the walls. But it didn't feel right.

"Dani?!" Knox called out, his voice echoing through the vast space.

No answer.

His heart felt like it was being held in an icy fist.

Harris moved in behind him, sweeping the area with his weapon drawn.

"Maybe not a good idea to shout her name, Captain," Harris growled, reminding Knox to rein it in and focus on the job at hand.

The last thing they needed was to announce they had arrived… just in case there was anyone else in the building waiting. Fuck, Knox knew that but he didn't fucking care, he just needed to see for his own eyes that Dani was there and she was alright!

They reached the elevator, after making their way through the old public house. The elevator was going to be a kill zone. And they both knew it, they had to get out ASAP if the shit hit the fan. Both men took stock of themselves as they waited for the ping and the doors to open. When the metal stainless steel protection split in two before them, they hugged the side walls of the elevator as much as possible to get as much cover as possible.

Knox scanned the loft. Everything was in place, the sleek kitchen, the low-slung sofa, the exposed brick walls. But no sign of Dani. His eyes darted up to the mezzanine bedroom, the glass roof casting a haunting reflection of the night sky. He had left her here. She was supposed to be safe. Fuck!

"We were too late," Knox muttered, the sick realisation settling into his chest. The pit of his stomach churned at the same time he started shaking his head as his nightmare was realised.

"Mac got to her," Knox ground out, causing Harris to close his eyes a moment in sympathy.

He was just about to open his mouth, no doubt ready to offer Knox false hope, when suddenly they heard movement. The sound of rapid footsteps echoed from the tunnel below as people flooded into the cellar and up the stairs. Knox's instincts flared, and he motioned for Harris to take cover. They moved silently behind the structural steel supports holding up the mezzanine floor, weapons at the ready.

A violent bang thundered overhead before black ropes fell from the oversized skylight, the shattered glass raining like diamonds in front of them. A tactical team, dressed in black combat gear, descended inside.

Knox's grip tightened on his SIG, his heart hammering in his chest. These weren't just any operatives. They were Mac's men, highly trained, heavily armed, and *fucking deadly.*

"They're here for Dani," Harris whispered, his voice laced with anger. But if that were the case, then at least that meant Dani had left on her own… *he hoped.*

The team of operatives spread out, unaware of the potential danger they had just descended into. Knox's eyes scanned their movements, calculating the odds. There were six of them, moving with practiced precision. Knox's home, once a haven, was about to become a battleground. He gave Harris a nod, and in the blink of an eye, all hell broke loose.

The first shot rang out, Harris taking down one of the operatives with a clean shot to the head. The room erupted into chaos, gunfire ricocheting off the metal beams and walls. Knox moved like a shadow, slipping between cover, his fire in controlled bursts aiming for kill shots. He dropped two more operatives with surgical precision, each bullet finding its mark. Thank fuck he was good with a gun.

But the enemy wasn't going down without a fight. Bullets shredded through the air, tearing into the once-pristine loft space. Knox's sleek kitchen was destroyed in an instant, granite countertops splintering into jagged shards as rounds tore through them. The flat-screen TV shattered, glass exploding onto the hardwood floor. A hail of bullets slammed into the steel framework, the sound deafening in the confined space.

Harris grunted as a bullet caught him in the shoulder, spinning him back. Blood sprayed from the wound, but he didn't falter. With a snarl of anger, he dropped to one knee, firing back at the advancing operatives. Harris's leg was hit next, but he kept fighting, ignoring the pain as he held his position.

Knox's mind raced as he maneuvered through the chaos. He knew every inch of this place, every piece of cover, every weak spot in the enemy's formation. Using that knowledge, he ducked behind the column once more and fired a shot that ricocheted off the steel, hitting an operative square in the temple.

Only two left.

Knox moved swiftly, taking out the next target with a messy shot to the throat, the operative crumpling to the ground in a heap and clutching at the wound pumping blood straight out the artery.

The remaining one advanced, firing blindly in a panic, all training lost in his savage attempt at surviving. Knox rolled to the side, taking cover behind what was left of the island in the kitchen just as bullets tore into the granite top above him.

He popped up from his cover, squeezing off a burst of fire. The last operative finally went down with a grunt as Knox hit him in the thigh, dropping him to the floor. With him being the only one left breathing, Knox was free to rise from his cover before walking over to him. Knox knew the man would bleed to death, he was useless already, so rather than try and get any information from him, he did him a mercy and delivered a single shot to the centre of his forehead.

The only sound now was the faint crackle of dust and debris in the air. The laboured breathing of Knox and Harris echoed as Knox lowered his gun, his pulse still hammering in his chest as he surveyed the wreckage. His home, his sanctuary, was in ruins.

As for the silence, it didn't last.

A faint mechanical hum could be heard before wheels set in motion as lift gears rotated, steadily growing louder. Knox's eyes darted toward the far wall, where the elevator stood behind a reinforced panel. The sound was unmistakable. The elevator was on its way up from the old public house below.

"More of them," Knox growled, his voice barely above a whisper.

Harris, bleeding heavily but still razor-sharp, rolled over toward one of the dead operatives. His fingers closed around the man's tactical vest, searching frantically until he found what he needed. A grenade. He pulled it free from the lifeless body, holding it up for Knox to see.

Knox gave a tight nod, signaling when the timing was right, before diving for cover. Without hesitation, Harris yanked the pin from the grenade and tossed it across the floor. It bounced once, twice, before rolling toward the elevator just as the doors began to slide open.

Time slowed.

The doors parted, revealing four more heavily armed men, their faces hidden behind ski masks. They barely registered the scene of carnage in front of them before their eyes fell to the small, round object rolling to a stop between their boots. The realisation hit them too late.

One of the men tried to scramble backwards, but in their panic, they collided with each other, each one now blocking the other's escape. It was chaos in a confined space as they desperately tried to escape the inevitable. But there was no room, no time.

The grenade went off.

A thunderous explosion ripped through the elevator, the sound deafening as fire and shrapnel tore through the enclosed space. The force of the blast sent a shockwave through the loft, shaking the walls and sending debris flying. The four men inside the elevator never stood a chance, caught in the blast, their bodies were torn apart in an instant.

Smoke billowed out of the elevator shaft, mingling with the dust already thick in the air. Knox and Harris crouched low, shielding themselves from the shockwave, but the job was done. The threat neutralized. For now.

As the fumes began to clear, Knox rose slowly, his eyes narrowing at the still-smoking elevator. Harris let out a strained laugh, wincing as he pressed a hand to his bleeding shoulder.

"That took care of them," Harris muttered through gritted teeth.

Knox knelt down next to him to assess his injuries, telling him, "Good job your aim isn't shit, Major."

Harris laughed the once before grimacing.

"Help me up, you funny fucker," Harris muttered.

Knox grinned, asking himself how many more attacks these two would survive together as he took Harris under the uninjured arm and helped him up with little difficulty.

"We better get moving," Harris added with a grunt of pain as his shoulder jarred with the movement.

Knox nodded, the weight of the moment settling in. They had survived yet again, but the real fight was just beginning. They needed to find Dani, before Mac sent anyone else.

Knox surveyed the wreckage. His once-beautiful home littered with broken furniture, bullet holes, and the bodies of Mac's men. Harris leaned against the wall, his shoulder and leg bleeding profusely, but he grinned through the pain.

"You always know how to throw a party," he quipped, his voice strained but steady.

Knox stepped over the body of an operative, his eyes cold.

"This isn't over," he said, his voice low, determined. "If

Mac sent these guys, he's coming for Dani. Which means we need to find her before he does."

Harris nodded grimly, gritting his teeth as he pushed himself off the wall he had been using to keep himself upright, blood dripping onto the floor.

"Then we better move fast," Harris agreed, although one look at his leg and Knox had to hold himself back from commenting because the first fucking thing the Major needed was a paramedic.

Knox helped Harris as they stepped over the debris and bodies. They were about to leave when a faint, ragged cough broke the stillness. Knox stopped, his eyes narrowing as he turned toward the source.

One of Mac's men, barely alive from the explosion, lay in a pool of his own blood, gasping for air, his chest heaving with laboured breaths. He was trying to drag himself to fuck knows where… Knox knew he wouldn't get far though now he was missing a leg. The man's eyes flickered with fading life, but there was a defiant glint still burning within them when he noticed his movements had been spotted.

Knox knelt beside him, his voice cold and unforgiving. "Mac sent you?"

The man coughed, blood bubbling from his lips as he struggled to speak. "Fu… ck… you."

Harris, still bleeding from his own wounds but ever the professional, stepped forward, his face a mask of fury.

"We don't have time for games," Harris growled, his voice low and dangerous. "Tell us where Mac is!"

The man's eyes darted between Knox and Harris, a flicker of fear breaking through his defiance.

Knox leaned in closer, his voice a deadly whisper. *"Talk, or you lose another leg."*

For a moment, the man hesitated, the shock to his system

starting to make his whole body shake. Then, with a grunt of pain, he spat blood onto the floor.

"You… you're too late," he rasped.

"And what of the girl?" Knox forced himself to ask.

"They need her…"

Knox's grip tightened, fury bubbling beneath the surface. "What!? What do they want with her? Fucking tell me!" Knox demanded, pulling his gun from his waistband and putting the tip of the barrel to his forehead. The man's eyes fluttered, his strength fading fast despite the threat.

"She's… *insurance.*"

Knox let the man fall back against the floor, his body sliding sideways, limp and broken. He wouldn't last much longer and Knox wanted him to suffer. As the operative's breathing grew shallower, Knox stood up, his mind racing, despite the comfort in knowing they hadn't taken her and she left here before they came. They needed to find Dani, fast, and since seeing that photograph in the prison, Knox had an idea of where to find her.

Lake Walchensee.

It wasn't much but it was all he had to go on. Rose had already been privately informed about some of what had happened at the prison and where they had been headed, because she could be trusted to keep it to herself. Knox knew that it didn't exactly sit right with her to keep such a secret, but it was necessary to keep Dani safe. As soon as the rest of T.I.7. found out, then they'd send a team for Dani, which inevitably could tip off Mac and that… well, that was something Knox wouldn't allow to happen.

So Knox pulled out his phone, quickly dialling Rose. The call connected after a single ring.

"Rose, it's Knox," he barked, the tense desperation easily

heard in his tone. "I need you to send a medical team to our location."

Rose quickly panicked, asking, "Harris? Is he… oh god, tell me, Knox… is he…" Rose couldn't finish her sentence and Knox could practically hear the tears already falling.

"He's going to be okay, two clean gunshot wounds, one to the shoulder and to the leg," Knox told her, putting her out of her misery and hopefully her head back in the game. She was the only one who could help him now.

"Rose, listen to me, Mac sent men after Dani, she was staying at my place."

"Oh shit," Rose muttered before Knox continued.

"She was already gone before they turned up. I don't have much to go on and I have no fucking idea if it'll work, but I have a lead I need you to check out."

Rose released a heavy sigh as she took in the situation, before asking him, "What do you need?"

"I need you to track down a cabin at Lake Walchensee. It's in a photo of Dani with Mark Thomas on her twenty-first birthday. I know Dani's not using her real name, but her surname should be Thomas. Cross-reference medical records. She had a burst appendix at the lake on her birthday, can you find me the hospital where she was treated. I'm hoping the records have the cabin's address."

"Okay, leave it with me, it might take me a few minutes." Rose's voice came back clear and determined.

Knox ended the call and pocketed the phone, his gaze shifting back to Harris. The big man was leaning heavily against the kitchen island, his face showing signs of pain he was trying to mask. A trail of blood dripped down his arm and he was trying to stay upright, but Knox could see the toll the wounds were taking on him.

"We need to stop the bleed to your leg," Knox said bluntly,

as he took his belt off to create a tourniquet. He secured it tight, making Harris grit his teeth.

"That should slow it down until medics get here," Knox told him, moving to his kitchen island where he kept a medical kit stashed. He hoped it didn't have too many bullet holes in it. "Sit your ass down before you pass out."

Harris grunted in response, lowering himself to the floor with a grimace.

"Had worse," he muttered, but his face told a different story.

Knox opened the kit and quickly set to work, pulling out gauze to plug the shoulder, knowing Rose wouldn't take long in getting people here.

The Major looked over to what was left of his elevator. "Please tell me there is another way out of here because it looks like your lift is out of service," Harris joked, just as Knox finished bandaging his leg.

"The good news is there's an emergency exit," Knox told him.

"And the bad news?" Harris dared to ask.

Knox looked down at his leg and with a smirk, told him, "It's down a fucking ladder."

TWENTY

ALPINE SHADOWS

Marie Thomas.

That had been the name Rose had given him.

She had called back when Knox had been upstairs changing out of his blood-stained clothes, periodically calling out to Harris to make sure the Major still remained conscious. He also grabbed anything else he needed to prepare for the trip so he couldn't be tracked. If he did find Dani, like he was hoping he would, the last fucking thing he wanted was to lead Mac straight to her.

This whole thing had been a clusterfuck from the beginning and including T.I.7 in this further would only make things worse. Their movements would be far easier to track than if Knox went off grid just like he intended to do.

"Tell me good news, Rose," Knox had answered, knowing time was of the essence here. Mac would soon realise his plan to retrieve Dani had failed and his men were all dead.

"I've got it," Rose said, her voice urgent.

"The cabin is registered to a family name that matches the medical records of Dani's appendix surgery. It's right by Lake Walchensee. If Mark Thomas has given Mac the location and they're headed there, then you better watch your back," Rose warned.

She was right, that could be where Mac was headed next. This was a race against time, where everything hinged on who could get there first. Knox had only one more thing to ask.

"What name was she born with?"

"Marie Thomas." After Rose told him Dani's original name, she then sent the address of the cabin to his phone. Knox looked down at it the second it pinged and heard her mutter, "Looks like you're headed back to Germany."

The hum of the jet engines still echoed in Knox's mind as he cleared customs at Zurich Airport, moving with the swift efficiency his high security clearance afforded him. No time for delays. He was a man on a private mission, and Dani or should he say Marie, a name he couldn't get used to yet, was at the centre of it. The only lead to her had led him back to Germany, and he wasn't going to waste a second.

He had flown in on a sleek, Honda Jet HA-420, known for its efficiency and compact design. The flight had been fast and smooth, the jet cutting through the skies like an arrow. It had cost him a fuck load of money, but he didn't give a shit because he needed the speed the private jet had awarded him. It also gave him some time for planning, which was why there would be a car at arrivals waiting for him.

Upon exiting the airport, ahead, a young rep dressed in a sharp, black suit stood waiting beside the sleek silhouette of a Bentley Continental GT Speed. The man glanced at Knox as he approached, no doubt having expected someone in a designer suit with a briefcase rather than a leather jacket with a duffle bag slung over his shoulder.

"Mr. Cini, sir. Your car is ready. Bentley Continental GT Speed, just as requested," the prestigious car hire rep addressed Knox under the name on the credit card he had used to book it. Then with a brisk nod, he stepped aside and gestured to the car.

Knox's eyes swept over the vehicle. It was a work of art and looked like a predator of the road. The polished black paint gleamed under the airport lights, its luxury lines betraying the beast within. The W12 engine was capable of hitting two hundred and eight miles per hour, more than enough to make up for lost time, and Knox didn't waste a second, holding his hand out and motioning for the keys.

He barely listened to the man's car hire scripted spiel about insurance, bringing it back with a full tank, etc. Knox just popped the boot with a quick press of a button, making it open with a smooth hydraulic hiss, before he slung in his bag that included extra ammunition, besides the usual essentials.

Slamming the trunk shut with one fluid motion, Knox signed on an iPad and muttered his thanks before sliding into the Bentley with ease. The interior was pure luxury. The sporty seats hugged his frame, and the Bentley's signature rotating screen flickered to life as he started the engine. It roared to life beneath him, the sound vibrating through the car's frame like a growling beast waiting to be unleashed.

Knox wasted no time selecting drive and pulling away from the airport, following the signs to Butzenbüelring with the car's GPS lighting up the route ahead.

The Continental surged forward as Knox hit the throttle, tearing down the highway, his mind already on the destination. Zurich fell away behind him as he merged onto the A4, then it was a clear run to the A3. He had over four hours of driving ahead of him. Four hours to reach Lake Walchensee, where the Thomas family cabin awaited.

Knox's mind churned with thoughts of Dani as he followed

the signs to Austria. The road led into long, sweeping bends, the countryside a blur of green fields and jagged mountain peaks. He pushed the car harder, watching the GPS for the next leg of his journey because he needed to make time, but the winding roads demanded focus.

After two hours, the signs pointed toward the heart of the Vorarlberg region of Austria. The Bentley hugged the curves of the road, the powerful engine propelling him forward effortlessly. The mountains loomed closer, and Knox could feel the tension rising as the landscape grew more rugged. He took exit 39-Langen, then merged onto the narrow roads leading him through the alpine valley.

Every mile brought him closer to Dani. But every time her name rippled through his thoughts, he wondered if he should try and get used to thinking of her as Marie. Was it her preferred name, did she just use the pseudonym of Dani for a job…? There were a lot of unanswered questions but, ultimately, he wanted to get to the cabin before Mac's men did because he had to assume they knew about the place.

Left with nothing but his thoughts as he drove through the mountainous landscape, he remembered back to the phone call that morning. Knox had said the prisoner's name, Mark Thomas, repeating it aloud after Harris had spoken to him on the phone. He even remembered the way she tensed by the refrigerator but, at the time, Knox hadn't picked up on it the way he should have. He also now understood why she seemed so upset when he left, because she had known that, soon after, she would be leaving too.

It had been her final goodbye.

His hands tightened on the steering wheel at the thought.

The road began to climb, the jagged summits of the Alps growing more imposing, and the GT handled the steep inclines with ease, the engine growling as Knox pushed the car toward the limit.

As he neared Sankt Anton am Arlberg, the road twisted and turned, snow-capped peaks casting long shadows over the highway. Knox barely registered the beauty of the scenery as his mind remained fixed on the mission ahead. He stayed on the road for twenty-six minutes, pushing to beat the time as he watched the GPS directing him towards the next section of the route.

He pasted through Telfs, the winding alpine roads opening up into brief stretches of straights before narrowing again. Knox veered off the main road, following the Möserer Landesstraße.

The drive grew more intense but the Bentley handled the tight curves with precision, the wide tyres giving tons of grip as its powerful engine roared. The urgency of the situation grew with every mile driven, and Knox could only hope that Mark Thomas kept the location from Mac.

Knox finally reached Kochel, Germany. The road opened up as he neared the lake, the waters of Lake Walchensee shimmering in the evening light. The Bavarian Alps surrounded the water, their rugged peaks reflected on the still surface.

The cabin's address was close, just a few more turns.

The GPS guided him towards the gravel driveway leading off the main road, and Knox slowed the Bentley as he turned off, the tires crunching over the gravel. The trees grew thicker as the car rolled deeper into the forest. His destination was still a quarter of a mile away, but the GPS put him right where he needed to be.

The Thomas family cabin was hidden somewhere within the dense woods surrounding the lake, but for now, Knox had his own rental cabin to stay in so he could do surveillance. As much as he wanted to storm inside and claim Dani back, Knox knew that she wasn't stupid. If she caught even a whiff of someone coming for her, she would be in the fucking wind and even worse this time, because she would leave Knox without a single fucking lead.

Knox pulled the car to a stop in the shadow of the tall pines. The air was cooler here, the scent of pine thick in the breeze making its way into the cockpit of the Bentley. He turned off the engine and let the silence settle over him as the tension coiled tighter in his chest. With his hands on the steering wheel he eyed the path leading to the cabin, needing a moment to decompress from the drive.

Dani. Marie. Whatever name she went by, Knox knew she was more than just a target now. She was a means for Mac to get what he wanted, and Knox had to protect her above all else.

The crisp evening air bit at his skin as he stepped out of the car, and scanned the tree line, his mind racing as he walked towards the rental cabin. The gravel crunched beneath his dark brown Timberland boots as he approached the old, rustic cabin. It stood alone, framed by tall pines that swayed gently in the evening breeze. The cabin had a weathered charm to it, with thick wooden beams and stone accents that gave it the appearance of something plucked straight from a Bavarian postcard. The roof was pitched steeply, built to withstand the heavy mountain snows that blanketed the area during the winter months.

He stepped up to the door, thoughts of spending time in a place like this with Dani under far different circumstances crossed his mind. The thoughts made him tense, the urge to go over there straight away riding him hard. But instead of doing what he knew was rash and impulsive, something that could get him killed, he took the key from a lock box and unlocked the front door. which creaked as Knox pushed it open.

The door creaked as Knox pushed it open and stepped into the dimly lit interior, the scent of aged wood and faint traces of smoke from an old fireplace greeting him. The space was cosy, almost too small for a man like Knox who was used to larger, more tactical surroundings. The floorboards groaned under his weight as he crossed the small living area, his eyes quickly assessing the cabin's layout.

A single bed, draped with a thick woollen blanket, was tucked into the corner of the room beneath a large window framed by simple wooden shutters. The walls were adorned with antlers, and faded black-and-white photographs of the surrounding mountains and the lake. Pictures likely taken decades ago. A stone hearth dominated the opposite wall, a stack of firewood neatly piled beside it. The cabin had a rustic simplicity, no frills, just functionality. It was the kind of place someone might come to disappear for a while.

Knox took what he needed from his bag before dropping it onto the worn leather armchair. One that sat near the small wooden table that served as both a dining area and work surface. A pair of sturdy chairs sat beside it, their seats worn from years of use. He moved methodically, his eyes continuously scanning every corner of the cabin, mentally preparing for what came next.

His attention shifted to the sliding door at the far end of the room, which led out onto a deck. Knox's boots echoed softly on the hardwood floor as he made his way towards it, and the light outside had begun to dim, casting long shadows through the glass.

He slid the door open, stepping out onto the deck. The air was even cooler out here rolling off the lake, and the sky had turned a deep shade of indigo as night began to fall over the mountains.

Lake Walchensee made for a breathtaking view, a serene, expanse of water that stretched out beneath the towering peaks of the Bavarian Alps. But Knox's eyes weren't drawn to the beauty of the landscape. His focus was on the distant cabin, barely visible through the trees around the shoreline.

The Thomas family cabin.

He was waiting until the cover of nightfall before getting closer, curious to see what he would find.

He could make out the rear deck that faced the water, tucked into the woods, blending almost seamlessly with the environment. It was quiet, still, as if no one was there, no lights. That made his stomach sink a little, but Knox knew better. Somewhere in that cabin, Dani could be hiding, trying to stay away from the storm that she no doubt feared was coming for her.

Knox leaned on the railing, his gaze locked on the distant property. The line of sight was perfect, hence why he had picked the cabin he was in, thankful that it had been empty this time of year. From his vantage point, he could also see the rear deck and a few windows, though the rest of the house was obscured by the dense trees surrounding it. The cabins were far enough apart that no casual observer would notice the connection between them, but Knox had no doubt that he'd have a clean view of any movement on the deck.

He lifted the compact night binoculars he had retrieved from his duffle bag and lifted them to his eyes, focusing on the Thomas cabin's deck.

No movement. No sign of life.

Knox lowered the binoculars, his mind running through the next steps. He needed to scope the area, plan his approach. This wasn't just a random cabin in the woods. No, this was a fortress of secrets, and somewhere within, Dani held the key to unravelling them all. There would most likely be security systems because he knew Dani well enough by now. Also, her father was a hacker too and therefore into shady shit. It would seem the apple didn't fall far from the tree in that regard. Dani must have been taught by him.

Knox exhaled slowly, the cold air clouding in front of him before disappearing into the evening sky. The lake was calm now, but Knox knew it wouldn't stay that way for long.

Turning from the railing, Knox walked back into the cabin, sliding the door shut behind him. He had work to do, starting with unpacking. The Thomas cabin was close, too close for comfort, and he needed to get over there because he was sure that Mac wouldn't be far behind.

If he hadn't of beaten him there already.

TWENTY-ONE

BENEATH THE SURFACE

K nox moved silently through the dark, the night enveloping him like a shroud. The cold air was heavy with the scent of the woodland, and the only sound was the distant ripple of water against the shoreline of the lake. Dressed in solid black tactical gear, he blended into the shadows, a wraith in the night. A Heckler & Koch MP5 hung securely from its strap, the collapsible stock tucked tightly against Knox's body for close-quarters use. His SIG 9mm was snug in its holster, within easy reach, along with his flashbang grenades and combat knife.

Through his night vision goggles, the ones he had packed and brought with him, the world glowed in hues of green and black. They revealed details the naked eye could never detect in the darkness. His sharp gaze locked on the Thomas family cabin nestled between the trees at the water's edge. It stood there in total darkness, no lights, no signs of life. At first glance, it looked abandoned, as if no one had been there for months.

He crouched behind a fallen tree, the perfect cover to study the structure through his goggles. The roof was barely visible through the canopy, but Knox's attention was drawn to three Starlink satellite dishes mounted on the stone chimney stack. That was a lot of bandwidth internet for a remote cabin like this. Too much. Dani's father would have been behind bars when that tech released so she had to have been responsible getting that installed. There was obviously serious computing power inside those walls.

His gaze shifted to the oversized air conditioning unit humming faintly at the side of the cabin. A single green LED light blinked on its side, the only visible sign that the cabin had power. Knox's instincts told him that this place was set up for heavy tech. Maybe even a makeshift server system hidden somewhere within the cabin's unassuming exterior.

Knox adjusted his position, moving low and careful. The closer he got to the cabin, the more his adrenaline grew. His night-vision goggles revealed thin, barely visible lines crisscrossing the perimeter; infra-red tripwires. Subtle, but effective. It was a network of security designed to catch anyone sneaking up too close. On top of that, several CCTV cameras were mounted around the property, small and painted to match the wood of the cabin, their dark lenses reflecting in the goggles sights being their only giveaway.

Knox moved with precision, his senses heightened, making sure to stay low, using the trees, bushes, and boulders for cover. He navigated carefully through the trip beams and around the cameras' blind spots. Every movement was measured, deliberate. One wrong step and maybe an alarm would trip or flood lights would expose him. Either way, Knox didn't want to find out. Besides, it wasn't like he hadn't done this before, countless times in fact. His experience with the SAS had trained him to be a predator in the darkness, moving undetected through enemy lines… Getting in, neutralising targets, getting out and being long gone before anyone was the wiser.

The cabin loomed closer, a solitary solid mass in the night. To the right, Knox spotted a stand-alone garage. No vehicles were parked outside, which was a good sign. He hoped Dani's was inside, out of sight, and not empty because she wasn't here.

Knox took comfort in the fact there were no signs of a kill team ever being here, no signs of a struggle. Everything looked untouched, there were no boot prints on the ground, it was all as it should be. Quiet and undisturbed. Knox exhaled silently, the weight of worry lifting enough to stop the pounding in his chest.

Several questions continued to linger in Knox's mind throughout all this. Was Dani inside, sleeping? Or had she not even come here? Or worse not made it here? Was all this for nothing? Had Mac already got to her somehow?

There was a possibility that Knox would have to stake out the cabin for days to see if Dani showed up. And in that time Dani could be in trouble somewhere else.

He stopped, mentally dressed himself down, and told himself to regain focus because that train of thought wasn't helping. There was only one way to find out what he needed to know for sure.

Knox circled the cabin, where the trip beams were laid out like a spider's web around the structure, and the CCTV cameras were positioned strategically, covering every angle except one. A side window. A small window that was slightly elevated off the ground, and the only part of the cabin not covered by sensors either. He found a weak spot… his entry point.

Knox crept toward it, his eyes scanning the surrounding area one last time before he moved in. He crouched beneath the window, carefully pulling his knife from its sheath. The window's catch was old, slightly rusted, and he slid the blade beneath the frame with practiced skill, lifting the latch with a quiet click as the old wood frame creaked. The sound was barely audible, but Knox paused, listening intently. His heartbeat slowed as he waited, ears straining for any signs of movement from inside.

Nothing. The cabin remained silent.

Satisfied, Knox gripped the bottom of the window and eased it open just enough to slip inside. He moved like a shadow, silently sliding through the opening and landing softly on the wooden floor. He expected the alarm to sound but it never came, making him frown in question. All of this security, yet having no alarm when a window was opened seemed off. He had fully been prepared to disable it once inside but there was nothing.

Still not trusting the silence, Knox moved deeper into the cabin, crossing the living space without making a sound. The room was cloaked in darkness, the faint scent of pine and wood smoke clinging to the air. Just as he picked up the first signs of life, he cut across to the far side of the room, positioning his back against the wall. He settled beside the opening that appeared to lead down a hallway, likely toward the bedrooms and bathroom. From here, he had a clear view of anyone approaching before they could see him.

It was the right move. Moments later, the barrel of a gun emerged from the hallway, its outline barely visible in the darkness, followed by a figure. Without hesitation, Knox sprang into action.

He lunged forward, grabbing the wrist holding the gun and twisting it sharply. A muffled groan escaped the person's lips as the weapon clattered to the floor. In one smooth motion, Knox pulled the figure close, slamming them against the wall, his forearm pinning them in place. His other hand was ready to strike, but he hesitated for a split second.

The soft scent of vanilla and jasmine hit him, a scent he knew all too well. His fingers, familiar with the shape and feel of this body, recognized the curves they had mapped out before. In that instant, Knox knew exactly who he had pinned against the wall.

He dipped his head close to her ear, the name on the tip of his tongue replaced by one more fitting. His voice was low, edged with tension.

"Hello, Marie." Knox's rich Scottish accent made Dani freeze in his arms, her struggle ceasing, no longer fighting him as his words sank in.

"Knox! What the bloody hell are you doing? Let me go!" Dani's voice rang out, sharp and incredulous, her body now shaking in his hold.

"Ssshh, it's okay, lass, it's okay, Marie," Knox said, pushing the foreign name through his lips so she heard it being said again. He made it impossible for her to ignore, wanting to hammer home the fact that she couldn't hide her true self from him.

"Don't call me that!" she snapped, pushing against him, fighting him enough that he let her go so she wouldn't accidently hurt herself.

She stormed away from him, flicking the lights on as she did. Now, he could see all of her. Dani was dressed for the cold, the autumn chill creeping into the log cabin despite the lingering warmth of the fire. She wore a thick, dark-grey woollen sweater that hugged her frame. Over it, a padded, olive-green body warmer added an extra layer of warmth. Her dark jeans were tucked into rugged black boots, and were scuffed at the toes from use. A knit beanie covered her head, stray strands of her blonde hair poking out. She looked both ready for the night and prepared to face the elements, the practical clothing a stark contrast to the tension in the air.

She ran her hands over her face in a frustrated gesture, no doubt upset to hear that Knox had discovered her true identity.

"Most people knock on the front door!" she shouted, whipping around to glare at him.

Knox let out a breath, a small grin tugging at the corner of his lips at her rant. *Fuck,* he was happy to find her alive and in one piece. He was also happy to see that Mac hadn't gotten to her like he feared.

"Didn't want to wake you, lass," he replied dryly, making her narrow her eyes at him.

"How did you even track me here? No one knows about this place," Dani asked after moving through her home, as if this was her sacred place and no one had ever stepped foot inside it before.

It was a large cabin, just as rustic on the inside as it was on the outside. Wooden beams crossed the ceiling, and a stone fireplace sat cold in the corner. There was a kitchen area, a table, and a few chairs occupying one side of the room, while a narrow hallway she had stepped out of earlier led to what he assumed were the bedrooms and bathroom.

But his eyes quickly returned to Dani. She looked tired, a little rough around the edges, but unharmed. Relief washed over him once more. She was safe. *Thank fuck she was safe.*

"I will get to that but first, we need to talk," Knox said, his voice low but urgent.

Dani started shaking her head, as if she wasn't ready to face the severity of all this. As if him being there now was too much reality for her to handle.

Well, it was tough shit, Knox thought, because they were talking about it and he was getting his answers.

Knox stood across the room, his arms crossed, tension crackling in the air between them both. She stared back at him, eyes flashing with a mixture of anger and something else, something softer, more conflicted. Her lips pressed into a thin line and, for a moment, neither of them spoke, the weight of everything unsaid hanging heavy between them.

"Why did you run, Dani?" Knox's voice was low, but the frustration was clear. "Why the hell didn't you tell me?" he added, because of course he knew the reason she had run, he just wanted to make her say it. A way to get her to start talking.

Dani folded her arms across her chest defensively, her expression hardening.

"You don't understand, Knox. I didn't 'run.' I had no choice but to leave."

"No choice?" Knox snapped, taking a step closer. "So, what? You were just going to disappear? You left me in the dark with not a single clue on where to find you. Do you know how fucking worried I have been about you!?" Knox unleashed on her, unable to stop his emotions bursting free.

"I couldn't tell you," Dani shot back, her voice trembling slightly, though she tried to keep her composure. "You wouldn't understand. And you… well, you didn't need to get involved."

Knox's jaw tightened at hearing that, his frustration and anger simmering just below the surface.

"Don't pull that bullshit. You knew why I was going to Werl Prison. You knew, and you pretended you knew nothing."

Dani opened her mouth to retort, but the words seemed to catch in her throat. She looked away, biting her lip, conflicted.

"You could have told me… you could have fucking trusted me, Dani," Knox argued, feeling the bitter pain rip through him now that he knew she was safe and he was free to be hurt and angry.

He stepped closer, his voice dropping when he saw her flinch against his outburst. The guilt easy to see on her face, and it was one of the only things strong enough to calm him down.

"I know now, Dani. I know your real name is Marie Thomas. Your father is Mark Thomas, the man I was sent to recover." At the mention of her father's name, Dani flinched again before lifting her chin, her eyes narrowing at Knox.

"So what?" she muttered with fake bravado. "You think you know everything now?"

"I know enough," Knox said, his voice tight with accusation.

Dani threw her hands up in the air dramatically and said, "Then come on, Knox, why don't you lay it all out for me? What exactly do you know!?" Dani shouted in a bitter tone.

"I know that your father must've taught you everything he knew, how to hack, how to set up fake accounts, ID's... everything. All the tricks you've been using. It's all because of him, right?"

Dani's anger flared, and she glared at him, stepping forward until they were almost face-to-face.

"My father?!" Her voice rose, a sharp edge cutting through it. "You think my father taught me any of this? He can barely turn on a fucking computer!"

Knox's eyes flickered with surprise, but he held his ground.

"Then explain it to me, Dani. Explain why you've been hiding all this. Why you lied to me," Knox asked, needing to know more than ever why Dani was the way she was.

The reasons he had assumed were the only thing to make any sense, but in that one sentence she had torn his reasoning to shreds... leaving him with even more unanswered questions.

Dani's hands clenched into fists at her sides.

"I didn't lie to you! I never lied about who I was. I haven't hidden all this from you, it was never any of your business to start with. There is a difference, Knox."

He gritted his teeth at that, unable to accept that her life wasn't his business when they both knew it was a lie. But before he could call her out on it, she carried on, shocking him further.

"My father had nothing to do with my skills, okay? I'm the hacker, Knox. *Me.*" Her voice trembled with frustration at the same time Knox frowned in confusion.

"*What?!*" he hissed, making her release a frustrated sigh.

"He took the blame for me... so I... so I wouldn't go to prison. He was the one who ended up behind bars... *because of me.*"

The sad regret in her tone cut Knox to the bone. He hated to see how much this affected her, how she clearly blamed herself for whatever it was that had happened.

Dani's breath hitched, her eyes filling with a mixture of guilt and sorrow.

"I lost everything when he took the fall for me. Everything. My life was destroyed, and I had nothing left but this cabin. No home, no family. I had to make a living, so I used the only skills I had, I did the one thing that I was good at. And eventually, that work led me to you," Dani said, raising her tear-soaked eyes to his.

His heart broke for her as he took a step closer but before he could reach her, she turned away from him, her gaze landing on a small photograph on the mantel.

It was a picture of her and a woman, who Knox instantly recognised as Dani's mother. The resemblance was striking. Dani's expression softened, her fingers brushing against the frame.

"My mother died just before my 21st birthday," she said quietly, her voice barely above a whisper.

"This cabin is all I had left of us. It's all I have left of my memories. So, I set it up to work from here. I didn't have a choice, Knox. I needed to survive."

Knox exhaled sharply, running a hand through his hair if only to stop himself from reaching out to her again, knowing she wanted space.

"Dani… I… damn. I didn't know, lass," Knox said in a sympathetic tone, one she clearly didn't appreciate.

"No, you didn't!" she snapped, though there was less venom in her voice now.

"You assumed it was my father. But like I said, he's in prison because of me. I was the one hacking, I was the one doing everything behind the scenes. He took the fall so I wouldn't go to jail."

Knox stared at her as the first of her tears fell. The weight of her words settling heavily on him. He felt a knot of guilt tighten in his chest, but he couldn't shake the frustration still gnawing at him.

Dani turned back to him, her expression softening.

"It's always been me. My father didn't teach me anything. I learned it all on my own. And when I met you, I thought maybe I could build a nest egg up so I could leave that life behind. But it's never that simple, is it?"

Knox sighed, rubbing the back of his neck. He looked at Dani, seeing her not just as the person who had helped him from behind a screen, but as someone who had been carrying a heavy burden… *alone.* It was something Knox could relate to because he had felt the same suffocating weight of loneliness.

The room fell into a tense silence, both of them lost in their own thoughts. Finally, Knox spoke, his voice low but sincere.

"I just wish you would've trusted me enough to tell me."

Dani's gaze softened at that, a mixture of vulnerability and frustration crossing her face.

"I wanted to. Fuck. You had no idea how much I wanted to open up… but I couldn't. I didn't know you cared like you did, and I was scared."

Knox took this moment of softness to step closer, his tone gentler now as he asked, "Scared of what?"

Dani was only an arm's width away from him now and he was pleased to see that she hadn't yet backed away from him.

"Of losing you," she whispered, the admission sinking in deep within his soul and staying there, rooted to his very being.

He loved this woman like no one else before her and to hear that her reason for not trusting him was through fear of losing him… It filled his heart with hope. Which was why he could take it no more, and quickly reached out to take her in his arms. She gasped in surprise but quickly melted into him, as if needing his strength and comfort.

She looked up at him, her eyes wide, her breath catching in her throat at the intense look he gave her in return. For a moment, neither of them moved, the air between them thick with unspoken emotions. Dani's lips parted slightly, but she quickly looked away, blinking back tears that threatened to fall once more.

"I'm sorry," she whispered, tugging at his heart once more and making him squeeze her tighter for a few seconds.

"We're in this together now. No more running. No more hiding," Knox told her, his words firm yet reassuring.

Dani nodded slowly, still conflicted but grateful for his presence.

"Okay," she said quietly, her voice barely above a whisper, but it was all Knox needed to hear before making the decision to prove to her just how much she could rely on him.

"We are going to get your dad back, Dani. I don't care what it takes, you're not going to lose another parent if I can help it."

His determined words made her cry out in a sob she had been holding back, the relief becoming a tangible thing he could feel as she threw her arms around him and clung on, burying her head in his chest as she cried. His hands created soothing circles on her back, and he made her a vow.

"You will never be alone ever again… *I promise."*

The cabin was quiet, the only sounds coming from a small propane stove where Dani was preparing coffee using an old moka maker. The worn wooden handle had darkened from years of use, and the aluminium body gleamed in the warm light of the kitchen. Steam hissed softly as the water heated, filling the air with the rich scent of fresh brewing coffee.

Knox stood in the living room area, lost in thought. He had pulled off his weapons, one by one, the MP5A3 resting against the wall, his SIG 9mm placed on a nearby table. He removed his tactical vest and sweater, revealing the tight-fitted black compression shirt underneath that hugged his muscular frame. The shirt clung to his broad shoulders and chest, defining every ridge of his powerful physique.

From the corner of her eye, Dani couldn't help but notice. She admired the way his muscles shifted beneath the fabric, the raw strength he carried with him everywhere. Her gaze lingered a moment longer than it should have before she quickly turned back to the stove, not wanting to be caught looking.

Knox, unaware of Dani's admiring glance, continued

moving through the room. His eyes drifted over the family photos displayed on the wall; pictures of Dani with her parents. *Damn*, Knox thought. She had always been beautiful.

One picture caught his attention, a younger Dani smiling between her father and mother, a snapshot of happier times. Her father, Mark Thomas, looked strong and proud, while Dani's mother, with kind eyes, had an undeniable warmth about her. Knox could see the resemblance between them.

Dani's mother had died before her 21st birthday, and Knox could see how that loss had shaped the bond between Dani and her father. There were more photos of them together; decorating the cabin at Christmas, fishing, traveling across Europe. The closeness between them was evident in every picture once they no longer included her mother.

"You spent a lot of time here, didn't you?" Knox asked, his voice soft as he continued to gaze at the photos. Dani glanced over her shoulder, her voice quieter now.

"Yeah, after Mom died, it was just the two of us. My dad and I, we became really close. He wanted me to have a connection to both sides of my family, so we split our time between Hereford and here at the cabin."

Knox listened and nodded, still studying the photos before replying.

"I would've never guessed you were half-German. There's no sign of it in the way you speak."

To this Dani smirked, turning back to the coffee.

"That's because you only know what I wanted you to know," she said dryly, waiting for Knox to bite, but he only raised an eyebrow. So, Dani told him that it wasn't fair looking that hot and it was too distracting wearing that shirt with all those muscles, and asked when the hell was he going to kiss her… all of which she rattled off in perfect German.

He turned to her with a smirk of his own.

"You think I don't understand you? How do you know I am not fluent in German, Dani?" Knox asked, teasing her. Of course, he didn't speak fluent German but he made out the word kiss, and the blush on her face told him all he needed to know.

Her eyes widened in surprise, a flash of embarrassment crossing her face making Knox laugh.

"Dani girl… *I love teasing you.*" He couldn't help but laugh again at the sound of her sigh, which now had him very curious to know what she had said exactly.

She muttered something that sounded like 'incorrigible' under her breath before turning back to focus on the coffee. She poured the espresso into two small cups, bringing them over to the table.

"I went to an all-girls private school in the UK," Dani explained, changing the subject back to her usual accent, or lack of a German one. "They drilled this posh, generic accent into me, and well, I guess it kind of stuck," Dani admitted with a shrug of her shoulders.

Knox picked up one of the cups, what little warmth of the tiny cup had spreading through his hands.

"In the briefing… when they talked about your father being the hacker, I didn't focus too much on what he was in prison for. I just figured he'd done something to get himself there and that was that. But now that I know he took the fall for you…" He let the sentence trail off, and she knew instantly what he wanted to know.

However, when she didn't speak, he prompted her to do so by asking, "What happened, Dani?"

For some reason she looked back towards the hallway, as if there was a room there that held all the answers. She then hesitated, her fingers tapping the side of her cup as she stared at the dark liquid inside, then she let out a small, humourless laugh.

"I hacked into Deutsche Bank," she admitted.

Knox blinked and thought he had misheard her for a second. The gravity of what she had done began sinking in as he sensed no teasing in her tone.

"You what?" Knox hissed incredulously. Dani looked up, her expression a mix of guilt and defiance.

"Yeah. It was… *a phase.*"

Knox frowned at this and repeated her once more, "A Phase?"

She cleared her throat awkwardly before telling him, "I was going through this whole animal rights thing. Vegetarian, saving the planet, you know?" She shook her head, almost laughing at her own foolish younger days before continuing. "I stole money from the bank to fund animal charities. I thought I was doing something noble."

Knox listened as he leaned back in his chair, still processing.

"You hacked into Germany's largest bank… for animal charities?" Knox asked, as if he needed what he'd just heard confirming again.

She nodded, his disbelief making her blush once more.

"Unfortunately, that wasn't the worst part," Dani admitted, her voice quieter now and obviously getting to the part that included her father.

"I accidentally hacked into a military account, one connected to NATO funds. That's what really set off alarms."

Knox's eyes widened at this before he blurted, "You hacked NATO?!"

Dani winced, nodding, making Knox whistle air through his teeth.

"Jesus," he muttered and again, Dani tensed.

"It wasn't NATO," she argued. "Just their bank account and not on purpose, trust me."

Knox felt bad for her, despite being in total awe of her skills. Rose hadn't been kidding when she said there were only three hackers in the world that could accomplish what Mac needed.

"What happened?" Knox asked, needing her to explain the rest.

"I triggered the security protocols, and before I knew it, they were hunting me down. The German government spun it as a terrorist cyber-attack, linking it to ISIS to cover their tracks. They couldn't admit that someone from within their own borders had hacked their flagship bank—it would've shattered their credibility. Imagine if they found out it was just a young, idealistic girl, thinking she could save the world?"

Knox stared at her, almost speechless.

"And your father…?"

Dani swallowed hard at hearing this, tears coating her eyes as she thought back to that day. The day her father begged her to let him go.

"He took the fall. He told them that he did it out of anger, low military pay, poor pensions. He made it sound like he was out for compensation. The authorities were eager to cover it up and even more eager to believe him rather than investigate me, just to make it go away quietly. They would've lost their biggest clients if that got out. So, my dad took the blame," she told him, swiping at her cheek as she felt the first tear fall.

A significant silence fell between them, heavy with the weight of what she'd confessed. Knox could see the pain in her haunted eyes from the guilt and blame she carried all these years. Because in the end, she hadn't just lost one parent, she had lost two. Knox didn't know how Dani's mother had died, but it had left her with just her dad and judging by all the pictures, someone who became her entire life and she now must feel she was losing him to.

Knox felt the pain like a laceration to the heart. She had been so alone and that made him feel like an even bigger bastard when turning her away back in Spain. *Fuck*, he should have been there for her from the start. From the very moment he began to develop feelings for her.

"I owe him everything," Dani said, eventually breaking the silence between them with a whisper, her voice cracking slightly as she continued. "He gave up his freedom so I wouldn't go to prison."

Knox's chest tightened further, a wave of empathy flooding over him as he reached out, placing a hand on hers.

"Dani…"

She looked up at him the second she heard him say her name, her eyes shimmering with even more unshed tears, but there was strength there, too.

"It's why I came here. To hide, to work, to survive. I didn't want you getting involved in all of this," she admitted, her emotions starting to get the better of her.

Knox's thumb brushed against her hand, the touch sending a surge of warmth between them. The tension in the air shifted from more than just frustration, but it was something deeper, something unspoken. The memories of their time together at Knox's loft, the night they spent wrapped in each other's arms, all of it flooded back to the surface.

Dani's breath hitched, and Knox's gaze dropped to her lips, the magnetic pull between them undeniable. He gently took her coffee cup and placed it down on the table next to his own. Then he moved closer, invading her space, needing to touch her. The fact that she didn't pull away only reaffirmed his movements.

Slowly, tentatively, he stood up, still holding her hand, and tenderly pulled her up to meet him. Then he leaned down, pressing his lips to hers in a soft, gentle kiss. One that she needed. *One that they both needed.*

Dani melted into him, her hands resting on his chest, feeling the heat of his body through the compression shirt. The kiss deepened, becoming more passionate, more urgent as the feelings they had both tried to suppress came rushing back. His hands slipped under her body warmer, fisting in her jumper as his need for her guided his actions, yanking her hard to him. *He never wanted to let go!*

Before they could lose themselves entirely, a sharp ping echoed through the room, a message notification from Dani's computer station. The sound made her suddenly freeze in his arms, then she pulled back, her breath coming in shallow gasps as she turned toward the sound.

"That'll be Mac," she said, her voice still breathless.

Knox stared at her in utter shock, his mouth opening before words quickly followed. *"What the... Fuck. I thought I had more time,"* he said in a dangerous tone that made it clear how unhappy he was with the situation.

"I reached out to him on the Dark Web," Dani interrupted his inner turmoil like what she said was completely normal, and that pissed him off even more.

With gritted teeth, he asked, *"You did what?!"*

TWENTY-THREE
BLOOD LOYALTY

Knox's eyes darkened and his mind raced at what he just heard. He pulled away from Dani and rubbed the back of his neck in frustration, trying to calm his temper. It didn't work.

"Fuck! FUCK! Dani, why the fuck would you put yourself at risk like that?!" Knox shouted, looking down at her computer like it was the enemy, as if Mac had the unearthly ability to reach through the screen and grab her.

"It's not a risk," she stated defiantly, making Knox groan aloud.

"Of course it fucking is!" he snapped.

Dani folded her arms across her chest and, usually, the sight would have calmed Knox down. Not only was she cute as fuck, but by God she had nice breasts. However, he was too busy being pissed at her.

"He can't track me, so no, it isn't a risk," she told him stubbornly, but he was having none of it,

"How the fuck do you know? He could have…"

"Because I am the best there fucking is, that's why!" she

shouted, obviously having enough of this argument, but Knox wasn't done yet.

"It's too much of a risk, Dani." However, after he said this, he watched as the fight drained out of her and her shoulders slumped. Then she said the only thing that calmed Knox enough to understand her reasons.

"He's my dad, Lucas… *my dad.* He's all I've got left and whether that's here in this cabin or in some shitty prison cell, it doesn't change how I feel. As long as he is alive somewhere in this world, then I have him with me and no one… I repeat, *no one is going to take that from me!"*

As she spoke, the emotion poured out of her, and Knox couldn't resist any longer. He took her in his arms when she burst into tears, cradling her head against his chest as he comforted her.

"Alright, lass… alright, I understand. Ssshh, it will be alright. Everything will be alright now."

Pulling back enough to look up at him, Dani asked, "But how? How will it be alright? Soon, Mac will discover that my dad's not the hacker and has no clue how to even work a computer, let alone hack anything. And then who knows what he will do to my dad… Knox, I am scared."

He pulled her close again, smoothing a hand down her hair and feeling her tears soak the material of his shirt.

"We will get him back… I promise. I will do everything in my power to help get him back, but you have to trust me, Dani. You have to trust me, and that means no more running… okay?"

When she looked up at him again, he framed her face and used his thumbs to rid her of her tears. Then she nodded, but he was quick to remind her,

"Words sweetheart… *I want your words."* He whispered

this last part down only an inch from her lips. Which was when she gifted him with all he wanted from her… *trust.*

"I promise."

Dani stared at the computer screen, her fingers trembling slightly as the first message from Mac appeared in the secure chat window. Knox stood behind her, silent but vigilant, watching the tension tighten in her frame as she read the name she had been born with.

"Hello, Marie Thomas."

She and Knox exchanged a knowing look before turning back to the screen, watching as more was being typed from Mac's end.

It was a single word this time,

"Hacker."

Dani was about to type a reply when Knox's hand covered hers, stopping her.

"Are you sure he can't trace you?" Knox asked, needing the extra confirmation.

"I'm positive. No one knows about this place other than my dad and I, and my dad wouldn't tell him knowing that it would lead to me… hell, I still don't know how you know about it," Dani said.

Knox shook his head and told her, "Later," then he nodded back to the screen, allowing her to get back to business.

"What do you want? "

Dani typed, the tightness in her jaw evident thanks to the tense situation.

"I want the real hacker, not the fake."

As Mac typed, each letter appeared in real time, making it a torturous process.

"Is my father alive?"

Dani typed next, this time her hands shaking as if too terrified to truly find out. It was why Knox placed a comforting hand on her shoulder, silently telling her that he had her back.

"For now, but whether he remains that way is down to you."

This was Mac's longest message yet and the hardest one to take so far.

Dani's breath hitched, her mind reeling. The image of her father, tortured and broken flashed in her mind. Mac's words were like a noose tightening around her neck. She didn't want to imagine the things Mac could have done to him.

"Ask him for proof of life. That way there may be something in the photograph we could use to find his whereabouts," Knox told her, despite knowing it was a long shot. All he could hope for was that Mac would get sloppy, underestimating Dani and her abilities to find people.

"I want proof of life."

Her breathing was heavy as she typed, then they both waited. She couldn't imagine how she was going to react if she saw a picture of her dad tied to a chair bleeding from a beating they had given him. A hundred horrifying images assaulted her mind all at once as the excruciating wait continued.

But it never came. No, instead, only one word was written: *"Goshawk."*

Dani sucked in a quick breath and her whole body tensed.

"What does that mean?" Knox asked, disappointed that Mac hadn't given them the clue they needed to find him first, but he also couldn't say that he was surprised.

"It means he just willingly gave that up as proof," Dani told him, and he was about to question it further when the next question she typed stopped him in his tracks.

"When and where for the exchange?"

"Wait, what are you doing?!" Knox shouted, knowing there was no way he was letting any fucking exchange happen! His emotions were clearly getting the better of him until Dani spoke again.

"It's the only way we are going to get the chance at getting both Mac and my dad."

Knox nodded, calming slightly because now the image of her being taken had been replaced with Mac walking into a trap.

"Hotel Belvédère. Come alone. No T.I.7. No Ambush. If I think you have double crossed me, your father is dead, so I suggest if he managed to find you that you leave your Scottish Knight at home. You have 48 hours."

The ominous tone in Mac's newest message made a shiver creep through her body, but she replied with confidence anyway.

"I will be there."

However, this wasn't enough for Mac because he clearly wanted to taunt her one last time.

"I know you will, Daddy's girl."

TWENTY-FOUR

COLLATERAL NEGOTIATIONS

Dani sat back, her mind racing as she stared at the last message. Knox could feel the tension radiating off her, but she kept her voice steady when she spoke.

"What are we going to do, Lucas? You heard what he said. I have to go alone."

He crouched beside her. "Listen to me now, we're going to get your father back. Whatever it takes, do you hear me? Whatever it takes… *except your life."* His voice was low but firm.

Dani swallowed hard, before saying his name with a sigh, "Lucas…"

"No, Dani, I will do what I can to save him, but I will not risk your life, do you understand me?" Knox's tone was unyielding and his expression tense. For him, this wasn't even debatable.

"But…" Dani tried again, but he shook his head, stopping her once more.

"No buts. For this to work we must play it my way and that means we need to move. Pack your things. I'm going to make a call to T.I.7. for backup. Carter needs to know what we're dealing with."

"He said no T.I.7., Lucas, we can't risk it!" The desperation in her voice was understandable, yet Knox was having none of it. If she thought for one moment that he was letting her walk into this dangerous situation ready to exchange herself for her father, then she could think again. *No fucking way.*

Which was why he stepped into her, now framing her face with his hands so she couldn't look away from him.

"Dani, we need them. Trust me, this is my world, and this is what I do," Knox said as he looked into her eyes, allowing her to see the sincerity in them. He needed her to understand that she couldn't take on Mac alone.

"Mac… fuck, you can't trust him. You can't trust that he will keep his word. I know it's hard, baby, I know it is, but I swear to you, only two things would happen if you gave him this exchange. The first is that they wouldn't let your dad go, instead they will keep him alive solely to have leverage on you, so Mac can force you to do what he needs you to do…" He felt Dani shiver in his hold, making him drop his hands down to her arms, rubbing the length of them once, twice, before holding her firm. "And the second is the worst. He would end up with a bullet in him so he can't tell T.I.7 anything. Information he would know after they believed him to be the hacker. He would know too much… he would know their plan, Dani, and Mac can't have him living long enough to tell anyone."

Dani closed her eyes at this, shaking her head but this time Knox knew it wasn't because she didn't believe what he was saying… *it was because she did.*

"Either way, neither of those options are what you want, and neither are going to fucking happen because I won't let them. *But you have to trust me, lass,"* Knox said after placing his forehead to hers, whispering the last plea for her to trust him and feeling it sink down into the core of him.

Nodding, she told him that she would trust him in this. That she would trust his ability to get her dad back if it was the last thing he did.

He held her tightly in his arms, letting her take the time she needed before gently releasing her. Her face was etched with fear, haunted by the endless possibilities playing out in her mind. Knox wished he could sit her down and give her space to process it all, but time wasn't on their side. With only forty-eight hours, the window to assemble a team was rapidly closing.

The one small comfort in Mac's deadline was that he didn't know Dani was already so close to the meeting point. Knox hoped that would give them the edge they needed. But first, there was a call he had to make.

"Pack light, anything you think you will need for a day or two," Knox told her, but when she reached over to grab the laptop, he added, "No tech, just in case they found some way of tracking you and we give them a way to ambush us."

He could see she was about to argue but something in his face must have told her to let it go. It wasn't that Knox didn't trust in her abilities, it was that he didn't want to leave anything to chance at this point. Not when it came to Dani. *Never again.*

Knox pulled out his phone, stepping out onto the rear deck and stood looking out onto the lake while Dani was inside packing. The surface of the water reflected the night sky as he dialled Carter, the Brigadier.

"Carter, it's Knox." His voice was sharp and concise as he spoke.

"Knox, what have you got for me?" Carter's voice cut straight to it and Knox did the same.

"I have Dani. Mac's made contact."

"What does he want?" Carter asked, clearly confused. Up until now, everyone assumed Mac had everything he needed after extracting the hacker. *If only it were that simple,* Knox thought bitterly.

"I want what I am about to tell you to remain confidential, off the books," Knox said, knowing he was taking a risk here, but he couldn't see any other way around it. Unfortunately, Knox knew he would need a team, or he would be going into this exchange completely outnumbered.

"Understood," Carter said firmly and, well, it wasn't exactly the solid reassurance Knox would have liked but he knew with a man like Carter, it was the best he was going to get.

So, despite his hands being tied, he looked back inside at Dani before telling the Brig, "Dani is the hacker."

"Come again, Captain?" Carter's shock was clear in his voice.

"Mark Thomas is Dani's father," Knox replied, his tone tight with frustration. "I don't have time for the full story, but she got herself into some serious shit, and he took the fall. It didn't take long for Mac to figure out he had the wrong hacker."

Knox gritted his teeth, expecting an outburst, but Carter's response was far more measured. No stream of profanities, just a heavy sigh as he quickly pieced everything together. Dani didn't mean anything to Carter, after all. To him, this was just another piece of the puzzle falling into place.

"So let me guess, now he wants to make a trade?" Carter dryly said.

"Yeah, but you've got to know now, I am not about to let that fucking happen. What it does mean is that we have a second chance here to get this fucker once and for all." Knox's words came out in a rumble of anger. No one wanted Mac dead more than him.

"Affirmative, Captain. Now what's our play?" Carter acknowledged before Knox told him the plan.

"We need to move fast. Mac has given Dani forty-eight hours until the exchange. As for the details, I will fill you in later, but for now, we're headed to Rhone Glacier in Switzerland. I need a team and we need an airtight plan. Mac isn't stupid, he will assume Dani isn't doing this alone and will have his own backup plan in place," Knox told him firmly, hoping he was making the right call by including T.I.7 in this.

"Then you should get your ass to Switzerland, Captain," the Brigadier ordered before abruptly hanging up.

Knox cursed under his breath. The day had spiralled in a direction he never anticipated. He had barely found Dani again, and now she was right back in the thick of danger, the very danger he'd been trying to keep her away from. But he knew there was no other option. He couldn't trust her to stay put, not when this could be another one of Mac's ploys. It could easily be a diversion to send them scrambling in one direction while Mac slipped in from the other, taking Dani when Knox's back was turned.

No, he wouldn't risk it.

He turned back to find Dani zipping up her duffel bag, her face fraught with worry. Her face lifted as he walked back in the cabin.

"We've got a plan in motion," Knox told her, grabbing his weapons and tactical gear.

She nodded, but still eyed her laptop as if it felt totally wrong for her not to take with her. Knox knew that this had been her weapon and to leave it behind now was like him leaving behind his guns.

"Let's get out of here. But first, cut the power to everything," Knox said before taking Dani's bag from her and leading her out the cabin.

A short walk away and they arrived at the nearby cabin that Knox was renting.

"Holiday home?" Dani quipped, and Knox winked at her in response.

They quickly loaded up the Continental GT with their gear, after Knox quickly and efficiently grabbed his stuff from inside. The car gleamed under the moonlight, and Knox slid into the driver's seat, glancing at Dani as she settled in beside him. Her face was still a mask of worry but also silent resolve. She was ready for whatever lay ahead.

Question was now… *was he?*

Knox turned the key, the engine roaring to life. As they pulled out of the driveway, the cabin shrank in the rear-view mirror, and Knox's mind raced. The road ahead was long, it was a six-hour, non-stop drive from Lake Walchensee to the hotel Belvédère, an abandoned hotel in the Swiss alps that Dani was quick to find the address of.

The danger they were heading in to was a dark unknown, the outcome hanging in the balance. Mac, unintentionally or not, had given them time to form a plan—but the tension gnawed at Knox. He knew this was only the beginning of a precarious situation that needed to be navigated with extreme caution. Revealing to T.I.7. that Dani was the real hacker was a move Knox hadn't wanted to make, but he'd been left with no choice. All he could do was hope that they'd prioritise her safety above everything else.

A chill ran down Knox's spine. Trusting T.I.7. with the Dani situation didn't sit well with him, but the thought of an ambush unnerved him even more.

This was a razor-thin line he had to walk, *and the stakes had never been higher.*

TWENTY-FIVE
MOUNTAIN SHADOWS

The Bentley Continental GT cut through the steep mountain road like a phantom, its sleek black crystal paint glistening in the dim light of dusk. Knox gripped the wheel tightly, the powerful engine purring beneath him as they sped through the desolate stone landscape. Taking the winding roads with pace and braking hard through the hairpins, he pushed them faster toward their destination.

Dani sat in the passenger seat, her face pale, her thoughts a million miles away. It had been twenty-four hours since they left her family's cabin, and despite the tension hanging thick in the car, they'd managed to steal some much-needed sleep at a roadside motel. Albeit broken sleep, with Dani waking from nightmares. Knox had held her through it, pulling her tight against his frame as he tried to soothe her fears with the sound of his voice.

But now, with only eighteen hours left until their meeting with Mac at the abandoned hotel, the time for rest was over. The towering snow-capped peaks of the Swiss Alps loomed around them. An imposing and isolated backdrop that seemed almost too perfect for the deadly game they were about to step in to.

Knox's mind raced with thoughts of the mission ahead, but he kept his eyes on the road. Next to him, Dani remained quiet, her hands clenched tightly in her lap. She hadn't spoken much since the motel, and Knox didn't push her. He knew she needed time to process what was coming but more so, the worry of the unknown happening to her father.

Ahead, a large metal building came into view, tucked away on a secluded mountain pass around twenty miles from their final meeting point. It was the location T.I.7. had sent him coordinates for… a staging area where they would finalise their plan before the exchange with Mac. The structure was unassuming, the type of place that housed snowploughs, road salt, and maintenance equipment. Dani glanced at it with uncertainty, her brow furrowed.

"This is the place?" she asked, her voice tense. Knox nodded, his eyes scanning the perimeter.

"Yeah. Looks like a standard storage facility, but trust me, it's more than that on the inside," he answered, before pulling the Bentley closer to the large roller doors at the front of the building.

With a quick press of the horn, the echo reverberated through the stillness of the early evenings icy air. For a few seconds, nothing happened and Dani shifted uncomfortably in her seat, her eyes darting around nervously. Then, with a loud mechanical whir, the doors began to roll open, the metal creaking as it slowly lifted.

The bright lights of the Bentley flooded inside the building, blinding the people watching them. Knox pulled the GT forward, the car's headlights cutting through the interior of the structure as they rolled into the makeshift base camp. As the roller doors shut behind them, the full scope of the operation revealed itself.

Several black SUVs and tactical vehicles were parked inside, and a group of T.I.7 agents stood around a long, makeshift table that was covered in maps, laptops, and comms equipment. Knox recognized the familiar faces immediately, and Carter, the Brigadier, stood tall and stern. Harris was now patched up and back on his feet after being shot, and he was leaning heavily on crutches. And Rose, her blonde hair was slightly dishevelled as she tapped away on a laptop, her fingers moving fast enough to believe the keyboard was on fire.

The headlights of the Bentley swept across the group, and they shielded their eyes from the glare as Knox killed the engine. Harris was the first to step forward, his hand raised in greeting.

"Bloody hell, Captain, you always know how to make an entrance," Harris called out, a wide grin on his face after Knox opened the door and stepped out.

Knox smirked, the weight of the situation momentarily lifting as he took in the sight of Harris, bandaged but standing strong.

"What's wrong, Harris? Thought you'd be lounging around with a cup of tea watching Coronation Street, not back in the field already."

Harris slapped him hard on the shoulder.

"Tea's for the weak. Besides, it's on catch up, and someone's gotta keep you in check."

Knox chuckled, shaking his head. "You sure you're up for this? Last time I saw you, you were bleeding all over my floor."

Harris laughed, then winced, rubbing his side. "What can I say? I'm just too damn tough to stay down. Besides, who would be there to save your arse if not for me?"

Knox laughed and was about to point out who out of the two of them had been shot. But before they could exchange more banter, Dani made her way from the car door she seemed rooted to. Her distrust of officials understandable, considering the way they so easily arrested and sent her father to jail to avoid their corruption being outed to the world. Her expression was tense as her eyes scanned the room, wary of all the activity. She continued to linger by the Bentley, her arms wrapped around herself as if trying to shield herself from the weight of what was coming.

Carter, standing with his arms crossed near the table, straightened as Knox approached,.

"Captain, Dani… good to see you both in one piece." His sharp, posh accent cut through the hum of the base camp.

"Brigadier, good to see you looking well after your injuries." Knox nodded in return, his voice carrying a hint of respect. Carter gave a slight nod back.

"Nothing that couldn't be fixed. Now, let's get to it. We don't have time to waste," Carter said, brushing off the mention of his past wounds, as if referring to such was a weakness he had no time for.

Knox nodded towards Dani, motioning for her to join them at the table, where Harris and Rose were already waiting for the briefing to start. Dani's tension grew as Carter began speaking, his tone serious and commanding.

"This situation has escalated," Carter began, glancing at the map of the abandoned hotel where the exchange was set to take place. Not that it ever would because Knox wanted it to be known that Dani was to be nowhere near that place. "Our primary goal is to secure the drive and neutralise the threat against national security. Ideally, we want to take Mac alive.

However, if this isn't possible, then I will give the order to shoot to kill."

Knox gritted his teeth at the thought of keeping Mac alive. He had his own agenda when it came to Mac, and at the first chance he had, he was taking him out. Naturally, Knox kept quiet about this because he knew to voice his opinions would only get him thrown off the team instead of leading it.

"And my father, what about my father?" Dani asked, frowning in annoyance and her voice strained as her anger burned brighter.

"And of course, we are to retrieve the hostage," Carter added, and even to Knox, this sounded more like an afterthought. But regardless, if it was, the whole point of getting T.I.7 involved was to provide Knox the manpower and therefore the opportunity to save Dani's father, as well as kill Mac.

"But we should be prepared for all outcomes. We still don't know if Mac will even be there, let alone your father, Dani. We have no confirmed intel on his location or the size of his force," Carter pointed out.

"We want Mac alive ideally," Rose said. "We need him for interrogation. The CIA's been hunting him, and they're eager to get their hands on him." The tech geek's voice was quiet but focused.

Carter's face darkened slightly.

"Yes well, after the mess back at the Nest in Spain, Agent Patricia Miller has another thing coming if she thinks she can fuck up my op again. Mac slipped through CIA's fingers once, and I am not about to let them get another opportunity to do so again. No, I've decided to keep the CIA in the dark about this operation. That said, capturing Mac would go a long way in rebuilding trust between our agencies if we eventually handed him over," Carter stated, the pain of how it went down and the cluster fuck it ended in clearly putting a dent in his pride. The Brig stood at the centre of the makeshift briefing area and motioned for the team to gather around. His commanding voice broke the tense silence.

"This new intel was just received a few hours ago. It's an update on the situation with the files stolen by Mac. The encrypted T.I.7. data was stolen using Dani's device aboard the Perez yacht." Carter paused for a second as he looked to Dani, who was tensed by Knox's side.

Knox's urge to wrap his arm around her was strong enough that he nearly did so without thought. But he also knew it would be a bad idea, no one knew about the type of relationship they had, despite Harris no doubt guessing. Knox wanted to keep it like that because after all this shit was done with, his plan was for them both to disappear.

"Mac used Isabella Perez, inside the Nest, as his pawn. She gained access to the Nest's encrypted servers and handed Mac everything. The only saving grace we have here, people, is those files are still encrypted. Right, Rose?" He finished after making the point he hoped.

"Yes, Sir, all indications are that my encryption hasn't yet been broken," Rose proudly said, but she also gave the slightest of looks to Knox, telling him silently that it wouldn't stay that way for long if they got their hands on Dani.

Obviously, Knox had no choice but to admit to the Brig that Dani was the real hacker, but he had done so in confidentiality and so far, it looked like Carter had kept his word... Making Knox wonder what exactly he had said to the team was the reason Mac wanted her.

Dani's face glared slightly as Carter talked about her device, failing to keep her expression neutral.

Carter continued, pacing slightly as he spoke. "That data contains sensitive information on hundreds of our government's assets and global connections. If Mac or anyone in his network open those files, we're looking at an international disaster. Their lives will be in immediate danger, not to mention the political fallout. We must retrieve the files, or at the very least, stop Mac before he decrypts them. If we fail, many heads will roll. Assets will be as good as dead." Carter's eyes swept over the group, his expression hard. There was no room for mistakes here, and they all knew it.

Harris stepped forward, rolling out large maps and blueprints of their target location. The abandoned Hotel Belvédère was perched high on the Furka Pass.

"Alright," Harris began, pointing to the maps. "We've got ourselves one hell of a location to deal with. The Hotel Belvédère was a historic place back in the day, luxury, panoramic views, and all that. It's been closed since 2015, and from what we can tell, it's now a perfect fortress for Mac and his men." Harris tapped the diagram, his finger tracing the layout of the hotel.

"The place has been renovated a few times since it was built in the late 19th century. First expanded in 1890, then again in the early 1900s. You've got the main building here, where the reception and dining halls used to be. Two additional floors were added during the renovations in the Belle Époque era, and it was a hit with travellers. By the mid-20th century, it was booming again after World War II, but the glacier's retreat and newer technology left the place abandoned."

Knox looked at the map, studying the layout closely. He knew what Harris was about to say. Even if most of what he had already said was like a history lesson.

"This place is a honeycomb for Mac's men to hide," Knox commented.

"Like fucking bees," Harris replied. "Yeah, they could be anywhere. You've got narrow corridors, plenty of blind spots, and areas that could easily be fortified. If Mac's holed up in there, he's picked a spot that makes recon nearly impossible. We think his men will be stationed across multiple floors, all with clear views of the surrounding area, meaning they'll spot any movement long before we even get close."

Knox's jaw tensed as he clenched his teeth. Of course there was a reason Mac picked this place.

Thankfully, Harris wasn't only full of bad news, and he began pointing out the weak spots.

"This area here, northern side, just past the old dining hall, was once used for deliveries. It's probably still a structural weak point. But make no mistake, getting inside undetected will be a challenge. This hotel is perched on a cliffside with only a few ways in, and like I said, Mac's going to see us coming a fucking mile off." Harris's words made Carter fold his arms, his expression grave.

"Our priority is to get in, secure the files, and take Mac alive if possible. We need him for questioning. Handing him over to the government intact is our goal, but we cannot let those files get decrypted. Failure isn't an option," Carter said, once again reiterating the objective.

Knox stepped closer, his eyes narrowing as he studied the maps. "Mac's smart. He'll know we'll be watching for a trap. If we can't take him by surprise, we need to make sure we're ready for whatever he's got planned."

Harris nodded, pointing again to the building layout. "This spot right here, the old guest rooms facing the glacier. Best vantage point Mac's men could ask for. We'll need to assume they'll have snipers posted up here, covering the entire approach."

Dani stood quietly, absorbing the information. Every piece of it brought them closer to the confrontation that had been brewing. She felt the weight of it all pressing down on her, but she couldn't afford to show it. Not now. Knox glanced at her briefly, catching her eye, and though they exchanged no words, she knew they were both thinking the same thing. Mac didn't want her father… *he wanted her.*

The briefing continued as Carter laid out more of the operation. "We'll deploy teams in a three-pronged approach. Recon will be done remotely for as long as we can manage without being detected. Once we're sure of the situation inside the hotel, we move in. 6:00am before day light. Everyone in position at 5:30am. But remember, we need Mac alive."

Knox's mind raced. They had to get Dani's father out alive too. Mac wasn't just a dangerous mercenary, he was a strategist, and the hotel would be the perfect arena for whatever game he was playing. The clock was ticking, and they couldn't afford to lose.

The team studied the maps and diagrams, knowing full well what awaited them at the hotel. Knox and Harris exchanged a brief glance, a silent understanding passing between them. They were walking into a trap, and the odds weren't in their favour, but they had no choice.

"Sir, I don't want Dani here when we are on the mission, I think…" Knox spoke out but was cut off by Carter as Dani glared at him.

"Yes, yes… Knox, we have a plan for that. Miss Thomas is going to be in safe hands," Carter said cold and clinical.

"Right, team, we have a lot to digest, and we all need to prepare. We will hit the target, we will succeed. I suggest everyone gets some scran and rest. Harris, a word please," Carter finished and motioned for Harris to follow.

Following the quick briefing, Knox couldn't shake the bad feeling in his gut. He knew there was something the Brig wasn't saying. No, not wasn't saying…

He just wasn't saying it to Knox.

TWENTY-SIX
AGAINST ORDERS

The cold mountain air bit at Knox's face as he crouched low behind a jagged boulder, his breath barely visible in the biting early morning darkness. He scanned the abandoned hotel ahead, its tall walls looming like a ghost against the sky. The Belvedere Furka Hotel, once a thriving retreat, was now a weather-beaten shell of itself. The only sound at 5:30 am was the faint whistle of wind slicing through the rocky terrain, and T.I.7. had the place surrounded.

Knox shifted his weight, his gut churning with unease. Something wasn't right. He'd had the feeling since they first set up their positions after working their way across a mile of harsh terrain, now hidden in the cover of night. The hotel sat still, too still. No lights, no movement. Nothing that gave any indication Mac or his men were inside yet.

Knox's mind drifted to Dani and the plan. It had been straightforward, Carter assigned a five-man Beta team to protect her. They had taken Dani to a barn, isolated and away from the base camp, a location Carter had pinpointed on the map during the briefing. It was supposed to keep her safe, hidden from Mac's reach.

But now, regret bothered Knox. He had a brief moment with her before leaving, saying goodbye, telling her to stay safe, pulling her into a quiet corner to steal a kiss. The memory of that kiss lingered, but it was tainted by the words he couldn't bring himself to say. The words I love you had stuck in his throat, trapped by the weight of everything else they were up against. He had let her go without saying them, and that haunted him more than the mission ahead.

"All units in position, status check," Carter's voice crackled in Knox's ear from the intercom, the Brigadier's tone calm but sharp. "Confirm eyes on Thomas, the drive, and most importantly, on Mac," Carter reiterated once again.

"Affirmative," Knox replied firmly, his grip tightening on his Heckler & Koch MP5, and his eyes narrowing as he studied the dark silhouette of the hotel.

There was nothing to confirm, though. No movement inside, no sign of life. He glanced to his side, where Harris lay prone on the ground, his injured shoulder bandaged but still sore. Harris wasn't part of the entry team. He was here to oversee the operation, and even though Knox knew his friend hated not being able to fight, in his condition, this was one he was forced to sit out on. The fact he was here at all was a testament to how tough the Green Beret Commando was. Knox leaned closer, lowering his voice after switching his comms mic off and signalling to Harris to do the same.

"Harris, you seeing anything?"

Harris let out a quiet grunt, his breath fogging in the cold air. "Nothing. Not a damn thing. I've got a bad feeling about this, mate."

Knox's gut twisted. "You and me both."

Harris glanced at him, his sharp eyes filled with understanding. He knew what Knox was thinking even before he spoke.

"This feels off, Harris. No movement, no signs of life. I promised Dani I'd get her father back, and I don't trust T.I.7. to care whether he makes it out of this alive."

Harris exhaled, nodding slowly. "You're right. They'll destroy the building without a second thought if they know Mac's in there. They don't care who else is inside." Harris told him something he already knew. It was what he had feared the most and was why he was second guessing his decision to involve them in the first place.

Why hadn't he just forced Dani's hand and took her somewhere safe first? Somewhere halfway around the world on some remote island somewhere while he had the time to find Mac himself. To hit him when he was least expecting it…

Because she had looked up at him with those beautiful tear-soaked eyes and practically begged for her father's life… *that's why.*

Knox's jaw clenched. T.I.7.'s orders were clear. Storm the hotel at 6 am sharp and eliminate the threat. They would blow the place to hell if they needed to. And Knox knew what that meant. Dani's father would be nothing more than collateral damage.

Knox wasn't about to let that happen.

Carter's voice came through the intercom again. "Knox, Harris, confirm positions. I want eyes on Mac before we move."

Knox cut the connection for a moment, his pulse quickening. He glanced at Harris, who met his gaze with a knowing look.

"You're thinking of breaking orders, aren't you?" Harris said, his voice laced with both disapproval and something akin to understanding.

"I don't have a choice, I can't let this happen," Knox said, his voice low but determined. "If I don't move in early, we might never get Thomas out alive," he added.

Harris sighed, his face hardening, but there was also a trace of sympathy in his eyes.

"You know I can't stop you, Captain, not with this shoulder or this leg. And honestly, I'm not eager to send these men in, knowing they could die at the hand of the same man who sent them."

"Didn't figure you'd try," Knox said with a smirk.

"Happily send you in there, though," Harris said with a rare smile. The major then shook his head and glanced back at the hotel. "Just be careful, Knox. You go in early, you're on your own. I'll cover for you with Carter, but you better make it out of there," Harris said, his tone serious.

Knox gave him a quick nod, the unspoken bond between them stronger than words.

"Thanks, Major. I'll see you on the other side. But one more favour?" Knox added with a grin, slapping Harris on his bad shoulder.

Harris groaned, gritting his teeth as he leaned back against the boulder.

"What favour, Captain?" Harris asked, giving Knox a look that said, *what now?*

"Hold off on sending the team in at six. Wait for my signal or until I call for backup," Knox replied, his voice firm and determined.

"For the record, you're a bloody fool for doing this, but okay," Harris said, grimacing from the aching burn resonating from under his bandages.

The major put his hand into his pocket and pulled out a hip flask and unscrewed the old cap, his eyes hard but filled with the weight of time spent in the trenches together. He raised the flask slightly, his voice low and steady.

"To the fight ahead, brother. May your aim be true, your steps be silent, and may we meet again in the light… or in the shadows where we belong," Harris toasted before having a good swig.

Knox took the flask, the worn, scratched up metal pressing against his palm. For a moment, he felt the weight of it, heavier than it should've been. Harris's words hung in the cold air between them, and the unspoken bond they shared felt more real than ever. Knox raised the flask, meeting Harris's gaze, and the shadows of the past reflected in both their eyes.

"To the fight," Knox said, his voice quieter than usual, but filled with the same steel that had gotten him through a lifetime of battles.

He took a slow swig, the burn of the whisky spreading warmth through his chest, grounding him for what was coming. As he handed the flask back, a rare flicker of emotion tightened his throat. He gave Harris a nod, one that said more than words ever could.

"I'll see you in the shadows, mate." Knox then turned away, the whisky warming his blood, but the gravity of what lay ahead settled on his shoulders. The chill of the mountain air returned, biting through the moment. Then with a final glance at Harris, Knox steeled himself and disappeared into the darkness… *alone.*

Knox navigated the shadows, moving quickly but silently across the uneven terrain. His breath came in controlled, shallow bursts as he darted between cover, each step taking him closer to the hotel. The icy ground crunched faintly beneath his boots, the cold stinging at any exposed skin.

The mountain loomed around him, its jagged peaks barely visible in the faint pre-dawn light. The wind howled as it whipped through the rocky outcrops, carrying with it a sense of foreboding. Knox's instincts screamed at him that this was a trap. But if it was, he had no choice but to spring it.

He approached the eastern side of the hotel, his eyes flicking to a section of the wall where the stone had crumbled. A small, flat section of the roof was just within reach if he could climb the wall. The hotel was old, the masonry weak, and there was a broken window near the top; an entry point.

Knox gripped the rough stone, hoisting himself upward, his muscles burning with the strain. The wall was slick and cold, makeshift footholds formed by rusted nails and old brackets barely supporting his weight. The wind bit at him with each movement, but he pressed on, his focus razor-sharp. With a final push, he reached the ledge, pulling himself onto the flat roof with a quiet grunt.

He crouched low, scanning the roof with a sharp gaze. The narrow path ahead led to the shattered window he had spotted from below, its jagged edges gleaming in the faint light. Moving cautiously, Knox pressed his body against the cold stone, every instinct on high alert as he inched closer.

The feeling that something was off still lingered. No guards. No signs of life. Where the hell were Mac's men? This wasn't right, none of it.

The glass was shattered, razor edges lining the frame, but the opening was large enough for him to slip through. He peered inside, his eyes adjusting to the darkness within. Still no movement, no sound. It was as if the entire building was holding its breath, waiting for something to happen.

Knox inhaled deeply, his instincts still screaming at him that something was wrong. But he had no choice now. He had to find Thomas. He had to keep his promise to Dani.

With one last look over his shoulder to the area Harris was positioned, Knox slipped through the window and into the darkness of the abandoned hotel, ready to face whatever waited for him inside…

243

TWENTY-SEVEN
INFERNO'S EDGE

Knox moved like a shadow through the darkened hallways of the abandoned hotel, his gun steady and at the ready. Every movement was precise and silent. Every corner, door, and shadow was a potential threat. It was all muscle memory for Knox, something he'd done countless times back at the Hereford training grounds. His instincts were honed to perfection and etched deep into his bones, guiding each step, never failing him.

The once-grand hotel was a ghost of its former self, its elegance long decayed and replaced by neglect. Layers of dust coated the worn furniture, faded paintings, and shattered mirrors, all ravaged by time and vandals. The musty air clung thick in his lungs, and every creak of the floorboards beneath his boots added to the eerie stillness, feeding the unease creeping up his spine.

It was too quiet, too empty.

This wasn't right. Where were Mac's men? His gut churned, that nagging feeling creeping back, telling him this was a trap. But he pressed forward, clearing every room, every hallway, gun aimed and finger on the trigger as he swept through the crumbling corridors. His senses were on high alert, every sound, every movement scrutinized. The stillness was oppressive, almost unnatural, as if the building itself was holding its breath, waiting for something to happen.

The further Knox went, the stronger the niggling in his gut gnawed at him. He passed through a dust-choked hallway, the faded grandeur of its old wallpaper and broken chandeliers giving way to a grand staircase. One that led down to a set of imposing double doors, slightly ajar. Beyond them, the ballroom, the heart of the hotel. His gut twisted as he approached, his steps quiet but deliberate, like a predator stalking its prey. With a final breath, he nudged the door open with the barrel of his gun.

Inside, the ballroom was a vast, dimly lit cavern. It was a cinematic scene of decayed elegance, once polished marble floors were now cracked, and the massive chandeliers above hung limp with cobwebs. The large windows lining the walls were caked with grime and boarded up. But at the centre of the room, in the pool of faint light from a high, broken window, sat a single man tied to a chair.

Knox's heart rate quickened. The man was slumped forward, barely moving, his head hung low, his face obscured by shadows. A faint stir of movement as Knox stepped into the room told him the man was still alive. As he approached, gun raised and ready, the man started to thrash weakly against his restraints, the muffled sound of gagged screams reaching Knox's ears.

Knox swept his gaze around the room, his instincts screaming at him. He was exposed in the wide, open space. Too easy to be ambushed. Too perfect a setup. But the man in the chair, Dani's father, Mark Thomas needed him. Knox moved closer, his eyes darting around the shadowed corners of the ballroom, searching for hidden threats. He reached Thomas, his gun still trained on the surrounding space.

The man was shaking his head violently now, his mumbled screams growing more desperate. Knox quickly knelt beside him, yanking off the gag and pulling the tape from his mouth.

"Where's Dani?" Thomas gasped, his voice laced with anger, his thick Herefordshire accent unmistakable. "Where's my daughter?!" he shouted this time, the panicked desperation twisting his features into something haunting.

Knox's eyes stayed sharp, still scanning the room as he responded.

"She's safe. We've got her. But we need to…"

"Get out!" Thomas interrupted, his voice hoarse but filled with alarming urgency. "This place is rigged to blow! It's a bloody trap!"

Knox's blood ran cold, but his focus remained razor-sharp. His instincts had been right all along. He glanced down at Thomas, who was shaking with anger and fear.

"Leave me! Get out now before it's too late! Its set to go off at 06:15am."

Knox looked at his watch, 06:13am. *Fucking Mac*, he thought with vehemence. But Knox wasn't leaving anyone behind. He reached into his tactical vest, pulling out his knife with a swift motion.

"Not happening, Sir," he cried, cutting through the ropes binding Thomas to the chair.

"You're a bloody fool, GET OUT OF HERE!" Thomas pleaded.

The honourable act of Thomas trying to save another wasn't lost on Knox. The second Dani's father was free, Knox grabbed him by the arm and yanked him to his feet.

"Move!" he barked, pointing to the nearest set of boarded-up windows.

The two of them sprinted across the ballroom, their boots pounding over the cracked floor as the heavy air grew thicker, every second feeling like a ticking clock counting down to disaster. When they reached the window, they didn't hesitate. Knox and Thomas both drove their boots into the boards with all their strength. The wood splintered and gave way after a few hits, the sharp crack echoing through the room.

"Go!" Knox shouted, ushering Thomas through the broken window. They both vaulted out of the opening, landing hard on the cold, rocky earth below. The moment they hit the ground, they scrambled to their feet, instincts pushing them to run.

They had barely made it a few steps before the hotel suddenly erupted behind them.

The blast hit with a deafening roar, the ground beneath them trembling as a fireball shot up from the basement. The explosion ripped through the building, blowing out windows, doors, and entire sections of the walls. Knox and Thomas were thrown forward, the heat of the explosion licking at their backs as debris showered down around them. They hit the ground again, their bodies rolling over the rocky earth, and they shielded themselves from the blast by throwing their arms over their faces.

Behind them, the hotel groaned as the force of the explosion travelled up through the structure. The roof buckled, timbers snapping before the entire building collapsed inward, a final, thunderous crash reverberating through the mountains.

Knox's eyes fluttered open, dazed and disoriented. The world around him spun, a thick fog clouding his senses as he tried to piece together what had just happened. For a moment, he could hear nothing, only a piercing, high-pitched ringing filled his ears, drowning out everything else. He blinked, his vision slowly clearing, but the ringing persisted, blocking out the chaos around him.

His chest heaved as he fought to steady his breathing. Dust swirled in the cold mountain air, and the wreckage of the exploded hotel smouldered around him. Pain throbbed through his body, but it was the disorienting quiet that threw him off balance. He shook his head, trying to clear the noise from his ears, the ringing fading slightly as the world came back into focus.

Knox groaned, forcing himself to sit up. His muscles ached, his ribs were bruised, but he was alive. Glancing to his side, he saw Thomas lying nearby, equally shaken, his face grimacing and covered in dust. The older man groaned as he stirred, his brow furrowed in pain and confusion.

"Thomas," Knox croaked, his voice hoarse, the words barely audible above the fading ring in his ears. He crawled over to him, grabbing the man's arm and shaking him gently. "You with me?" he yelled.

Thomas blinked, disoriented, his breathing shallow as he struggled to come to his senses. He coughed, shaking his head, his eyes still glazed over with shock.

"Dani… *my daughter…*" His voice cracked, desperation flooding his words as his gaze sharpened, locking onto Knox. "Where's Dani? I need to see her, now!" Thomas demanded.

Knox's heart clenched as he heard the fear in Thomas's voice. He helped the man sit up, gripping his arm firmly.

"She's safe. I will take you to her, I promise. But we need to move."

Thomas's eyes, though clouded with pain, were filled with an intense urgency.

"Are you sure? I need to see her… I have to see her… that bastard… fuck… he *knows*," he muttered, his voice barely above a whisper, but Knox could hear the deep need, a father's plea cutting through the haze of their escape.

Knox nodded, his jaw tightening, because once his senses

returned to him so did the questions that followed. Why had Mac blown up the hotel? Was it a trap? What was the point in arranging an exchange? How could he have been so sure that Dani wouldn't be there?

Panic hit Knox, now matching that of her father's.

"We will. We're getting out of here and I'll take you to her. But we've got to go now, before this place falls on us or we cook." Knox held a hand up to his own face as he looked back at the ruin, the fires burning with a growing intensity.

Then the situation became clearer as his mind whirred with the questions… and now possibly some answers.

Mac had to know about T.I.7.'s plan.

His chest still heaved from the blast as he helped Thomas to his feet, their movements sluggish from the impact. The weight of the explosion still rang in Knox's bones, and he wasn't sure if they were out of the woods yet. Just as he was about to speak, he saw the hurried crunch of boots on gravel. The shadows weren't easy to focus on and his muscle memory tried to kick in as he reached for his gun but faltered.

Then they came into view. A struggling Harris, followed by several T.I.7. agents, came running across the road, their faces tense with urgency. Harris's eyes locked onto Knox's, relief flooding his features when he saw them both alive. He skidded to a halt, reaching out to steady Knox while the other agents helped Thomas, pulling him upright.

"Bloody hell, Knox," Harris said, panting slightly. "You alright? You been playing with matches again, Captain… Captain?" Harris said, shaking Knox, trying to reach him through his brain fog.

Knox gave a half-nod as Harris brushed off the dust from him.

Some clarity came back to Knox as the situation unfolded and he shouted, "They fucking blew it, Harris! Dani… he wants

Dani… coming for her." Knox panted, his body feeling like it had been put through a grinder.

Harris, still catching his breath, glanced over his shoulder, already reaching for his comms unit because Knox didn't need to say anything else. His dark eyes narrowed, knowing exactly what this had fucking been… *a distraction!*

"Team Beta, come in. What's the status on the asset at the barn? Is Miss Thomas secure?" For a moment, the only sound was the cold wind whistling through the mountains.

Knox's heart was in his fucking throat as he waited through the silence. It was the longest fucking wait in his entire life, he couldn't get his hands to stop shaking. Harris cutting him a look, one that would have mirrored Knox's had he been in love with what he had just called the asset.

But to Knox, she was his Dani girl. And as the torturous silence continued, she quickly became something else…

A fucking target.

"Team Beta, this is Harris. Report. What's the status on Dani Thomas? Over." Harris's hard command came and went as the deadly quiet ensued.

Until it didn't.

A crackle of life was soon followed by the sound of a dying man saying a single word, *"Ambush…"*

This was followed by the fatal sound a single gunshot, and what came next filled Knox's veins with an icy dread.

A woman's scream…

It was Dani's.

TWENTY-EIGHT
NO WAY BACK

"Fuck… FUCK!" Knox bellowed, his heart close to fucking stopping. A cold knot of tension twisted inside him as the sound of her scream echoed through his mind.

His jaw clenched, his hands curling into fists. Before he could say anything else, the sharp crackle of Carter's voice cut through the dead air.

"Knox! Harris! Report. What the bloody hell just happened? Knox, you were ordered to hold position!" Knox's features twisted, anger gripping him in a vice so tight, he couldn't fucking speak!

"Carter, it was a trap. The place was rigged to blow. Thomas has been retrieved, but had Knox not entered early, then all our men would be dead," Harris informed him, nodding to Knox, having his back.

But right then it didn't fucking matter. None of it did, because Knox needed to get to Dani and didn't have time for this shit!

"Mac? The drive? Report, Captain," Carter's voice snapped

through the radio, each word heavy with anger. Knox's pulse quickened, frustration boiling up.

"There's no fucking sign of him. No damn drive! We need to get a team to the barn, to Dani ASAP!" Knox raked his hands through his hair, pacing, his mind racing for ways to get to the barn, to Dani. He felt the tension thickening in the air as silence stretched over the radio, the weight of Carter's fury palpable even through the radio static. When Carter's voice finally came back, it was cold, cutting like a blade.

"You disobeyed a direct order. You went in alone. Did you even confirm Mac was there?"

Knox's teeth ground together and his jaw tightened before grabbing the radio and gripping it hard enough that he heard the casting groan.

"I got Thomas out alive, you piece of shit! The place went up before I could find anything else. Mac fucking played us, Carter! This wasn't about the drive. Or a hand over… it was about creating a fucking distraction!" Knox snapped, his fury willing him to throw the radio down the damn mountain.

Carter's reply came fast, sharper than before.

"Damn it, Knox! We needed Mac alive, and we needed that drive. Now everything's gone to hell, and you've got nothing to fucking show for it."

Harris, standing beside Knox, stepped in, trying to diffuse the tension. His voice was calm but firm. "Brig, with all due respect, Sir, it was a fucking setup. Knox saved Thomas. We'd have lost him and our men if we followed protocol. And we still don't know if Mac's dead or alive. There's no proof either way."

Knox couldn't hold back any longer. Time was running out and he was losing his window to save Dani.

His voice was thick with urgency as he shouted into the radio, "I need to get to Dani. We've lost comms with Beta team, the last contact included the word ambush and ended with a fucking bullet. I need a fucking vehicle!"

For a long, tense moment, there was nothing but silence on the other end. When Carter spoke again, his frustration simmered beneath the surface. He was more clinical now.

"No. Knox, get back to base. Arrest Thomas. We need to debrief and question both of you. Mac's still out there. We'll send Alpha team to check on Miss Thomas. Radios might just be down, no one knows where she is, Captain, and she has a five-man team guarding her. You better pray we still have a chance to salvage this."

Knox looked at Harris incredulously.

"Did you not fucking hear a word I said?! The location has been taken, there is no fucking team left, you dumb shit, and they have Dani!" Knox bellowed.

Harris took the radio off him, hoping to defuse the situation, but Knox was fuming. He should have listened to his instincts and kept T.I.7. out of the whole thing. Trusting Carter had been a mistake.

Meanwhile. Thomas watched this all playing out, the same pain etched to his own features as what he could read on Knox's.

"Vehicles are already on route to you. See you *both* at base. Carter out." The crackle of the radio silenced after the last transmission, and Knox exploded.

"Fuck! This is fucking bullshit!" Knox roared, only calming enough when he saw four T.I.7. vehicles come into view, pulling up fast and coming to a sharp halt. Without missing a beat, Knox stormed toward the lead vehicle, his eyes burning with determination.

"Knox, you heard the Brig! Knox, stop!" Harris called after him, but Knox was already set on his course.

Going back to base was not a fucking option, not when

Dani was still out there. His mind raced, heart thudding in his chest. There was no way he was leaving her fate up to luck. If he had even the barest hint of a chance at saving her then he would fucking die trying to do just that.

"Harris, take Thomas. I'm getting Dani," Knox barked, yanking open the driver's door of the lead vehicle. The driver hesitated, wide-eyed, but before they could react, Knox pulled his gun, pointing it at the grunt's head.

"Get the fuck out of the car, soldier!"

The driver looked to Harris, who subtly gave him the okay before he extracted himself from the tense situation, now backing away.

"I can only cover for you so much, Knox," Harris said, his voice edged with concern.

"If she's been taken, it won't fucking matter," Knox told him, his tone cold and deadly.

"Stay safe, and for God's sake, don't get dead."

Knox nodded, his jaw clenched as he slammed his foot on the accelerator, the Land Rover Defender tires screeching as he sped away, gravel spitting in his wake.

His adrenaline went into overdrive as he tore down the mountain road, hands gripping the wheel with white-knuckled intensity. The morning sun was just beginning to rise, casting an eerie orange glow over the mountains, but Knox's world was a blur. Still recovering from the blast, his head pounding, his thoughts were consumed with one thing… Dani. The woman he loved. She was out there, in danger, and every second that passed without reaching her felt like a blade twisting deeper into his gut.

The tactical vehicle roared down the winding road, reckless speed sending it skidding dangerously around the sharp bends. Knox didn't care, he pushed harder, his foot slamming the accelerator as the tires screeched against the asphalt. The vehicle fishtailed, barely holding the line because the vehicle wasn't designed for this speed, but Knox kept control. He could feel time slipping away and his desperation was mounting.

"Please, God, let her be okay," he said out load, as if God would hear his pleas better.

The terrain shifted, the road levelling out as the old barn came into view in the distance. His heart lurched in his chest. There it was, a weather-beaten, red barn, standing crooked in the middle of overgrown grass and twisted trees. The place looked deserted, but as the tactical vehicle's headlights illuminated the scene, Knox's stomach dropped to its deepest pits.

A body lay in front of the barn.

Knox slammed the brakes, the vehicle skidding to a halt, headlights casting a long shadow over the still figure. His heart was in his throat as he threw open the door, jumping out and hitting the floor running. Gun in hand, he sprinted across the uneven ground, the cold morning air slicing through him as he neared the fallen figure.

It was one of the Beta team agents, his body limp, eyes lifeless, a bullet hole clean through his chest at close range just below the neck. Blood pooled beneath him, dark against the overgrown grass. Knox tried to swallow but his throat was too tight and panic clawed at his insides. His breath came in ragged gasps as he scanned the area. There was no sign of the other team members.

"Dani!" Knox shouted, his voice raw, filled with desperation. There was no response. No movement. Just the eerie silence of the dawn and the creak of the barn's old wooden beams from the wind pushing on the side walls.

He rushed forward towards the barn entrance, instincts overwhelmed by fear and panic and the weight of his gun barely registered in his grip. He had to find her, there was no time to think. No time for caution.

Knox reached the barn's small side door and kicked it open with all his strength, the heavy wood splintering as it flew inward. His heart raced as he charged inside, scanning the dark, cluttered space. Old farming equipment and bales of hay filled the area. The contents casted long, ghostly shadows from the rising sun cascading down from the hayloft opening above. But there was no movement.

No sign of Dani.

He ran deeper inside, calling her name again, his voice echoing off the barn's rotting walls.

"Dani!" Still nothing. His chest heaved with every breath as his mind raced with horrible possibilities. He wouldn't stop. He couldn't stop. He had to find her.

Knox ran through the barn, pushing away the pain of a stitch in his side. He scanned the dark corners, hoping, praying, for a sign of Dani. He stepped into a sticky wetness on the dirt floor and looked down to his boots… blood. Then he saw them, three more bodies. T.I.7.'s Beta Team. Executed, each one from close range by the look of their wounds.

Panic clawed at his chest and he flipped on his comms unit, his voice shaking as he called in to base.

"Base, this is Knox! How many men were in Team Beta? I've got four dead. Was there a fifth? Dani isn't here, have they called in?" Knox rasped, the wait from a reply taking an eternity.

Static crackled through his earpiece before Harris responded, his voice clipped.

"There were five men in Beta. What's going on, Knox?"

Knox wiped the sweat from his brow, the weight of it all crashing down on him. Four bodies, but no sign of Dani.

Carter's voice cut through the comms, laced with frustration.

"Knox, you didn't follow orders, again! Dammit, this is exactly why I didn't want…"

Knox tuned the asshole out as the distant sound of helicopter rotors reached his ears. His stomach twisted, and without thinking, he sprinted toward the noise, frantically pushing through the debris in the barn. He reached the massive doors and without hesitation, raised his gun and shot off the chain and lock. The metal clattered to the ground before he swung the doors open and burst into the open air, his eyes scanning the horizon.

In the far distance, illuminated by the rising light, Knox saw a helicopter prepping for take-off and his heart plummeted. Then he saw her… the blonde hair… was it Dani? He couldn't fucking tell from this distance, but it had to be!

"Dani…!" Knox bellowed with every last breath in his lungs, before drawing in more.

The figure turned their head towards his desperate call and it was like a punch to his gut. She was being dragged toward the helicopter by two men. He couldn't make out their faces clearly, but one of them was wearing T.I.7. gear.

A double cross. And the other… *Mac.*

Knox's vision tunnelled as he sprinted full speed, yelling into his comms.

"I've got eyes on Dani! Eyes on Mac! They're getting into a chopper!"

But even has he ran, *he knew. He knew he wasn't going to fucking make it!* The distance was too great, and the helicopter's rotors were already spinning faster. His legs burned as he pushed harder, faster, desperation fuelling him. He wouldn't stop, he couldn't stop. Shots were fired at him, but the distance was too great to be accurate and they buzzed past him, nothing but a vibration through the air.

Carter's voice came through his earpiece again. "Knox, hold your position. Is the team in place?"

A voice crackled in response. "Roger that, target locked."

Knox skidded to a stop, his lungs burning, his eyes darting to the high mountain road to his left. A single T.I.7. vehicle was parked there, two operatives stood out with a surface-to-air launcher. Knox's breath caught in his throat as the realisation hit him like the icy touch of death on his shoulder.

"Carter… Carter what are you… No, No, don't fucking do this!" Knox stuttered through the horror of what Carter was now planning and his voice cracked with panic. For he was currently battling against the devil and this time,

It was one he had invited into the fight.

"Take the shot," Carter's voice came coldly over the comms.

"NO!" Knox's desperate cry soon became a rolling echo as his world slowed to a crawl. His eyes locked onto the helicopter as it lifted off the ground with Dani now inside, the rotors cutting through the air giving it lift as it tilted forward. One of the T.I.7. operatives raised the launcher, tracking the chopper's ascent.

"NO!" Knox screamed again, sprinting toward the helicopter, helpless to stop what was coming but running all the same.

In the distance, a streak of light shot from the launcher, carving through the air with deadly precision. Time froze as the missile found its mark, and for a heartbeat, everything was silent.

Then the explosion ripped through the sky.

The helicopter was engulfed in a fireball, the deafening roar of the blast echoing off the mountains. Metal twisted and shattered, debris raining down like fire from the heavens. The chopper spun wildly, the wreckage spiralling as smoke billowed into the darkening sky. The orange glow of the flames illuminated the entire valley into a twisted torch of destruction.

Knox's legs gave out beneath him, his knees hitting the cold, hard ground. He stared at the fiery wreckage, his mind unable to process what had just happened. His vision blurred, and his throat constricted as a gut-wrenching scream tore from his chest.

"ARRRRHHHH!" His voice ripped his throat raw, filled with agony as he pounded his fists into the dirt.

"NO! DANI! FUCK NO! *No… no… no.*" His voice became thick and filled with desperation. But as the flames crackled and rumbled in the distance, no matter how much he wished it hadn't fucking happened, there was too much proof that it had.

It was his worst fucking nightmare, the smoke rising like a grim cloud, marking the place where Dani had been taken from him. Knox's heart shattered, the weight of failure crushing him. His breaths came in shallow, ragged gasps, his body trembling as he stared at the inferno. It felt like the entire world was collapsing around him, and there was nothing left to hold on to.

Tears blurred his vision, but all he could see was the orange fire. The echo of the explosion still rang in his ears, drowning out everything else. *He had lost her.*

As the destruction raged on in the distance, Knox rolled onto his back, his hands clutching his face, his body shaking with the grief and fury of a man who had been pushed beyond his breaking point.

Knox reached for his weapon and pulled it up to his head, his finger on the trigger… It could all be over in an instant. Just one squeeze of his finger and he could join her.

As the gun fired, he realised his arm was up in the air, bullets firing above him until the clip was empty.

His heart shattered to pieces with no hope of repair as her name slipped from his lips.

"Dani."

EPILOGUE

After Knox had come to his senses a little, nothing but pure anger pumped through his veins. A storm brewed within him… and he knew exactly where he would unleash it… *or should he say, who he would unleash it upon.*

Furious footsteps took Knox into the base camp, rage boiling over, threatening to consume him entirely. The cold warehouse air bit at his skin, but he didn't feel it. Knox didn't feel anything except the fury and grief that pulsed through every cell of his being.

He spotted Carter standing at the briefing table, barking orders and asking his men how Dani's father had escaped. The knowledge barely just registered, but not enough to stop his wrath. Carter was in Knox's sights, going over maps with his team, oblivious to Knox's approach.

Without hesitation, Knox grabbed Carter by the shoulder, spun him around, and slammed his fist into his face. The punch landed square, knocking Carter back onto the table, scattering papers and equipment as he crashed down hard.

Knox stepped back, drawing his gun in one seamless

motion, the cold steel now trained on Carter. His chest heaved, his vision tunnelled, every muscle in his body tensed with pure, unfiltered rage. This man, the one who gave the orders to kill… the one who kept Knox from saving Dani. He was the reason she was truly gone.

It was all his fault.

No… *it was Knox's own stupidity… for trusting in Carter.*

Knox tightened his finger on the trigger, fighting himself for control as rage boiled over and a scream ripped from his throat.

"You!"

Before Knox could take the shot, Harris appeared, standing between Knox and Carter. His friend. His comrade.

"You can't do this, Knox. I won't let you," Harris said firmly, his voice steady but laced with tension as other T.I.7. operatives trained their weapons on Knox.

"You want to kill Carter, I get it. I do. But listen to me when I tell you that his death won't bring her back, Lucas. And I am not going to see you dead, meaning you'll have to kill me first. So come on, brother, lower the weapon."

Knox's hand trembled, his grip tight on the gun, the weight of everything crushing him. His heart raced, but Harris's words cut through the storm. Slowly, Knox's resolve cracked, and he lowered the gun.

However, rage was quick to take over again and Knox lunged at Carter, trying to get his hands around the man's throat. Harris wrestled him back, pulling him away before he could land another blow. Carter, still recovering from the punch, wiped blood from his mouth, his voice cold and venomous.

"I should have you shot for insubordination, Knox. The only reason I won't is that you saved the lives of one of our teams today. Now get out of my command centre before I change my mind!"

Knox, breathing heavily, glared at Carter, his eyes burning with hatred. Then he looked to the guns aimed at him.

"This isn't over, Carter," he promised, voice low and full of vengeance before he kicked a tactical box across the room. Then he turned, storming out of the camp without another word.

T.I.7. and everything it once stood for were dead to him.

Many hours later, Knox stood at the door of Dani's family cabin, the quiet surroundings mocking the storm of emotions raging through his body. He stepped inside, the familiar smell of wood and pine filling the air as he scanned the room, lingering on everything that reminded him of her. Her laughter, her fire, her life.

But Dani was gone. And the silence felt like a knife in his chest.

Knox's balled his hands into fists and looked around, his mind consumed by guilt and anger. He had promised to protect her. He had promised to get her back. And now, all that was left was the echo of those broken promises.

There was no logic in his mind for why he went to her cabin instead of his own, but he just needed to be somewhere close to her. It was like a memory he was grasping on to, fearing every second spent with her would suddenly evaporate and leave him with nothing.

Hollow and empty.

As his gaze fell on the old laptop sitting on Dani's desk, a notification sounded and broke the painful silence. Knox frowned, walking over and running his hand over the smooth surface of the laptop, the cold metal a sharp contrast to the heat of his emotions.

A second notification pinged, pulling Knox's attention. He opened the laptop, only to be met with a password screen. But before he could react, the password field began to auto-fill, unlocking on its own. Knox frowned, questioning how.

The question died when he witnessed the impossible…

The screen flickered and revealed a message. Knox's heart stopped as he read the words:

'Hello old friend.'

His breath caught in his throat as the message continued, the mocking tone so tangible it could almost be heard, like a fucking ghost whispering over his shoulder.

'Come now, you didn't really think I was dead, did you?'

Suddenly, Knox's world tipped on its fucking axis and Knox couldn't breathe.

A photo loaded on the screen.

It was an impossible sight and the disbelief exited Knox's body in a gasp as all the blood drained from his face. He gripped the screen so hard he was surprised it didn't crack, because there she was, with fear in her stunning blue eyes and a gun to her head.

Dani.

'I'll be in touch… old friend.'

Knox read this last message before the screen went blank and left him with his own murderous reflection staring back at him.

A flurry of emotions warred inside Knox, from relief that Dani was alive, to rage that she had been captured. It was difficult to pinpoint exactly where his head was at, but what he did know for sure was that this was far from over.

The battle to save Dani had become a war.

And Knox would soon be the one to deliver his own form of…

Blood Vengeance.

To be continued in Book 3

Blood Vengeance
Release date February 12th
Pre – order now

ACKNOWLEDGMENTS

I would like to thank close friends for their massive support, words of encouragement and belief they have shown.

To my beta readers, their views and ideas have improved and helped my writing, in no order thank you.

Claire Boyle, Kathy & Tony Cini,

The editing team Stephanie, Claire, and Sarah without you this book would not have been published.

And thank you to all the people who joined the Lucas Knox Series FaceBook group and follow the Page.

ALSO BY BLAKE HUDSON

Lucas Knox Series

Blood Retribution

Blood Ties

Blood Vengeance

ABOUT THE AUTHOR

Blake Hudson is an English action adventure/romance writer. He was born in Birmingham England, raised in Worcestershire, and now lives in the Costa del Sol, Spain. From a humble background, he originally aspired to be a film score composer after his studies in audio engineering. After years of working in the audio world as a technician, he then joined the TA alongside his work and served one tour in Iraq.

Returning home and having a change in life's direction, Blake found himself in the highly challenging and stressful work as a HGV driver around the City of London. After this, he was soon ready for relocation to a slower and more peaceful way of life, so he moved to Spain with his beautiful family to pursue his new dream of writing the stories he wanted to read. This was made possible with the added confidence and belief from his wife, bestselling author of the Afterlife Saga, Stephanie Hudson. She inspired him to overcome his dyslexia, as she had once done.

Blake started with his first venture into the world of action adventure novels, with Lucas Knox: Blood Retribution Book 1 of the Lucas Knox series.

OTHER AUTHORS AT HUDSON INDIE INK

<u>Paranormal Romance/Urban Fantasy</u>

Stephanie Hudson

Tatum Rayne

Sorcha Dawn

Georgia Seren Mills

<u>Crime/Action</u>

Blake Hudson

Jack Walker

<u>Contemporary Romance</u>

N.O. One

Gemma Weir

Nicky Priest

Jax Knight